RIDING TEMPTATION

JACI BURTON

HEAT | NEW YORK

THE BERKLEY PUBLISHING GROUP
Published by the Penguin Group
Penguin Group (USA) Inc.
375 Hudson Street, New York, New York 10014, USA

Penguin Group (Canada), 90 Eglinton Avenue East, Suite 700, Toronto, Ontario M4P 2Y3, Canada
(a division of Pearson Penguin Canada Inc.)
Penguin Books Ltd., 80 Strand, London WC2R 0RL, England
Penguin Group Ireland, 25 St. Stephen's Green, Dublin 2, Ireland (a division of Penguin Books Ltd.)
Penguin Group (Australia), 250 Camberwell Road, Camberwell, Victoria 3124, Australia
(a division of Pearson Australia Group Pty. Ltd.)
Penguin Books India Pvt. Ltd., 11 Community Centre, Panchsheel Park, New Delhi—110 017, India
Penguin Group (NZ), 67 Apollo Drive, Rosedale, North Shore 0632, New Zealand
(a division of Pearson New Zealand Ltd.)
Penguin Books (South Africa) (Pty.) Ltd., 24 Sturdee Avenue, Rosebank, Johannesburg 2196,
South Africa

Penguin Books Ltd., Registered Offices: 80 Strand, London WC2R 0RL, England

This is an original publication of The Berkley Publishing Group.

Copyright © 2008 by Jaci Burton, Inc.
Excerpt from *Riding on Instinct* by Jaci Burton copyright © 2008 by Jaci Burton, Inc.
Cover art by axb group.
Cover photograph by Corbis.
Cover design by Rita Frangie.
Text design by Kristin del Rosario.

ISBN-13: 978-1-60751-112-0

PRINTED IN THE UNITED STATES OF AMERICA

To my kids, who realize that deadlines equal madness. I appreciate your indulgence and understanding more than I can ever say. And as always, to Charlie, for filling my world with love.

acknowledgments

To my editor, Kate Seaver. Thank you for your enthusiasm about my books, and your willingness to discuss plot and characters. Your excitement about my stories always fuels my enthusiasm, and I'm most appreciative.

To my agent, Deidre Knight. As always, thank you for the sanity checks.

To my wonderful friend Lora Leigh. Thank you for reading and for loving my Wild Riders as much as I do. Your advice is worth a million.

one

DALLAS, TEXAS

TO SAY JESSIE MATTHEW'S PULSE WAS JACKED WAS an understatement. The Wild Riders were all assembled downstairs in General Grange Lee's office. An assignment was forthcoming, and Jessie was excited. No matter how much convincing it took, she was going to be in on this one. She was, after all, one of the guys. Even if she was female.

Her friend and Mac's girlfriend Lily was a Wild Rider now, and she'd been given assignments. Just because Lily was older and a former cop and private investigator didn't mean squat. So what if Jessie was only twenty-three and didn't have beaucoup years of formal training? She had street experience, and that was way more useful in the jobs they did. Besides, the Wild Riders had trained her. Former thieves, hard-core bikers and now government agents, the Wild Riders were the best at what they did—undercover work.

And Grange had trained her. She'd been in training one way or another for this since she was fifteen years old. She was ready.

Jessie slid into one of the chairs at the front of the room. The rest of the guys straggled in, some looking haggard and tired. She'd heard bikes roar in late into the night. Since she lived at Wild Riders' headquarters, along with General Lee, being called in for assignment would be easy for her. Mac used to live here, too, until he hooked up with Lily. Now the two of them shared an apartment in Dallas so they could have some privacy. Totally understandable. Most of the guys lived elsewhere and only came in when there was an assignment, like now. Typically, they dragged themselves in at the last possible minute, too, which meant wee hours of the morning. She grinned at all the yawns.

"Okay," Grange said, dressed as usual in his military camos and combat boots, his gray hair buzz cut was typical military style. "Grab some coffee and wake the hell up. We've got several jobs to work on, so you've got five minutes to infuse caffeine, and I want you sharp."

Excitement coupled with nervousness had woken Jessie before dawn. Giving up on going back to sleep, she'd showered, dressed, and had breakfast. Now she eagerly awaited an assignment, certain this time she wouldn't be left out. Grange had promised the "next time" would be her turn. This was the next time, dammit. She wasn't going to let him forget.

"Do you think he'll put you on a mission this time?"

Lily slid into the chair next to her, cupping a steaming mug of coffee between her hands.

"He'd better."

"He did promise the last time he doled out assignments," Mac said, taking a seat on Lily's other side.

The two of them were perfect together. Jessie's heart squeezed each time she saw them. They were so obviously in love it was adorable to see them interact. And since they cared so much about each other, Grange never assigned them to the same case. He said it would affect their judgment. He was probably right. Too much emotion could wreck an assignment. Too bad. But work was work. Fun was for after work.

Not that Jessie knew about either.

"All right." Grange stood and started talking. There was a lot going on, and he started splitting up teams. Mac, AJ, and Pax were heading to Las Vegas. Lily would be working with Rick in D.C.

"Vegas?" Lily asked, turning to Mac.

Mac just grinned.

"You suck," Lily mumbled. "Don't spend the rent money gambling."

"Want me to hold his wallet for him?" AJ asked.

"Bite me," Mac replied.

Pax snorted. "I'll keep good watch over your boy, Lily. Don't worry."

"I don't trust any of you," she said, then grinned. It was obvious she cared about them all.

Just like Jessie did. These guys were her family.

"Diaz and Spence, you're on assignment in Arkansas," Grange said. "There's a biker gang suspected of selling arms to a dangerous survivalist group up there. And we aren't talking your run-of-the-mill type of survivalists who avoid government interference and want to be left alone. These are extremists. Dangerous. The kind that could easily start a war if they had the weaponry to do it with."

"Oh, great," Spence said.

Diaz stood and grabbed the packet Grange handed him. "Who's the gang?"

"The Devil's Skulls, led by Crush Daniels."

Jessie's ears perked up at the name. "I know him."

Grange frowned. "You know Crush Daniels?"

"Yeah."

"I've heard of him," Spence said. "And the Skulls. Rough group of bikers."

She shrugged. "They seemed nice enough."

Diaz leaned back in his chair and scowled at her. "How the hell did you get mixed up with them?"

"I was out riding in Louisiana several months back before I got my new bike. You know how the old one kept cutting out on me? It died by the side of the road. They came by, helped me get it started again, asked me if I wanted to ride into the nearest town with them. So I did. I spent some time with him and his gang, riding around."

"Jesus," Diaz mumbled. "You were alone."

She kept her gaze on Diaz. "Well, yeah. But it's not like I just rode with one person. And there are other women in his group. We all had fun."

Diaz ran his fingers through his thick, dark hair. Jessie swallowed, watching the movement and clasping her hands together.

"Are you out of your mind, Jess? How many times have we told you to ride with someone?"

"I'm not a child, Diaz. I can take care of myself. And there wasn't more than twenty miles between towns on that ride anyway."

"On a beat-up, piece of shit bike. You know better."

Her ire rising by the second, Jessie tapped her foot. "In case you haven't noticed, I've grown up in the past few years. I'm an adult now. I don't have a curfew. I can ride when I want and where I want. It gives me something to do while I'm waiting for an assignment." She finished off the last sentence by slanting a look at Grange.

Grange cleared his throat. "Yes, about that . . ."

"You promised."

He inhaled, sighed. "I did, didn't I?"

"If Jessie knows this Crush Daniels, she'd be a perfect addition to Diaz and Spencer's assignment," Lily said.

"No."

Jessie glared at Diaz. "Why the hell not?"

"You're not ready," Diaz said.

She cast a pleading look toward Spence, who shrugged. "I think Jessie's more than capable and has been for a while."

"You did promise," AJ said to the general. "We all heard it during the last round of assignments."

"I agree," Lily said. "Give her a chance, Grange."

"Maybe you want to hear about the assignment first before you jump on it," Grange said to her.

"Fine. Hit me." Though she didn't care if she had to climb a flagpole naked in front of a million people. She wanted the case.

"The Devil's Skulls hold their annual initiation for new members every year right after the bike rally in Fayetteville."

"What kind of initiation?" Diaz asked.

"From what we understand, it can be anything from fighting their current members—both for the male and female initiates—to public acts of sex."

"Yippie ki yay," Spence said with a wink.

"You get all the fun assignments," Rick grumbled.

"Trade you," Pax said.

Diaz snorted. "That leaves Jessie out."

"It does not," she protested. "I can handle initiation." It was no worse than the life she'd led before she came to the Wild Riders.

"No." Diaz shook his head, crossed his arms. "This is a bad idea, Grange. She's just a kid."

She'd like to brain him upside the head with her boot. Or lift her shirt and flash her boobs at him. Geez, was he blind? "I am not a child. I wish you'd quit treating me like one. All of you."

Grange raised his hand. "Okay, let me think. Jessie, you have a point. I did promise you an assignment, but I do think this one has the potential to be dangerous. I don't like the idea of you initiating with Crush's gang, considering what could happen. However, you are an adult now and capable of making that decision for yourself."

She folded her arms across her chest. "Thank you."

"Is this what you want, knowing what you might be facing? Because once you're in, you're in. You can't back out."

"I understand, Grange. I've been trained. By you. I know what I might have to do. I can handle it."

"Okay. You're on the case. Since you said Crush already knows you that will give us an 'in' with them. And you'll have Diaz and Spence to protect you. But do not—I repeat, do not—go off by yourself or do anything without them, do you understand?"

She nodded, excitement drilling through her veins. "I got it."

"That's it, then. You all need to get together with your teams and read your assignments, then get packed and on the road first thing in the morning," Grange said, effectively dismissing them.

Jessie resisted jumping up and down. But holy cow, she had an assignment!

Cases in hand, everyone began piling out of the office. Once the room was empty, Diaz grabbed Jessie's arm. She paused, tilting her head back at him. She felt the tension in his coiled fingers, though they were warm and held her loosely.

"Rethink this."

She shook her head. "I know what I'm doing."

"Right. Like you did when you went riding with Crush Daniels and the Devil's Skulls?"

"He was nice to me. There was no problem."

"Hell, yeah, he was nice to you. He has a thing for you, that's why he was nice."

"A thing? What kind of thing?"

"He wanted you."

Wow, was Diaz off base. "He did not."

"See, that's your problem, Jess. You're naïve."

"I'm not naïve. And you're cynical."

"No, I'm realistic, and my eyes are always open while yours are in the clouds. You know what Crush wanted from you, don't you?"

"You weren't even there. He and his gang were friendly. They helped me out. I rode with them for the day and then I took off. Nobody hit on me."

"Uh huh. I'll bet."

She pulled her arm away from his grasp and leaned against the table. "Okay, Diaz. You tell me what you think Crush wanted."

"Isn't it obvious? He wanted in your pants."

She rolled her eyes. "Not every guy is a lecherous pervert."

"Honey, trust me. If a guy has a dick, he's going to want in your pants. Wake up, Jess. Before you end up in trouble that you can't get out of."

Diaz turned and walked away. Jessie watched his broad back and jeans-clad ass leave the room, pondering what he'd said.

He gave her so little credit. She'd been around grown men since she was a child, knew what some wanted. She could tell the good ones from the bad ones within seconds, knew instantly when to be wary. She'd felt no danger signals from Crush Daniels. Yeah, he was a rough biker and led a tough gang, but she'd been a fellow biker in distress and he'd helped her out. End of story.

Diaz? Now he was something entirely different, and so was her reaction to him. She couldn't breathe around Diaz. He made her uncomfortable. Not in a bad way, but in a God-that-man-is-gorgeous-and-makes-my-panties-wet kind of way. From the time her hormones had burst onto the scene at the age of sixteen, they'd zeroed in on Diaz and hadn't deviated since.

And in all these years Diaz had never once even noticed she was female. When Mac had brought her in, Diaz had at worst ignored her completely, at best treated her like a little kid. It had remained that way for the past eight years. Or at least she'd thought so, until today. But his comments and the way he looked at her made her wonder if her secret lust wasn't quite as one-sided as she'd always thought it had been.

How long had he been noticing her? Was he even aware of it? Because he wasn't doing the typical little sister protecting thing like the other guys did. No, this was different.

Interesting. And a little off balancing. Being given an assignment was exciting enough. Assigned a case with Diaz? Bonus.

He'd always avoided her. Now he wouldn't be able to.

Not only was she finally going to be working a case—and a fascinating case at that—but this was her chance to get to know the man who had fueled her fantasies for a number of years.

DIAZ DELGADO THREW THE PACKET DOWN ON THE TABLE IN THE library, muttering curses under his breath.

Jessie. What the hell was Grange thinking letting her tag along on this case? He jammed his hand through his hair, trying to fight the annoyance coursing through his veins. Maybe an hour or so with the punching bag in the gym would help release some of the fire fueling his anger. He needed an outlet for the rage he could barely contain right now.

If it was up to him, Jessie would have been sent to college far away from the dangers the Wild Riders represented. She had no business being a part of their life. From the moment Mac had brought her in—a scared young teen trying to act tough—Diaz had known this wasn't the kind of life for her. Oh, she talked the talk and walked the walk, but there was a hint of vulnerability about her—a sweet innocence that Diaz had wanted to lock in a closet and protect.

Shit. He didn't want her to go to Arkansas with Spencer and him. And that was the bottom line.

"Need someone to beat the shit out of?"

He whirled at the sound of Spence's voice. "Maybe. You volunteering?"

Spence slid into one of the wide leather chairs, crossing his ankles together. "I might if you keep acting like Jessie's old man instead of her friend."

"Somebody needs to have some sense. She's just a kid."

"She's twenty-three. She's capable. Have you gone a few rounds with her in the boxing ring?"

"No."

Spence worked his jaw back and forth. "That *kid*, as you call her, throws one hell of a punch. As well as a kick. She's a damn good shot with a gun, and pretty handy with a blade, too. I'd say she can hold her own just fine. Hell, she came to us with that knowledge. She's street-smart and savvy. She's wise beyond her years and a good judge of character."

"Really."

"Yeah. If you'd pull your head out of your ass and quit tiptoeing around her, maybe you'd notice."

Oh, he noticed. All the wrong things. Like her curves. Her breasts. Her long legs and sexy voice. Her mouth. Her laugh and her quick wit.

She made his dick hard. And he'd known her since she was a kid.

Yeah, he noticed her all right. He'd tried to avoid her since her eighteenth birthday when she turned those gorgeous green eyes on him in a way that made his balls quiver.

She was smart—too damn smart for her own good. Jessie was one hellaciously sexy package that he couldn't touch. She made him crazy.

He wasn't going to survive this assignment.

"I don't think it's safe for her. You know what these tough biker gang initiations can be like, Spence. Do you want that for Jessie?"

Spence shrugged. "Not my call. She's an adult now, and she's been training for a long time. This is her chance and she wants it."

"Are you willing to watch her have sex?"

Spence swallowed, looking as uncomfortable as Diaz felt. "Hell, I don't know. But we all have to let her grow up and stop thinking of her as our kid sister. She's not related to any of us. She's a woman and she can make her own choices, even if that includes sex as part of an assignment. You know it goes down that way sometimes. She's always wanted to be a Wild Rider. And that's part of the deal."

No shit. The thought of watching her fuck another man made his blood boil. He knew nothing about her private life, but with her sexy, cropped-short platinum blond hair, full lips, bright green eyes, and killer body, he imagined she'd had as much practice with fucking as she'd had with weapons and hand-to-hand combat. And *that* he didn't want to think about.

"This sucks," he said, sinking into the chair across from Spence.

"What sucks?"

He looked up at the sound of Jessie's voice, his pulse racing when she stepped into the room. She wore leather pants, boots, and a skintight top that revealed just a hint of her smooth stomach. The glittering jewel of the piercing at her navel—emerald to match her eyes—tantalized him and made him itch to lick around the little gem on his way down to the treasure below.

Jessie looked at both Spence and Diaz. "You two were talking about me, weren't you? Still debating whether you think I can handle this assignment?"

"I wasn't the one doing the debating," Spence said.

She turned her attention on Diaz. "For someone who has completely ignored me since I got to Wild Riders, you sure picked one hell of a time to start paying attention." She walked into the room and grabbed the packet from his hands. After dumping the papers out on the table between his and Spence's chair, she spread them out and picked up one piece at a time, studying the documents carefully.

"This is Crush Daniels," she said, handing one pic to Diaz and one to Spence. "You might want to know what he looks like."

Diaz took the picture she held over her shoulder. Crush looked to be in his early thirties, with short black hair, a goatee, and intense gray eyes. The picture was a close-up, no doubt taken with a telephoto lens. He sat on his bike—nice bike, too—his expression intense as he studied something off in the distance.

"Christopher 'Crush' Daniels, thirty-three years old. Six feet tall, weighing in at approximately two hundred and twenty-five pounds. Well muscled, works out regularly," Jessie reported, reading from the intel.

"What does he do for a living?" Spence asked.

"He owns a garage in his hometown of Little Rock. Correction. Co-owns it with his older brother, Donald. I guess that's how he has time to take all these road trips on his bike. His brother must mind the store while he's out riding. Says here that his brother isn't a rider."

"Lucky for Crush," Diaz muttered.

"Not exactly a rich guy, but certainly not poor, either," Jessie reported. "Has enough money to do what he wants, when he wants."

"Single?" Diaz asked.

"Yes. Never married. Gets around. Lots of different women."

"And no doubt wanting to add you as one of them."

Jessie craned her neck to look at Diaz, then rolled her eyes. "Not."

"Naïve."

"Pervert." She turned away and resumed reading. "High school education, then two years of community college. Got his associate's degree in business before opening up the garage with his brother. They've been running it for ten years now and it's pretty popular. I guess their parents left them money."

"Where are the parents?"

"Both dead. Natural causes."

"So, inheritance money to maybe fund some survivalist activities," Spence added.

Diaz nodded and scanned the sheet Jessie handed him. "Possibly. Says he likes to take a lot of trips into the Ozarks. Several times a year, in fact."

"It could mean he likes to hunt. Or fish. Or maybe he goes camping," Jessie said.

"And it could mean he likes to hang out with his fellow survivalists," Diaz countered. "Keep your mind open to the possibilities, Jess. Don't give the bad guy an out."

She shifted to look up at him, her eyes so trusting it pained him. "So, guilty until proven innocent?"

"Something like that."

She shook her head. "Sorry, my mind doesn't work that way. We'll have to prove him guilty."

"You're not a lawyer. It's not your job to find him innocent. He's our suspect. We need to prove him dirty."

"I don't agree."

"And trying to protect some guy just because he was nice to you once could get you killed."

"I'm not trying to protect him. I'm keeping an open mind, that's all."

"Close it. It's safer."

She arched a brow. "I think you're just jealous."

Spence snorted. Diaz shot a glare in his direction, and Spence resumed careful study of the papers, but the smirk on his face lingered.

"Honey, for me to be jealous, I'd have to care. And since I'm not the one with my hand in your panties at the moment, I have nothing to care about. But I am team leader on this assignment. That means it's my responsibility to make sure no one on my team acts like a fool and fucks up this case."

Her smile died. She looked down, then back up again, her voice lowered. "I know what I'm doing, Diaz."

His face tightened with tension as his gaze penetrated hers. He really hated laying down the law to her, but it was better to do it now rather than later. She needed to know this wasn't fun and games. This was dead serious business.

"You'd better, or you'll be back here faster than a bullet travels, explaining to Grange why you screwed up your first—and last—assignment."

TWO

DAWN FILTERED ACROSS THE WILD RIDERS COMPOUND, CLOUD-less and blazing hot already. It was going to be a blistering day for a ride. There wasn't a leaf blowing in the windless morning, nothing rustling the trees sheltering the garage area behind the massive house where all the cars and bikes were stored. Jessie looked out the window, watching Grange and Diaz step out of the garage, stop for a brief conversation, then head toward the house.

Jessie hadn't slept at all last night, her mind occupied with the case and her annoyance with Diaz.

Damn, he got on her last nerve. In more ways than the obvious, too. He had absolutely no sense of humor, couldn't take teasing at all, and was dead serious about this case.

Not that she wasn't. She really was. But could Diaz lighten up at all? Spence could. Diaz? Apparently not. Did he think for one second that she wasn't going to take this assignment seriously? She'd been waiting years for this chance. Ever since she turned eighteen, she'd wanted the opportunity to work for the Wild Riders. Before that, actually, but Grange said no way until she was legal age. And then he'd forced her to attend the local college, telling her she needed some education along with training. Still, he'd never assigned her to a case, instead making her train at headquarters, day in and day out, working with the guys on weapons, ops, intel, computers, body conditioning and endurance, martial arts, and, of course, the bikes.

She loved the bikes, had always loved them the most. She'd been riding since she got her license at sixteen, and she was damn good at it.

Actually, she was good at everything she did. Even the guys said so. How come Diaz gave her no credit? He treated her like a brainless dimwit, a blond bimbo with big boobs. Just because a girl was pretty and had a great body didn't mean she was stupid.

That was going to stop today. She'd prove to him she could handle this case.

Her bags were packed. She was dressed and ready to go. She grabbed everything she'd need for this trip and went downstairs to meet Diaz and Spencer.

She found Diaz, Spencer, and Grange in the kitchen. Trying to act nonchalant even though her heart was pounding, she brushed past Diaz to grab a cup from the cupboard and slid it underneath the coffeepot, filling it halfway. She'd already been up for two hours and had drunk three cups. She was wired.

"Morning," Grange said. "You ready for this?"

She nodded while she sipped. "I've been ready for a long time."

"If at any time you feel like you can't handle it—any of it—you're welcome to drop this case. There'll be others."

She leaned against the counter, weary from having to say the same thing over and over again. Their protectiveness was wearing her patience thin. "I'll be fine."

"Ready to ride?" Diaz asked.

"Whenever you are." She was still touchy over his comments last night, but buried her feelings. Diaz was lead on this case. She didn't want to appear childish, especially in front of Grange. They were in work mode now. She had to put her personal issues aside and work with him.

"Let's go."

She grabbed her bag and followed Spence, Diaz, and Grange outside and into the garage. But when she went for her bike, it wasn't in its usual spot.

"Uh, where's my bike?"

Grange smiled. So did Spence.

"Diaz traded it in."

She whirled around to face Diaz. "You what?"

Diaz wore no expression on his face. "Your 883 was too small for a road trip. We'd be stopping every hundred miles for gas."

She almost broke down in tears. "Do you know how hard I worked to save money to buy that bike?" It wasn't brand-new, but it was hers. She'd picked it out herself. She loved that bike.

"I know. But you have to be realistic. This is for the job." He dug into his pocket and pulled out a set of keys. "It's over in Stall Four."

She blinked, then frowned. "What's in Stall Four?"

"Your new bike."

Still not understanding, all she could do was cock her head to the side and stare at Diaz. He finally had to grasp her by the shoulders and spin her around.

"Look, Jess."

She did. But she didn't believe what she saw. Her jaw gaped open. There, in Stall Four, was a bright, beautiful, brand-spankin'-new Harley 1200 Sportster, a bigger and more powerful bike than the one she'd had before.

"That's mine?"

"Yeah."

"It's blue." A beautiful pacific blue paint job. "And all that chrome."

"Yeah. Figured you'd like that."

She walked around the bike, gaping at all the features. The quick-release detachable windshield, the pillow-look touring seat—her butt was already saying "ahhh" at the sight of it. Air cleaner, pipes, cables, grips, handlebars, pegs—everything was upgraded from standard, all chromed out, gleaming and gorgeous.

"It's beautiful," she said, unable to keep the awe out of her voice.

Diaz came up next to her and her gaze shot up to his. He quickly turned away to look at the bike, but in that brief second she'd seen something in his eyes. Something hot.

"When did you do this?" she asked.

"Last night."

"How?"

"I have friends in all the right places. And you need a bigger bike if you're going to work cases. It would be inconvenient for us to pull over every couple of hours so you could fill the 883's gas tank."

That's not why he'd done this. She wanted to hug him. Kiss him. And so much more.

"Thank you, Diaz," she said, stepping between him and the bike, forcing him to look at her.

He shrugged, shoved his hands in the pocket of his pants. "No big deal. You ready to try it out?"

She grinned. "You know it."

Grange wrapped an arm around her shoulder. "Be careful."

She nodded. "I will."

She stowed her bag, climbed onto the bike, and fired it up, her entire body vibrating to the thrum of the engine. The immense power between her thighs never failed to turn her on. That Diaz had gifted her with this bike was more than she could fathom. Why had he done this? It wasn't that much of an inconvenience to gas up more frequently. Her 883 would have sufficed. But this new bike? It was heaven. She wasn't going to complain.

She'd find an appropriate way to thank him.

They took off, and she waved to Grange as they pulled down the long drive and through the gates. The Sportster had a lot of power behind it—much more than her smaller bike had. She had to rein in the urge to let the throttle out and see what this baby could really do. Especially while they were still within the confines of Dallas city limits. Instead, she followed Diaz, with Spence behind her, obeying the speed limit as they moved through the city. They took the highway the entire way, so no enjoying of scenery, just weaving in and out between cars and semis.

It didn't matter. Jessie had a new bike, the wind in her face, the hum of the engine surrounding her, and she got to watch Diaz's back in front of her, which gave her hours of uninterrupted time to ponder. And she had plenty to think about.

Like why he'd question her ability to handle this case one minute, and the next buy her a brand-new bike—one with some muscle behind it. If he had no confidence in her, why reward her with something like this beautiful machine?

And what was up with his sudden attention, when previously he hadn't seemed to care what she did, or even paid attention to her when she was around? It wasn't even like he was acting as a father figure—so not Diaz's style anyway. No, it was more than that. Something different, intriguing. Exciting. Yet he acted as if he was irritated with her.

The man made her crazy.

Diaz signaled for them to pull over at a combination gas station/restaurant, which was a good thing because Jessie was getting hungry. She climbed off her bike, leaned back to stretch her legs, and watched Diaz frown over her shoulder.

"What?"

"Nothing."

He wasn't looking at her, so she pivoted, saw two guys in a pickup leering and elbowing each other.

"What were they doing?"

"From what I could tell, checking out your ass."

She grinned. "Oh. Ignore them. I do."

"I don't." He started over to them, but Jessie stepped up, blocking his path.

"Are you serious? If you're going to take on every guy who looks at me, this is going to be a long trip. Let it go, Diaz."

"They're assholes and they have no business looking at you that way."

"Yes. But isn't that what guys do?"

"Not this guy."

She raised her brows. "Seriously. You've never given a girl with a nice ass a second look?"

He finally dragged his gaze away from the Neanderthals at the gas pump, and looked at her. "Not in the way they were checking you out."

She rolled her eyes. "Whatever. Come on. I'm hungry. Come protect me from the leering diner patrons."

Spence snorted and Diaz turned, shooting one last I-still-might-kill-you look at the two men before opening the door for Jessie.

Since it was about an hour and a half after the traditional lunch hour, the diner was practically empty. They slid into a booth at the corner of the restaurant. Jessie ordered coffee when the waitress stopped at their table to deliver menus. Diaz and Spence did the same.

"We've got about two hours before we arrive in Fayetteville," Diaz said. "Why don't you fill us in on what you know about the Devil's Skulls?"

Jessie nodded. "Not much, really. My old bike broke down on one of the back roads outside Shreveport while I was on an early morning ride. I was about ready to hoof it to the nearest gas station when I heard the thunder of bikes approaching, so I stayed put. There were about thirty of them, Crush in the lead and his best friend Rex riding next to him. They pulled off while the rest of his gang continued into the next town. Crush and Rex helped me fix the bike, then escorted me into town. I ate breakfast with their gang."

"Don't you carry your cell phone?" Spence asked.

She nodded. "It didn't work in that remote area. So I intended to start walking until I either reached a town or until my phone worked."

"You shouldn't ride by yourself, Jess. It's too dangerous."

"Yes, Daddy," she replied, finishing off by sticking her tongue out at Diaz.

Diaz frowned. "Don't call me that."

"Then stop treating me like a kid. It's pissing me off."

Spence laughed.

"Shut up, Spence," she said.

He held his hands up. "Can we help it if we still see you as the skinny little kid who first came to us?"

"I wasn't skinny."

"You were, too. And you had an attitude. Thought you knew everything about everything."

"Did not."

"Oh hell yes you did. You were our little diva with a chip on her shoulder. You didn't want to be there, didn't want to take classes and finish your education. You fought Grange every step of the way."

He was right. She did. God, had she ever had an attitude back then. She'd been so lost. Thank God for Mac and the rest of the Wild Riders. God only knows what would have happened to her. "I did a damn fine job stealing that car."

"Bullshit," Spence said. "You might as well have called the police before breaking the driver's side window. Mac said you made enough noise to wake the whole neighborhood. If he hadn't grabbed you and hightailed your ass out of there, you'd have done time in juvie."

"No, if he hadn't scared the shit out of me by coming up behind me and jerking me away, I'd have hot-wired that Chevy and hauled ass out of there before anyone found me."

Spence shook his head. "Brat. You'd have been toast."

She smirked. "I'd have been gone. With wheels under me."

"You'd have been caught at the next corner."

She paused, laughed. "You're probably right. I was so green." *So desperate.* "But look how much I've learned since then."

"Yeah. Now you're a great thief," Spence teased.

She snorted, turned to Diaz, who only frowned. He never did join in with the other guys' teasing her, even when she was just a kid. Always remote, always quiet. Oh, he was boisterous enough with the other guys, just not with her. Never with her. He kept his distance, muttered a few words now and then. She always thought he disliked her.

Now? She wasn't so sure.

"From our research into the Skulls, they have a rep as trouble-makers. Fights here and there, a bit of gun and knife activity during altercations, normal gang stuff," Diaz said, obviously changing the subject. "From the packet Grange gave us we know they're based out of Arkansas. So we start there as far as checking them out."

Spence nodded. "Notoriety is a big thing. But they must be pretty low profile because I haven't heard any bad news on them and I travel a lot in Arkansas."

"We ran into some other biker groups when I rode with them," Jessie said. "No altercations. Everyone kept their distance, but Crush and his gang didn't seem to be looking for trouble."

"And didn't start any with you," Spence noted.

"No, they didn't. They found me on a fairly deserted stretch of road, too, so if they'd wanted to mess with me, they could have."

Diaz heaved a heavy sigh. Jessie knew he was frustrated with her again, no doubt because he thought she took too many chances with her own safety. She supposed she should appreciate his con-cern, but she wished he was more confident in her abilities to take care of herself. She wasn't some sheltered rich girl who didn't know the ways of the world. She was streetwise, had grown up seeing and experiencing the worst. She knew what was up and how to avoid getting into dangerous situations. And if she somehow got into one, she knew how to get herself out.

"So maybe they were having an off day and decided to be nice," Diaz said, not sounding convinced. "Because the intel we have managed to get on the Skulls said they're brawlers, carry guns and knives, and spend a lot of time on the wrong side of the law."

"That could be PR and nothing more," Jessie argued. "You know how that goes with biker gangs. The same could be said of the Hells Angels, and they do more good things than bad. Sometimes the law spins things their way to make bikers look bad."

"True enough. But what we need to find out is if their gang is a front for a group of survivalists who are buying and stockpiling illegal arms. We know for sure there are illegal arms shipments coming into this area, and intelligence says the arms are connected to Crush's gang somehow. So let's meet up with them and see for ourselves what side of the law the Devil's Skulls are straddling."

She nodded. That made sense, though her interactions with the Devil's Skulls had only been positive. Crush and Rex had been good to her, had helped her out when she'd desperately needed it.

Though that didn't mean they weren't the bad guys, and it was important she remember that. She had to keep an open mind, not be too trusting or too wary.

Diaz had his way of doing things. She had hers. Perhaps the mission would benefit from the two different approaches. She supposed that remained to be seen.

They finished eating and got on their bikes again, heading up north the last couple of hours into Fayetteville. The rally was already underway. Over thirty thousand bikers were expected in for the weekend's festivities. The roads were crowded with motorcycles already and Jessie thrilled to be surrounded by her fellow bikers. Alone and on the streets at fifteen, starving and desperate, she'd never foreseen this kind of future for herself. Thanks to Mac and Grange and the Wild Riders, she had an exciting life ahead of her, and now she had her first assignment as a government agent.

Who would have thought that could happen, when she could have ended up dead, or in jail—or even worse, if she'd stayed at home with her mother?

It was too early to check in to the hotel rooms Grange had managed to wrangle on their behalf, so they hit the main drag first. Bikes lined both sides of the street, all parked in neat rows. Bikers walked along, watching other bikers ride up and down the road. People waved and checked out the custom bikes. It was like a circus or party atmosphere.

Jessie loved bike rallies, never missed an opportunity to come to one. She always met new people or caught up with old friends. This one would be even more exciting because she was working— on a case. She couldn't help the tiny shiver of excitement skittering down her spine. She felt like Bond, Jane Bond, secret agent girl.

At a stoplight, she pulled up alongside Diaz, with Spence on her other side.

"You're our eyes here," Diaz said to her. "Since you've met him, you'll be the primary lookout for Crush and his gang. Signal if you spot them."

She nodded and they took off when the light turned green, cruising through the town, blending in with everyone else as if they were just another couple of bikers checking out the action. Vendors here and there, lots to see and do, which was great, since no one paid any attention to them. They could get lost in a massive crowd like this, gawk as much as they wanted, and search for Crush.

By the time they had ridden for two hours, it was obvious Crush and the Skulls weren't there. They found a place to park at the top of the hill near the beer garden and went in for a cold drink.

"You sure you didn't spot him?" Spence asked.

Jessie shook her head. "They wear distinctive patches, and a lot of them have special jackets with their gang symbol on the back. Skulls with devil horns. You can't miss them."

"Rally starts today," Diaz said. "Maybe they aren't coming."

"He's coming," Jessie said, propping her feet up on the vacant chair at their table. "He asked me if I'd be here."

Diaz frowned. "When?"

"That day he rescued my bike. We stopped and ate together, re-member? I told him I was on my way back home after a bike rally, and he told me about this one in Fayetteville because it was near where he lived. He gave me the details on location, what went down around here, and what time of year it was, then asked if I'd come. I told him I would. So I assumed his gang would be here, es-pecially since this is Devil's Skulls territory. Trust me, he'll be here."

"He'd better, or this will be one short assignment."

"We could always head into the hills and look for them," Spence suggested.

Diaz nodded. "We'll do that if we have to, but I think Jessie meeting up with him should look more like chance than design."

They sat at the beer tent for a while and nursed a few beers, listened to the band, and watched bikes cruise down the main drag. Jessie focused on keeping watch for Crush or anyone else wearing the Devil's Skulls insignia.

After a couple of hours they'd seen nothing, and it was getting late. They got up and did a bit of walking, venturing into the main activity area, into the buildings and tents, hoping to find Crush there. He wasn't.

"Let's go," Diaz said. "We'll grab our bikes and take another ride around and see if we can spot them. Maybe they're all parked somewhere else."

They looked everywhere, then swung back around and rode the main streets again, but finally Diaz called it quits and they headed to the hotel where they'd made reservations and checked in. As they walked down the hallway toward their rooms, Jessie's stomach gnawed with disappointment.

Her first day of her first assignment and absolutely nothing had happened.

She reached her door and turned to the two of them. "You want to get something to eat?"

Spence shook his head. "I'm going to stow my stuff, then head back to one of the bars on the main drag and keep watch for any of the Skulls."

"I'm going to do some research into their gang, so I'll stay here," Diaz said. "Jess, you can go with him if you want."

Research? What kind of research was Diaz going to do in his room?

"I'm tired. I think I'll just hang here," she said.

Spence nodded and moved down the hall to his room while Diaz unlocked the door across the hall from hers.

Jessie went into her room and closed the door, quickly unpacking her things. She sat on the bed, staring out the window. Pent-up anxiety kept her from relaxing.

It was early. She had nothing to do. She needed some action.

Research. That's what she needed to do, find out what kind of research Diaz was doing. She picked up the phone, called down to the hotel restaurant and ordered two sandwiches, then took a quick shower and changed clothes.

Thirty minutes later she stood in front of Diaz's door with a bag of sandwiches and sodas. She raised her hand to knock, then paused.

What if he had a girlfriend in this town and he'd just made up the research excuse so he could be alone with her?

No. That was stupid. Why would he lie? Because they were supposed to be working and he was goofing off instead? What difference would that make? If Diaz wanted to get laid, he'd just say so. Wouldn't he?

Her stomach panged at the thought. Had to be hunger. What right did she have to be jealous? She had no claim on Diaz. They didn't even have a relationship. They had . . . nothing.

He was definitely researching. But what? And how?

She meant to find out. Besides, she'd brought him dinner, a legitimate excuse for knocking on his door.

Oh, quit debating and knock, dumbass.

She rapped three times, hoping like hell some half-naked woman didn't answer. Her instincts were usually right. Diaz would be working, not screwing some biker babe.

She'd hate for this to be the first time she was wrong about something.

THREE

DIAZ CURSED WHEN HE HEARD THE KNOCK AT THE DOOR. HE pushed back from the too-small desk, cursed again when he bumped his leg, and hobbled to the door, mentally letting loose another string of obscenities when he saw who it was through the peephole.

Jessie.

He unlocked the dead bolt and pulled the door open.

"What?"

She arched a brow. "Wow, you're grumpy. Do you need a nap?"

"No. Just some solitude."

"Too bad." She slid her way past, carrying a bag and two cans of soda, which she put on the nightstand next to his bed. "I brought dinner, figuring you wouldn't order anything since you had some sort of *research* to do."

She kicked off her sandals and climbed onto his bed, pulling one of the pillows out from the bedspread and tucking it behind her back. "Hope you like turkey."

"What are you doing here?"

"Weren't you listening? I brought dinner." She opened the bag and laid two sandwiches on the nightstand, then popped open the top of one of the soda cans. "I'll take care of setting things up, so, don't let me disturb you."

Too late. One look at her and he was distracted. One whiff of her as she passed by, her breasts brushing his chest, and he was definitely disturbed. Deeply, profoundly disturbed. She smelled like sunshine, outdoors, and Jessie. He wanted to lick her neck.

How the hell was he supposed to work with her in the room?

"Are you hungry yet?" she asked.

Yeah, he was hungry all right. But not for a turkey sandwich. "No."

"Is that a laptop?"

He took the chair and resumed his spot at the desk again. "Master of the obvious, aren't you."

"Smartass. I didn't know you brought one. What are you doing?"

"I told you. Research."

She slid off the bed and came up behind him. He tried not to breathe her in, but he couldn't avoid it. The scent of her was right there, as was her body as she leaned over him.

"The Devil's Skulls have a website?"

"Yeah," he managed, though he wasn't concentrating on the screen anymore. "Most of the prominent groups have their own websites so they can show off pictures, list their activities and where they're going to be. I figured if the Skulls were big enough, they would, too."

"Show me."

He flipped through the pages of the website, showing her pictures of bike rallies and fund-raisers, lists of their officers and members, some of the charities they gave to.

"Do they have a calendar of events?"

"Yeah." He clicked on it. "It brings up the current month as well as future months and what's happening."

"It says they're going to be at the rally."

"Yup."

"Hmm. Wonder why they weren't there today?"

"No clue."

She laid her hand on his shoulder, leaned farther in, her breasts pillowed against his back. For the love of God, the government could use her as a torture device. She could break a man in less than ten minutes by rubbing her breasts across his back. His balls were already twisting up in a knot.

Diaz always prided himself on his self-discipline. Torture him? Fine. He could handle it. He had a high threshold for pain, could tune it out and focus inward on something else. There wasn't much that could faze him once he decided to power his concentration on the task at hand.

He tried that now, focusing his attention on the computer screen, trying to cull as much information as he could about the Skulls so they could come into the group well informed.

It wasn't working. Jessie was devastating to his senses, and the information on the laptop was a total blur.

"Well, this is surprising," she whispered, her breath warm against his neck.

"What is?" He hoped he hadn't missed critical information. How would he explain something right in front of him? *I'm sorry but your breasts distracted me?*

"You. A laptop. I never took you for an Internet geek. You're always outside, riding, or working on the bikes. You never spend time in the tech room."

"You know very little about me, Jessie."

She pulled away, much to his relief. Now he could exhale.

"Well, fill me in. I'm dying to know." She flounced on his bed and grabbed her sandwich. "Tell me all about yourself while I eat."

He half turned in his chair. Was she joking? "What is it that you think I'm going to tell you?"

She shrugged. "Oh, I don't know. Since you're a complete mystery to me, how about everything?"

Giving up, he grabbed the turkey sandwich and took a bite, chewing thoughtfully. What could he say that would get rid of her? "I was born. I grew up. I screwed up. You know the drill. I came to the Wild Riders in the same way the rest of the guys did. You've been around me for years. You know who I am and what I do. End of story."

"Oh, come on. Out of all the guys I know the least about you. Why is that?"

"Because there's nothing to tell." Nothing he'd want her to know about, anyway.

"I don't believe that. Everyone's told their story about who they were before Grange dragged them into Wild Riders, what kind of trouble they were in. I never heard yours, though."

He shrugged. "It's not that eventful."

"So are you going to tell me, or am I going to have to fantasize and make up my own horrible stories about you knocking off a couple of banks, terrorizing small towns, on the run from the Feds . . ."

Anything to shut her up. Even the truth. "I was seventeen. I liked to hijack money out of ATMs and use stolen cars to get away."

She raised both brows and lifted her lips. "Really. So I was accurate about knocking off banks. You stud."

He shook his head at her teasing remark. "Some of the ATM machine and bank cameras showed vehicles and license plates, so I typically stole a car before I broke into an ATM."

She nodded. "Rather industrious of you. Where did you lift the ATM cards?"

"Pickpocket. Easy to grab a wallet or purse on a busy street. Business people talking or a woman distracted while shopping. And then the cars were easy to grab. I went for older model vehicles—usually beat-up, left unlocked, and a no-brainer to hot-wire. Since I used them once and abandoned them, I didn't need them to be in top condition."

"How did you bypass PIN numbers?"

"I know computer stuff."

Her brows lifted. "I'm intrigued."

She really had no idea. "I picked up things here and there. I didn't just steal cars."

"So, you had it made, did you?"

"I thought so. Until I got caught and tossed in jail. No money, public defender who couldn't give a rat's ass about me or whether I ended up in prison for life or not. When Grange showed up and offered the deal, I would have sold my soul to take it."

"You were grateful for the second chance."

"Eventually, sure. But not at first. You know how it is. You were the same way. At that age you think you're hot stuff, that no adult is going to save you from yourself. All you want is out, so you can get back on the street, be independent, and do things your way."

Jessie nodded with a smile. "I remember. Grange had other ideas, though. Didn't take any crap from us."

"No, he didn't. Worked me hard from the first day and never

let up. Told me it was either his way, or prison. For the first few months I wondered if prison wasn't the easier way to go."

Jessie laughed. "I know. He didn't cut me any slack because I was a girl, either. Made me study, eat well, exercise, lights out early, no phone, no friends . . . all these damn rules. And here I thought I had slipped away from school. It was worse being under his care."

"Yeah. School first, then all the physical workouts, plus shop—learning more about cars and bikes than I had ever known before. Stripping them down to the chassis and building them back up again. I learned a lot." At first he'd hated every second of being flattened under Grange's thumb, but then he started to respect General Lee. The man ruled with an iron fist, took no shit from the smartassed kids he'd taken under his wing. Eventually, Diaz came to appreciate three meals a day, no abuse, and being taught that if you wanted to be respected, you had to earn it and show respect in turn. He'd learned how to be a man from Grange Lee, something his own father had never taught him.

"I'd fall into bed at night—nine p.m., no less—completely exhausted," Jessie said.

"He'd drag us out of bed at dawn. No wonder we had no problem going to bed at nine." Diaz hadn't gone to bed that early since he was five years old. But working under Grange's laws made it easy.

"I had family," Jessie said. "A hard taskmaster for a father figure, but for the first time in my life, I finally had a family who cared about me. A father, and brothers who looked after me."

Brothers. There it was. That chasm he couldn't cross.

"Yeah. Family is good." He finished his sandwich, crumpled up the napkin and tossed it in the trash, then turned back to the laptop, hoping Jessie would get the hint and leave his room.

She didn't say anything for a few minutes, but then he heard her move behind him, her breasts once again pressed against his back as she studied the laptop screen. He sucked in a quick breath, heat surging through his veins.

Christ. Just being near her sent his nervous system haywire. And she thought of him as a brother. He was such a fucking pervert. He had to get her out of his room.

"I think I can finish this up now." He shut the lid on the laptop and pushed the chair back, forcing her to move away from him.

Jessie backed up a couple of steps, a confused frown on her face. "That's it? You're done with your research?"

"Yeah." He moved to the door, hoping she'd follow.

She didn't.

"Diaz."

He hovered near the door. *Come on, Jess. Get the hint.*

"What?"

She walked toward him. He watched the way she moved. So graceful, so slow, so seductive. She stopped in front of him, tilting her head back to look him in the eyes. Her lips were parted a fraction of an inch, revealing just the tip of her tongue as she studied him.

He was beginning to sweat. His cock twitched. His heart pounded.

Fuck. He wasn't seventeen. He was thirty-one goddamn years old, too old to let a young woman affect him this way.

She inched closer, so close that the tips of her breasts nearly brushed his shirt. His knees almost buckled.

"Why are you so afraid of me?"

He tilted his chin down and stared at her. "What?"

"You're afraid of me. It's obvious. You've been avoiding me for years. You never talk to me. I enter a room, you leave. I try to talk to you, and you mumble a few unintelligible phrases, but otherwise, you won't engage and then you make up some excuse to get away from me."

"That's not true."

"It is, too." Her gaze swept his body, from his feet to the top of his head. "Now you're, what? Six-two or so?"

"Six-four."

"Fine then. I'm five-six, so you're almost a foot taller than me. And you have to outweigh me by over a hundred pounds, if not more, so I don't think my mere presence scares the shit out of you."

Darlin', you have no idea.

"I just can't figure out what it is about me that makes you keep your distance."

"You don't scare me, Jessie."

"Yeah, I do."

She moved in on him, and he backed up a step.

"Otherwise, you wouldn't be backing away from me. So, see, I'm right. You *are* scared of me."

"I'm not afraid of anything, or anyone."

A small smile teased the corners of her mouth. "That kind of false bravado could get a guy killed in our line of work. Everyone is afraid of something. With me, it's cliffs—looking over one and that fear of falling. Gives me a vicious case of vertigo. Oh, and I hate spiders in a major way. A girlie thing, I know, but I can't help it. And I'm really not too keen about sleeping alone in the dark. I like a light on. So what about you? What scares you?"

"I told you. Nothing."

He flattened his back against the door, but Jessie kept coming, pressing her palms against his chest and leveling him with a teasing grin. "Nothing except me. Big, bad Jessie scares you."

She was playing a game. He wasn't. "Stop."

She did. She had to—there was nowhere else to go unless she climbed up on him. He smothered a groan at the visual that presented. Naked, her full breasts pressed against his chest. Her legs wrapped around him, his hands filled with her sweet ass as she bounced up and down on his cock. Her pussy would be wet, tight, gripping and squeezing him until he shot loads of come inside her.

Shit. "Get out of here, Jess."

"Why?"

He inhaled. Big mistake. The scent of her filled the air around him. Intoxicating, sensual. He went hard in an instant.

"Because you're playing with fire, little girl."

Her eyes went smoky. "I'm not a little girl. And I like a little heat, Diaz."

Invitation was written all over her face, her body. *Tempting.* Oh, so tempting.

But that's not what they were here for. And this was Jessie, not some random woman to fuck. It was Jessie. He had no right. She belonged to all of them, all the Wild Riders. All the guys who counted on him to take care of her. Because they all loved her.

Like a sister.

He grasped her by the shoulders, taking in and memorizing the small surprised gasp she made. He wanted to put his lips on hers, to swallow her gasp, to slide his tongue inside her mouth and taste her.

God, he wanted that bad.

He pushed her back the few inches it took to open the door and set her on the other side of it.

"Go to your room, Jess."

He shut the door in her face, not hearing as she opened her mouth to speak. He threw the dead bolt, feeling like a coward, which he was. He turned around and leaned his back against the door, blowing out a breath.

Not afraid? Yeah, right. Jessie had called it right. She scared the shit out of him.

It took him a few minutes to regain the ability to breathe normally.

One woman. One small woman, and she sent his entire nervous system haywire. He should be able to handle her, to ignore her. But he couldn't, because one look at her, one whiff of her unique scent and he was like a freakin' bloodhound, salivating and on the hunt. How was he going to do this assignment, be an effective leader, with Jessie underfoot? How was he going to remain immune?

He dragged both hands through his hair, pushing off from the door to pace the small confines of his room.

Priorities. Taking down the gunrunners was his objective. He'd have to compartmentalize Jessie to that place in his mind where she didn't exist. Or jack off a lot while he was alone, to ease the stress of having her near. His cock twitched, aching for touch, but it wasn't his hands it wanted. It was Jessie's. Her hands, her mouth, her pussy.

Tough. His dick was just going to have to suffer, because he wasn't going to fuck her. Even though it seemed she'd wanted that tonight. She'd put one hell of a move on him. Any other guy would have taken what she'd so obviously offered.

She was playing a dangerous game with him. But Jessie was a kid. She didn't know what she wanted. It was going to be up to Diaz to show restraint.

He groaned. This assignment was going to be like a long ride into hell.

FOUR

Jessie paced her room, staring at the clock, waiting for the appropriate time to meet up with Diaz and Spence. The roaring sounds of bikers zipping up and down the street woke her early, though she hadn't managed much sleep anyway. Her thoughts had been occupied with Diaz most of the night. She'd tossed and turned, her body on fire from being close to him.

Close, but not close enough.

Diaz was a man. All man. Loaded with testosterone. She'd all but impaled herself on him, and what had he done? Tossed her out the door, politely but firmly, and sent her to her room.

Her cheeks flamed in embarrassment at the memory of being rejected.

Maybe she just didn't turn him on.

No, that wasn't it. She'd gotten a look between his legs, at the hard ridge of his erection so prominently outlined against his jeans. She shuddered at the thought of his hard cock riding between her legs, stroking the flame that burned incessantly inside her. She'd made no secret of her desire for him last night, so why hadn't he taken what she offered? Why had he held back, pushed her away?

Jessie was determined to find out. She never had been one to give up easily.

She turned at the knock at her door and opened it to find Spence leaning against the doorjamb.

"Diaz says we ride. You ready?"

She grinned. "Always."

They rode into the main part of town and found a cozy little restaurant overlooking the main drag to eat breakfast. There, they could watch all the bikers ride up and down the street. Perfect venue to catch a glimpse of Crush and his gang in case they rode by.

"See anything last night?" Diaz asked Spence.

"Yeah. Bikes. Lots of them. And chicks. Lots of those, too. But no Devil's Skulls and no Crush Daniels."

Jessie smiled and scooped up another forkful of scrambled eggs.

Diaz frowned, which seemed to be his favorite expression. "Let's hope we haven't wasted our time coming here."

"We haven't. He'll be here," Jessie said.

"How do you know?" Diaz countered.

"Because he told me he'd be here, and because it said so on the Skulls' website last night."

"Y'all were on the Internet?" Spence asked.

"Yeah. Diaz brought his laptop."

"Geek," Spence said before lifting his coffee cup to his lips for a long swallow.

"Someone has to do the research around here."

"Yeah, but someone who looks like you should be kicking ass, not burying your head in a computer."

"I can kick ass, too. Want me to show you?"

Jessie shook her head. She was used to this constant bickering among all the guys. It was typically more a show of bravado and teasing than anger at each other, though she'd seen some rousing displays of machismo in the boxing ring at the Wild Riders' work-out room, one of her favorite pastimes. Nothing like bare-chested, sweaty men going at it, with straining muscles and oozing testos-terone while they worked on their skills. *Yumm*. She might think of most of these guys as family, but the fact of the matter was, none of them were blood relatives and she didn't at all mind ogling their fine bodies.

In fact, she made sure to be in the gym when Diaz was working out with the guys. Seeing his body straining with effort as he lifted weights or boxed, his face and torso dripping with sweat, the lines of concentration on his face as he worked hard to master whatever skill he targeted . . . it was droolworthy. She'd go in the gym on the pretense of using the weight equipment, run on the treadmill or go a few rounds punching the speed bag, but her gaze would in-evitably shift to Diaz, to admire the bunching of his muscles in the ring as he and Spence went a few rounds, wishing it was Diaz and her in the ring alone . . . playing together.

The guys would often box with her, though not seriously since any one of them could knock her flat. But it was good practice for her footwork, stamina, and learning to duck a punch and give one back. These guys were tough and they'd taught her how to be even tougher than she'd been on the street. Unfortunately, Diaz never offered to work out with her. As was typical, he avoided her.

She was determined to figure out why.

Her breakfast finished, she sipped her coffee and gazed out the window. That's when she caught sight of the white skull with the red devil eyes on the T-shirt of a biker zooming by. She sat up straighter, focused, and watched as a few more rode by the restaurant.

"They're here," she said, keeping her voice low, not tearing her gaze away from the window.

"Where?" Diaz asked.

"A few just rode by."

"Did you see Crush?"

"Not yet."

"Let's go."

They paid the bill and hopped on their bikes, joining in with the throng of bikers cruising up and down the main street. Riding the main drag was a chance to see and be seen, to show off your bike and look for friends.

"Be casual," Diaz said at a red light. "If you spot Crush, just let us know but don't be too obvious."

She nodded. That was her plan, to make sure Crush saw her, to make him come to her.

Bikes rode in both directions, and Jessie watched. The Devil's Skulls were a big group, and she started seeing a lot of jackets, vests, and T-shirts with the Skulls' insignia. It didn't take long to find Crush leading a pack of riders. She played oblivious, but then as they rode the strip, he spotted her, waved, turned his bike around, and rode up next to her, motioning her to pull over onto a side street. She followed, as did Diaz, Spence, and a few of Crush's people. She acted surprised to see him.

"Hey. Didn't think you and your gang were coming," she said, straddling her bike.

Crush was a really good-looking guy, not the kind of man you'd think would lead a rough gang of bikers. Inky black hair cut short and spiky, and his face was gorgeous, with sharp-angled cheekbones, full lips, and the most beautiful storm gray eyes she'd ever seen. His body was lean, his clothes always clean . . . he just didn't fit the profile of some backwoods survivalist. But what did she know? She was the novice here.

"We had some other stuff to do yesterday so we rode over early this morning. Did we miss much?"

"Not really. Quite a few bikers came in yesterday, but it was quiet last night. Looks like a lot more are wandering in this morning."

Jessie wondered what that other "stuff" was that they'd been doing, and if it had anything to do with illegal arms. She decided to reserve judgment. She flipped her thumb behind her at Diaz and Spence and introduced them to Crush.

Crush arched a brow. "Are these two your lovers?"

She choked back a laugh at the thought of having two men. Hell, she'd be happy to have one. Instead, she flashed Crush a grin. "Maybe."

"Are you part of a gang?"

"No," Diaz said. "We travel alone."

"The three of you ride together a lot?"

Diaz nodded, then said, "But we're thinking of hooking up with a bike group. We do a lot of riding together, like to travel. We like the Ozarks area, so maybe we'll join up with a gang around here, settle in this area."

Crush studied Diaz and Spence. "Lots of undesirables around here. You need to be careful about riding alone. If you want to keep your woman safe, you should join a gang. There's safety in numbers."

"I think we can take care of Jessie just fine on our own," Diaz said.

Spence nodded at Diaz, but his smile was directed at Jessie. "I think Jessie can take care of herself."

Jessie grinned at Spence's compliment, and wondered what the hell Diaz was doing. Weren't they supposed to play into Crush's hands? Then again, she supposed it would be a sign of weakness to indicate they couldn't take care of themselves, or each other, alone.

She had a lot to learn.

"I'm sure y'all do a fine job looking out for each other. Still, I grew up around here and trust me, it's not safe to travel some areas with just a few of you."

"Is that an invitation to join the Devil's Skulls?" Diaz asked.

"Maybe," Crush said, his lips lifting in a lazy smile. "But in order to join with us—that is, if I invite you—you'd have to handle initiation. And that's not easy. Think you've got the balls for it?"

"Hell yeah," Spence said.

Diaz didn't even smile. "We can handle it."

"And what about Jessie?" Crush asked, this time not looking at her but addressing the question to Diaz. "Can she deal with it?"

Wasn't that just so typical? "I can speak for myself, and I can handle anything you dish out, Crush."

Crush's gaze drifted her way, and he nodded, his lips lifting. "I'll just bet you can."

He was challenging her, teasing her. After spending most of her formative years with a group of tough, streetwise guys, she wasn't a bit fazed by Crush Daniels. She grinned at Crush. Diaz, however, looked ready to hop off his bike and strangle Crush.

Interesting. She'd almost think he was jealous if she didn't know him so well.

"You can ride with us for the next few days. Get to know us, and we'll get to know you. Then we'll decide if you've got the stuff. When the weekend is over, we'll let you know if we want you to go through initiation."

Diaz nodded. "Sounds fine."

Crush looked over at Jessie. "New bike, huh?"

"Yes."

"Fits you perfectly. You picked a good one."

Warmth filled her. Diaz chose a good one—one that fit her. But she didn't tell Crush that.

Crush fired up his bike. "Let's ride."

They followed, mixing with his gang, who seemed to come out of nowhere and grow in numbers as they entered the main drag. By the time they exited the general area of the bike rally, the Devil's Skulls had swelled to over fifty members. Diaz, Spence, and Jessie stayed near the front, riding close to Crush and a few other people. He led them out of the city, heading northeast and off the main highways.

It was a beautiful ride, and a perfect day for letting the breeze blow against your skin. This was Jessie's favorite part of being a biker—being around other bikers who loved riding as much as she did—and the freedom of the open road. It wasn't just being able to see the trees zipping along the roadside, bending toward you as if in greeting. It was being able to smell them—the tangy scent of pine as you breezed by, the musky smell of earth, and whenever they had a chance to idle or stop, to listen to the sound of rushing water from the nearby rivers. It was nature in all its glory, and if you rode in a car you'd miss it all. There was nothing like being a biker. She loved this part of her life.

Crush took the back roads into the hills—winding, curving roads where you could really test yourself in the turns. They stopped at a gas station along the road and took a break. One of the Skulls girls came up to Spence and started talking to him and Jessie grinned, shaking her head. Spence was a girl magnet. If there was an unattached female around, she gravitated to Spencer. Of course with his height, killer body, and good looks, it was no surprise women flocked to him like a gaggle of geese. He was a master at charming the ladies.

"Glad we managed to hook up."

Jessie spun around to face Crush. "Oh. Me, too. I was afraid I wasn't going to see you."

"Told you I'd be here, didn't I?"

"Yes, you did. But sometimes things come up."

He grinned. "I'm never that busy."

"So what do you do for a living, Crush?" Even though she already knew his background from the intel they got, she wanted to hear it from him.

"This and that. Mostly mechanical stuff. My brother and I own a garage, so we work on cars and things."

"Really. And that gives you a lot of free time for riding?"

"Plenty. He's the hard worker."

"And you're just the investor?" she teased, hoping he'd reveal something about his financial situation.

Crush laughed. "I work when I want to. But my brother likes to stay put. I'm more of a wanderer. So I pour a lot of my share of the profits back into the shop, and he's content to do the labor."

"While you ride."

"Exactly."

"Sounds like a perfect life, as long as you can afford it."

"What about you, Jessie? Can you afford to ride when you want?"

She shrugged. "I make do. Pick up jobs here and there. I don't have much trouble making ends meet."

He looked her up and down. "I'll just bet you don't."

She felt Diaz's presence behind her.

"What's up?" he asked.

"Just talking," Crush said.

"We're discussing how we manage to have free time to ride," Jessie offered, then told Diaz about Crush's ownership of a garage with his brother. She hoped Diaz would grab a clue that she was fishing for information.

"Ah. Nice gig."

"What about you, Diaz? What do you do?" Crush asked.

"I'm independently wealthy. I don't need to work."

Crush arched a brow, studied Diaz for a minute, then tilted his head back and laughed. "That's a good one."

He'd been purposely vague. Crush probably appreciated it. And if Crush was, in fact, involved with the survivalists hiding out in these hills, that would be a perfect answer to give. Diaz had played it well.

They rode east for half the day, stopped at a burger joint to eat, then rode back. By then it was past nightfall and they enjoyed the festivities put on by the bike rally sponsors. It was well beyond midnight by the time Jessie, Spence, and Diaz escaped from Crush and his gang, with the promise they'd meet up in the morning and ride again.

When they got back to the hotel and parked their bikes, Spence said, "Look. There's a girl who's pretty tight with the upper echelon of Crush's gang. She used to be the girlfriend of Rex, who's Crush's second in command or something. Anyway, she's put her eye on me, so I'm going to follow up on that."

"For business or for pleasure?" Diaz teased.

Spence flashed a wide grin. "A little of both, probably."

Jessie laughed. "More pleasure with you, isn't it, Spence?"

"Hey, there are always perks to the job, babe," he answered with a wink. "But the word is that Crush and the others think the two of you are a couple."

"Why?" Diaz shot out.

Spence shrugged. "No idea, but that's the way it's going down. So you should play it out that way. And anyway, it's protection for Jessie so she isn't alone."

Oh, she'd love to hear Diaz's answer on that one. Now he was on the spot. He couldn't very well back away from it.

"Sounds like a good idea to me," she said.

Diaz frowned. "I guess."

"We should share a room, then. Couples don't have separate rooms. I'll check out of mine while you notify the front desk we'll be bunking up together."

Before Diaz could object, she said good night to Spence, who said he was going to ride back to the main street and hook up with Stephanie. Then she went up to her room to pack. By the time she opened the door to her room, Diaz was standing there.

"What?" she asked. "I was just coming over."

"I changed rooms."

She cocked her head to the side. "Why?"

"My room only had one bed."

"So?"

He rolled his eyes and grabbed her bag. "Come on."

When he opened the door to the new room, she smothered her laugh.

Two double beds. She tossed her bag on one of the beds and turned to him.

"What's the matter, Diaz? Don't trust yourself to sleep in the same bed with me?"

He stalked over to her, one slow step at a time while she admired the way he moved. When he stopped, he was mere inches away.

"Jessie, if I was in the same bed with you, there'd be very little sleeping going on."

Oh. My. God. There it was, exactly what she'd wanted to hear. Her heart slammed against her chest and her entire body went liquid. She couldn't catch her breath, and she was pretty certain her toes curled. And didn't it just figure, he'd tossed out the perfect line and she couldn't find her voice for a comeback.

"Oh."

That was it? That was all she could manage?

His eyes, so dark and sexy and giving her that look . . . *that look . . .* spoke volumes. But then he backed up a few steps and turned around, breaking the sensual spell he'd wound around her.

She finally exhaled.

Well, that seemed like a good start. But he'd stopped, and that wasn't good. Time to step things up a bit. She unpacked and grabbed a couple of things. "I'm going to take a shower."

From the look on Diaz's face one would think she said she was about to perform brain surgery on herself in the bathroom. He looked a little green. She closed the door to the bathroom, undressed, and turned the water on, taking her time washing up, hoping Diaz was out there thinking about what she was doing in here.

She even hummed a tune, making sure he could hear her, that she had his attention and he wouldn't forget about her and where she was. She finished her shower, dried off and dressed, then grabbed the lotion bottle and stepped out of the bathroom.

Diaz was at the desk, his back turned to her. She moved to the bed, came around to the side closest to him, and sat, setting the lotion on the table. She poured some lotion onto her hands and spread it over her legs.

It didn't take long. Diaz lifted his head, inhaled, and took a slow glance over his shoulder, almost as if he was afraid what he might see.

His brows knit in a tight frown.

"What are you doing?" he asked, his tone more accusatory than curious.

She paused. "Um, putting on lotion?"

His gaze narrowed further. "Why?"

"Because my skin will get dry if I don't."

She had to fight hard not to burst out laughing as he stared her down like she was an international spy and lying through her teeth.

"Couldn't you put some clothes on? Geez, Jessie."

She looked down at her terry cloth shorts and tank top. "What? This is what I sleep in."

"Nearly everything is showing."

"Really?" She looked down. She was covered. Granted, not by much, but that was the intent. "I can't see anything."

"Those shorts are so high up on your legs they damn near show a road map of the Promised Land. And that top hardly covers your . . . your . . ."

"Breasts?" she finished for him, biting the inside of her cheek to smother a laugh.

"Yes. Those. Hell, Jess, you might as well sleep naked," he said, turning around and facing his laptop once again.

"I usually do," she said to his back.

His fingers stilled on the laptop keys.

Gotcha.

She refused to be ignored. They were sharing a room—this was her chance. He was going to notice her, even if she *did* have to parade around naked. Hopefully, it wouldn't come to that, though if he continued to avoid her like she was poison, she might have to resort to drastic measures. Because if initiation into the Devil's Skulls meant what she thought it did, then she was going to need a favor from Diaz.

A huge, intimate favor. One she'd never ask of anyone else, because she wanted Diaz to do the honors.

She stood, bent over the bed, and propped one foot on the mattress, pouring more lotion onto her hands, her butt pointed in Diaz's direction. A few seconds later she heard him breathing. Heavily. Then he pushed back from the desk and walked by her, grabbing his jacket.

"Where are you going?"

"Out."

"Hang on a second and I'll get dressed." She hurried to the closet by the front door, blocking his exit, which didn't seem to make him too happy. He slung the jacket over his shoulder.

"I'm going out alone, Jess."

She slid the closet door closed and looked up at him. "Why?"

"Because I need some space."

"That's not what we're supposed to be doing. We need to be seen together. We're supposed to be a couple."

"Even couples take breaks from each other. We're not glued together."

"Agreed, but we haven't established ourselves as a couple yet. So why don't you give me a second to change clothes and I'll go with you."

"No."

That sounded rather final, and pretty much like an order. Jessie bristled as Diaz tried to push by her. She backed up against the door and crossed her arms.

"Move," he said.

"I don't think so. Not until you tell me what bug crawled up your ass tonight."

"Not in the mood for this, Jess. Now get out of my way."

"This is stupid. Talk to me, Diaz. Let me go with you. Let's do our job together."

"This isn't about the job."

"Then what is it about?"

"It's about . . . just move or I'll move you. I need out."

It was about her. "Then move me."

"Goddammit Jessie." Though he'd almost whispered the words, he slammed his hands up against the door, placing them on either side of her shoulders, pinning her there between the door and his huge body.

Tension, thick and hot, coiled around her middle. Her belly did flip-flops, her clit trembling at being so near to him. She swallowed, her throat gone dry as her entire body became aware of him, his scent, the need to reach out and touch him. Every nerve ending tingled.

She wanted this, wanted him to lean in and take her. Couldn't he see that, couldn't he read the signals?

Do it, Diaz. Take what you want. Because she damn well knew he wanted her, that he was fighting it. She could feel it in the coiled-up muscles bunching against his T-shirt, the way he shifted, leaning in just a fraction of an inch closer to her. She tilted her head back, her gaze meeting his head-on.

I want you. Oh, God, why couldn't she just say it? But she couldn't make her mouth work, couldn't make the words spill from her lips. She knew why—because she wanted *him* to do it, needed him to make that first move.

The first glide of his hands along her upper arms made her tremble with excitement.

Followed by the crush of disappointment as he pulled her out of the way, opened the door, and closed it behind him.

She stared at that door for a few long minutes, stunned that he'd just walked out on her. On them. On what could have been.

For the second time, they'd been *this* close, and he'd slammed the door in her face.

What the hell was wrong with that man?

DIAZ RODE HIS BIKE LIKE DEMONS FROM THE BOWELS OF HELL were after him.

Maybe they were.

He'd caught up and rode with a few other bikers, then found a deserted stretch of road, let the throttle out, and just flew, trying to clear his head. He rode for over an hour, then turned around and headed back, pulling over when he arrived back in town. He found a bar and parked his bike, located a nice dark corner, and ordered a beer, content with the loud music and no one bothering him.

Though that wasn't true. He was bothered, all right.

When he'd closed the door on Jessie earlier he'd been shaking. Shaking! A man like him wasn't supposed to fall apart just because some sweet young thing shook her ass at him. Where was his god-damn self-control?

Nowhere to be found, apparently, whenever Jess was around.

Parading around half naked, teasing him like that. Did she do that with all the guys she met?

Don't. Go. There. He didn't want to think about Jessie and other guys, didn't want to know what she'd done with any other man. His mind conjured up plenty of things he'd like to do with her. He didn't need any other visuals. Walking around with a perpetual hard-on was torture. He was going to have to figure out a way to survive this mission.

To survive Jessie.

Tonight he'd come close to taking her, to stripping off her skimpy excuse for clothing and licking every inch of her skin, starting at her toes and ending with her sweet, sassy little mouth.

God, the things he'd like to do with her mouth.

His cock twitched. He groaned and took another long pull from the bottle of beer, hoping the icy drink would cool his libido before he had to head back to the hotel.

And sleep in the same room with her.

Where he'd hear her, shifting underneath her covers, where he could smell her, see her, be almost close enough to touch her. He really wanted to touch her. He wanted to do a hell of a lot more than touch her.

He wanted to fuck her.

And no way was he going to do that. Tomorrow, he and Jessie were going to have a talk, set some things straight. He didn't know what kind of game she was playing with him, but it was going to stop.

They were on a mission, and there was no fucking on a mission. At least not each other. Or anyone else for that matter.

Fuck. He didn't know what he was talking about. His brain was like scrambled eggs. He was supposed to be in charge here, figuring out strategy, studying Crush and his gang. Instead, he was hiding out in the corner of this dark cave of a bar, nursing a beer and avoiding one hell of a sexy woman because she was first and foremost on his mind.

Yeah, he and Jessie definitely needed to talk.

Tomorrow. It could wait until tomorrow.

He drained the beer and signaled the waitress for another.

FIVE

Diaz's talk with Jessie had yet to materialize. When he got back to the room last night, she was asleep, huddled under the covers, which suited him just fine. He undressed and climbed into his bed, promptly passing out. The next morning she was up and out of the room before he got out of bed.

Maybe she was angry at him. Good. If she decided to start avoiding him, it couldn't work out better. He could concentrate on the job at hand, and not on fending her off.

Because a man only had so much control.

He found her downstairs having breakfast with Spence, who filled them in on Stephanie, the woman he'd hooked up with the night before. She was not only Rex's ex-girlfriend, she was also Crush's cousin. Figuring that Stephanie had an in with the Devil's Skulls, Spence told them he decided to get close and hang tight with Stephanie, who was currently unattached and seemed to have taken a liking to him.

Not surprising. All women seemed to like Spence. Spence seemed to like all women. And if it worked for the mission, it was all good.

Over breakfast, Jessie barely spoke to him. She was civil, but not overly friendly. Avoided eye contact, scooted her chair away from his.

Yeah, she was pissed.

He should have been happy about it. Strangely, he wasn't. He tried to joke with her but she grabbed her jacket, slung it on, and bumped her hips against Spence, teasing him about his latest conquest, ignoring Diaz as the two of them walked out the door toward the bikes.

Okay. That's how it was going to be. And she bitched at him about how they were supposed to give the outward appearance of a couple? He rolled his eyes.

It didn't take long for Crush to hook up with them as they wandered around the tents and exhibition areas of the rally. Jessie seemed really happy to see him, looping her arm into his and walking away with him, her platinum blond head tilted toward Crush's dark one, whispering and laughing.

"What the fuck?" Diaz muttered.

"She's doing a good job getting close to him," Spence said. "He seems really taken with her."

"He's old enough to be her . . ."

Spence grinned. "He's about your age, moron."

"Fuck you."

Spence laughed. "Jealous, huh?" Spence leaned back and studied Diaz. "This is a new side to you."

"Do you really want to brawl with me out here, Spence?"

Spence arched a brow. "Do you really want me to kick your ass again?"

"Again? You were the one with the broken arm."

"You needed stitches. That's why you're so ugly now."

Diaz's lips quirked. Leave it to Spence to shake him out of this mood. "The stitches were in the back of my head."

"That's why you have no fucking sense."

Diaz laughed. "Smartass. Let's go. I want to keep an eye on them."

"You go. I see Stephanie. I'm going to do a little intel of my own."

"Pussy is not intel, Spence."

"That's what you think. You'd be amazed what a woman will tell you when you're giving her an orgasm." Spence winked and moved off to catch up to the petite redhead waving in their direction.

Which left Diaz to follow along behind Jessie and Crush like a lost puppy, a position he didn't like at all. Not that Jessie left him much choice since she stuck to Crush like glue while they wandered around the vendor tents, laughing and whispering to each other. She didn't once turn around to see if he was behind her.

Which wasn't how they were supposed to play this gig.

Yeah, they were going to have a talk, all right. About a lot of things, the least of which was her inability to follow orders. She could leave her personal feelings in the hotel room. If she was pissed at him for something, tough. This was an assignment. They were supposed to be a couple. She was doing a shitty job acting like part of one right now.

They turned a corner and Crush spotted him.

"Hey, Diaz. Jessie was just telling me about you."

He caught up to them, acting surprised to see them. "Yeah? What was she saying?"

Jessie smiled, but it wasn't a happy smile.

"She was telling me that you do your own work on bikes."

He shrugged. "I've done some."

"That's not what she said. She said she's seen you take one apart and build one from the ground up. That true?"

Diaz gave Jessie a frown. She continued to plaster on that fake smile.

"I guess. I just tinker."

"Hey, if you ever need a job, our garage could use a guy like you."

"Thanks for the offer. I'll keep it in mind. Never know when I might need a job."

What was that all about? And what else had Jessie been telling him? He needed to pull her away from Crush and have a chat with her about what she could and couldn't say, though he thought she already knew the rules.

Unfortunately, she seemed to be glued to Crush's hip today, because she saw something at another vendor tent and dragged Crush along to see. Crush gave Diaz a helpless look and followed. Diaz kept a watchful distance, fuming inside. He couldn't exactly jerk Jessie away from Crush. Then again, wasn't he supposed to be her . . . boyfriend or something? Shouldn't he be jealous or possessive about her spending her time with Crush, hanging so close to him?

Shit. He wasn't very good at this. He supposed if they were going to put on an act, he'd better start acting.

He stalked over to them and grabbed Jessie's arm. "We need to talk."

She tilted her head back, her eyes unreadable behind her sunglasses. "I'm busy."

She turned away, but he jerked her back around. "Now, Jessie."

Ignoring Crush, who simply grinned and nodded, he dragged

Jessie away from the vendor tent. She wasn't exactly coming along willingly, either. As soon as he pulled her far enough away from anyone who could hear, he stopped.

"What the hell are you doing?"

She pulled her shades on top of her head. "I was shopping. What did it look like I was doing?"

"Flirting with Crush."

She arched one brow. "Hardly. I was gathering information. Isn't that what we're supposed to be doing here?"

"Looked more to me like you were flirting."

"Flirting."

"Yes. With Crush."

"I was not."

"We're supposed to be a couple."

She snorted. "Yeah, you do that couple thing so well, don't you Diaz?" She moved to push past him, but he stopped her.

"Jessie, we're on a mission here," he whispered, casting his gaze around to be sure no one else could hear. "Don't forget that. And we set it up so the two of us are supposed to be a couple. You hanging all over Crush isn't making us look like a twosome."

"Crush and I have a friendship started. He's comfortable with me. We were talking. That's it. Now if you don't mind, I'll go back to doing what I was doing and see if I can get him to open up to me. Unless you think I need to hold your hand, talk only to you, be only with you, which will get us absolutely nowhere in this assignment."

She crossed her arms and stared up at him, as if daring him to argue her point.

Fuck it. Let her go hump Crush's leg if she wanted to. It wasn't like he cared, and if the end result was information, it was great, right? "Go for it."

She nodded and walked away, finding Crush and greeting him with a giant smile. They whispered, and Crush looked over at Diaz. Jessie said something and Crush tilted his head back and laughed. Diaz could only imagine what joke was being told at his expense.

He could feel his blood pressure rising, the pounding in his temples, the headache beginning to form.

Diaz searched out the beer tent, determined to let Jessie do her information gathering. He'd watch the other Skulls, see if anyone looked to be doing anything suspicious.

Which was a complete bust, but at least Crush ended up finding him and sharing a beer and bratwurst with him. And that meant Jessie had no choice but to follow, which didn't seem to make her happy.

"Having fun?" Crush asked while Jessie excused herself to go off to find one of the Porta-Johns.

Diaz mumbled something noncommittal.

"Your lady seems to be irritated with you today."

"So it seems."

"Hey, I read the hands-off signals loud and clear, man. She and I are just talking."

Diaz shrugged, but his blood was boiling.

"I respect a man's property. You have nothing to worry about."

Yeah, right. A woman like Jessie throwing herself at Crush, letting him know she was available and interested? As soon as Diaz's back was turned, Crush would be in her pants.

"She's spent the entire time with me talking about you," Crush added.

Diaz tilted his sunglasses down his nose. "I'll bet she has."

"No bullshit. She told me about how you build bikes, how good you are at riding and working on them, how much she admires your ability, both mentally and physically, to look at a bike and know exactly how to put it together. She really loves those Harleys. And the lady's crazy about *you*, man. She can't stop talking about you. It's kind of annoying," Crush finished with a smirk.

Diaz had nothing to say about that.

"I admire a woman who's that loyal to her man, even when she's mad as hell at him."

He really had no comeback for that statement, especially since Jessie returned just then, sitting down next to Crush, of course. She smiled at Crush and took a long swallow of beer.

"It's hot today," she said. "I hadn't expected the weather to be so warm."

"It'll cool off at night," Crush said. "It usually does."

"You do this every year?" Diaz asked.

Crush nodded. "We do a lot of bike events, but this one every year since it's in our backyard, so to speak. We do several weekend rallies in different states, but this is our big event of the year. After this weekend, we'll head east into the Ozarks, ride the mountain roads, hang out at the lake, soak in the fall color."

"Oh, that should be fun," Jessie said. "I looked at the roads on the map. Awesome riding."

"It is. Some of the curves get pretty intense."

"Sounds like my kind of adventure. I love those wild and crazy rides," Jessie said with a grin.

Crush nodded. "You may have found the right gang to ride with, then. That's our kind of road."

"If we survive initiation, can we ride with you after the rally?" Jessie asked.

"Yeah. *If* we invite you to initiation."

"Then we'll all have to be on our best behavior, won't we?" Jessie said with a pointed look at Diaz.

Crush snorted. "I'm tired of sitting. Let's ride."

They cruised the rally area for a while, Crush picking up his gang here and there, then they rode north into the hills, taking some winding roads where they could really turn their bikes on edge. Diaz was content to ride behind Jessie, since most of the roads were two lane and they had to ride single file. This way he could keep an eye on her as well as where they were and where they were going.

This was Devil's Skulls territory, and he'd already rode up next to Spence and told him to keep watch for anything that looked suspicious. So far, it was only asphalt in front of them and forest on either side. A few houses here and there, but they'd ridden pretty remote and deep into a dense forested area, so not much housing to be seen. Mainly resort cabins, the kind people bought and used for vacations. It was too isolated an area for general living purposes, unless you retired and enjoyed roughing it.

As the breeze blew by, Diaz inhaled. It was woody here, the smell of pine and earth heavy in his senses. He loved the open road, always had. Even when he was a kid he liked to hop on his minibike, take the back roads from home, and just get lost, as far and as fast as he could. Dirt spraying in his face, he'd sail over the mounds and fly so he could forget. He could relax, and pretend he was someplace else. Someone else. Someone free.

Of course back then he'd eventually had to go home, had to face reality.

Now, this was his reality. This was his job.

He was damn lucky, and he had General Lee to thank for it. He pushed the throttle and roared past several bikers, including Jessie, so he could catch up with Crush, who nodded as they rode next to each other for a few miles.

Diaz spotted a trail of smoke back in the deep woods. He pointed it out to Crush, who nodded. When they stopped at a bar several miles down the road, he decided to test Crush.

"Did you see that smoke back there?"

Crush narrowed his gaze "Yeah. So?"

"What did you think that was?"

He shrugged. "Campers, probably."

"In those dense woods? How do you get back there? There are no roads that I saw."

"Hell if I know. Maybe there are bikers camping out. I need a beer."

Interesting that Crush blew him off, almost as if he didn't want to continue the conversation. Diaz had caught a glimpse of a flag as they'd ridden by that spot. Maybe it was a marker of sorts. They'd breezed past it quickly, though.

He'd also made a mental note of the mile marker they passed. They might have to come back and investigate this area. It could be a hidden survivalist camp nestled back in the woods. The location was perfect—seldom traveled back road, deep in the forest, and no discernible path leading into it. Too bad they couldn't do it now, but there was no way they could go off road without arousing Crush's suspicion, and it was vital they get in his good graces.

Which Jessie certainly had done today.

And was still doing, making a pointed effort to ignore him and hang with Crush. *Whatever.* She could do what she wanted as long as it didn't compromise the assignment. He intended to sit back, enjoy his beer, and watch.

Which was why he was the closest to the door when it banged open. He sat forward, his senses on immediate danger alert.

A group of bikers strolled in, and the first thing Diaz caught was the scowl on Crush's face. Then the other Devil's Skulls turned slowly around.

The tension in the room increased, and the small bar had just become way too overcrowded. The leather jackets the gang wore said Dustriders. Not good. The Dustriders were a bad gang out of Texas. Diaz was familiar with them. Half the members ended up tossed in jail at every bike rally they attended, and they made it a habit to brawl with other bikers at any opportunity.

The Dustriders didn't play well with others.

Diaz needed to get to Jessie, to be sure she was safe. She stood next to Crush, but Spence was on the other side of her. A short shake of Spence's head told Diaz it was a bad idea to make any sudden moves. At least Spence would be there to see to Jessie's safety. Diaz gripped his bottle of beer, his entire body ready to spring into action.

"My guys want a beer and you're in our way."

That statement had been spoken by a big, burly guy. He looked like a damn wrestler, all muscle and brawn with a thick red beard and thighs like tree trunks.

Crush leaned against the bar and shrugged, seemingly unaffected. "No one's stopping you, Meat."

Meat? The dude's name was Meat? Diaz resisted the urge to laugh. Probably not a good idea, all things considered.

"You're stopping me, Crush. You and all these pansies you like to call the Skulls."

Crush didn't budge, seemingly unaffected by the insult. "Don't start shit you can't handle, Meat."

"I can handle anything and you know it."

"You want a beer or do you want to rumble today?"

Meat grinned. Missing a few teeth on the top, too. *Nice.* "I think we'll just work up a good thirst first."

"Okay, all of you. Take it outside." The bartender and owner of the bar was a big enough guy on his own. "Or I'll call the sheriff and no one will get to fight."

This wasn't going to go well. Diaz made eye contact with

Spence, hoping Spence was a good mind reader. He wanted Jessie out of the middle of this and now. Spence inched in front of Jess. Jess frowned at Spence, then shot a mutinous glare at Diaz as if to tell him she could take care of herself.

She could be pissed at him if she wanted to, but no way would he let her get hurt. This was going to get ugly.

Crush gave a short tilt of his head. "No problem, Bill. Come on Skulls, outside."

Diaz shot out of his chair and moved to the door. If they were going to be asked to go through initiation, they'd have to prove they deserved it. Besides, he had enough anger boiling up inside him that it would be a pleasure to release a little of it by skinning his knuckles on a few jaws.

Half the group hadn't made it out the door before fists went flying. Meat had shoved Crush in the back, sending him sprawling onto the ground, a cloud of dirt in his wake. Crush rolled and lifted his booted foot into Meat's ample stomach, and with a hard kick Meat crashed onto the bar's porch, temporarily blocking the doorway.

Then all hell broke loose and Diaz could only concentrate on himself, because he was shoved through the doorway and jumped from behind. A fist connected with the side of his head, sending his anger and frustration into full-on fury. He whirled on his attacker and sent a fist into his nose. Blood spurted, the guy went down, replaced immediately by another.

It didn't take long to figure out the Dustriders fought dirty. Fine with him. He'd grown up with street fighting. No rules—made brawling more interesting that way.

He was so occupied he couldn't stop to look for Jess. The only thing he could hope for was that she had the sense to stay inside, though he doubted it. There were women in the parking lot tearing each other's hair out, biting, kicking, and scratching.

He knew Jessie. No way would she meekly wait inside like a coward, because she was street tough too. She'd want to be right in the middle of this.

Opponents began to wear down. Heaving, panting breaths of exhaustion became the prominent sounds, replacing the initial battle cries.

When it became evident the Skulls weren't going to yield the bar, the Dustriders grudgingly climbed onto their bikes and headed out, dragging their wounded with them. As soon as they were gone and the billowing dust settled, Diaz looked around for Spence. He found him near the porch, sporting a bloody lip and a wide grin.

"That was some serious fucking fun," Spence said, glancing over Diaz. "Anything broken?"

Diaz licked his own blood off the corner of his mouth. He had some cuts and bruises, but otherwise he was fine. "Hell no. They were pussies."

Spence laughed.

"Have you seen Jessie?"

Spence shook his head. "I was too busy kicking ass."

"Me too." Diaz turned in a circle, searching, finally saw her walking toward them. Dusty, her face dirty, her hair disheveled, with a wide grin on her face.

"Kick their asses, honey?" Spence asked, throwing his arm around her shoulders.

She tilted her head back and graced Spencer with a smile Diaz hadn't seen directed at him all day long. "You know it."

Spence kissed her on the forehead. Diaz sighed, then masked his emotions as Crush came toward them.

"Y'all are good fighters," Crush said, extending his hand to shake theirs.

"Hey, it was fun," Spence said. "We get bored if there's no ass to kick."

Crush laughed. "That's what I like to hear."

They went back into the bar, cleaned up a bit, and really enjoyed their beers. By the time the sun had set, they'd made their way back to the rally and the main drag, goosing their engines as they rode up and down the street, much to the delight of the crowds lining the sidewalks. Bikers by the thousands rode well into the night hours, stopping occasionally at bars along the way—if they could manage to find a parking place. Crush and his gang seemed to be content to simply ride and be seen. Diaz could almost believe Crush was looking for something, or maybe someone, but they finally broke off when the crowds began to die down. They closed down the street, the Devil's Skulls one of the last gangs left.

"I need to find Rex," Crush said. "He and a few of the others went riding north into one of the other towns. Said there was a hot babe review at one of the bars. Wanna come?" Crush asked them.

"Sounds great to me," Spence said.

"Me too," Jessie chimed in with a teasing grin. "But only if the review includes guys."

Diaz shook his head. Hadn't she had enough for the day, or was she deliberately trying to provoke him? Knowing Jess, it was probably the latter.

Crush laughed. "Not sure about that. I think it's all girls, but there'll be plenty of guys there watching."

"Good enough for me," she said. "I'm in."

That was Diaz's cue to put an end to Jessie's bullshit. "I don't think so."

"You're not coming along, Diaz?" Jessie asked.

"No. I mean you aren't going either."

"Huh. Last time I looked I was over twenty-one. And you aren't my dad."

"And I'm taking that as a clue to hightail it the hell out of here before there's more bloodshed. Let's ride." Crush took off and the rest of them followed, leaving Diaz and Jessie on a side street, staring at each other.

"Let's go back to the hotel."

She shook her head. "I think we should go with Crush."

"I think Spence has it covered. You and I need to talk."

"Is that an order?"

She was really pushing it, but if that's how she wanted to play it . . . "As a matter of fact, it is."

She shrugged, started up her bike and they rode back to the hotel.

Jessie didn't speak to him on the ride or on the elevator to the room, instead staying a couple of steps ahead of him, using her key to walk into the room. She tossed her things onto the desk without a backward glance in his direction. With every silent step she took, Diaz's temper rose.

"Enough, Jessie."

Ignoring him, she peeled off her jacket and sat on the bed, toeing off her boots, concentrating her attention on her feet. She wouldn't even look at him. Diaz shrugged out of his jacket and threw it over a chair, crossing his arms as he stood in front of her, willing her to make eye contact.

She didn't. Instead, she grabbed a change of clothes and went into the bathroom. He heard the shower turn on.

Fine. They both needed to clean up after that brawl at the bar today. He'd wait her out, but he wasn't going to let this go. Instead, he paced the room, trying to block out visuals of her naked in the shower, water streaming down her body in rivulets, then stepping out to smooth lotion over her creamy skin.

Okay, that wasn't helping. She'd hardly take him seriously as her superior if he had a raging hard-on when he talked to her. He focused instead on the mission, on everything they'd discovered so far, on questions unanswered. Like that flag and the smoke he'd spotted today.

Jessie opened the door. The scent of her shampoo filled the room as she walked by. He yanked clean clothes out of the drawer and went into the bathroom, took a hot shower, finishing it off with cool water to clear his head. When he came out, she was sitting on the bed, staring at the darkness outside.

"We need to talk."

No answer. She stood and inched around him, heading toward the bathroom again. Oh, no, she wasn't going to hide anymore. He grabbed her wrist before she could slip by.

"Jessie."

She stopped, angled her head so her gaze met his.

"What?"

"Sit down."

"Is this about work?"

"Yes."

"Fine, then." She took a seat at the foot of the bed.

"What the hell is wrong with you?"

She stood and walked toward the bathroom again. "We're done."

He blocked her way. "We're not done. Sit down."

"You said we were going to talk about work. That wasn't work."

"It sure as hell was. Now sit."

She took a step forward, but he refused to move. She didn't back up. "I am not a dog, Diaz. You can't order me around."

"On this assignment I'm your superior, and if I say climb the goddamn walls, you'll climb them. Got it?"

She gave him a military salute. "Yes, Captain. Can I go now?"

"No. We need to talk." Good God she was making this difficult. Who knew Jessie had this much of an attitude.

She crossed her arms and leaned against the bathroom doorway. "Talk away."

This was going to go well. "What were you doing today with Crush?"

"Uh, talking?"

"About?"

"I was trying to get to know him, to gain his confidence. He likes me, so I was playing on that. I already told you what I was doing. Why are we going over this again?"

"It looked to me like you were trying to do more than your job."

"What did you think I was doing?"

"I think you like Crush and maybe you want to get something romantic going with him."

She rolled her eyes. "Jesus, Diaz."

"This assignment isn't about you finding your way into Crush's leathers, Jessie."

She threw her hands in the air. "Are you really that stupid? I'm not the least bit interested in what's in Crush's leathers or beyond that. I spent some time getting to know him, trying to figure him out, see if he'd trust me. Some guys like talking to girls because they think we're harmless. He's likely to reveal more to me than he will to you or Spence, so I thought I'd give it a try."

"Uh huh. We're supposed to be playing this together."

She lifted her chin, clearly not liking the direction of the conversation. "I tried a different tactic, and it worked out just fine."

He leaned into her. "You're the junior member of this team, Jess. If you want to strategize a move, clear it through me first. In the meantime, stay the hell out of Crush's pants."

JESSIE HAD TAKEN ALL SHE WAS GOING TO FROM DIAZ. HE WAS bullying and berating her for something she hadn't done. Yes, she might have used Crush today because she was pissed at Diaz. She'd been honest, too, though. It was also a tactic to see if she could find some information about him and the Devil's Skulls. She wanted to do a good job on this assignment, not just be an extra body Grange had forced on Diaz. She wanted to do something productive, and she had.

But it was more than that. Diaz was being an ass, and she'd had enough.

"You didn't seem to have a problem with Spence using Stephanie to gain information."

"That's different."

"How?"

He didn't have an answer, exactly what she figured. This had nothing to do with the mission and everything to do with what had been happening—or rather not happening—between them. And since he started this tonight . . .

"Stop pushing me away."

Diaz leaned back. "What?"

"You heard me. Stop pushing me away. Stop running whenever we get close."

"I don't know what the hell you're talking about."

"Don't you? What is it about me that makes you run like hell, Diaz? I mean, I know I'm not hideous looking, and I have a decent body." Now it was her turn to advance on him. He started backing up. "But I'm getting tired of you and me getting close and you slamming the door in my face."

"Yeah. I could see today how brokenhearted you are over it."

Men were such babies sometimes. He'd started this game. Too bad for him that he didn't like it when the rules changed. She'd had enough. "Maybe if you had a working dick of your own and knew what to do with it, I wouldn't have to go searching in Crush's pants for one."

Diaz's gaze narrowed, his eyes going dark. She felt the fury coming off him in waves, saw the way the muscles bunched under his T-shirt. He advanced on her and Jessie backed up a step, realizing she might have just said the wrong thing.

SIX

Jessie could tell Diaz was pissed because he kept coming at her, his face a tight mask of utter fury.

Never insult a guy's manhood. Big, huge mistake.

Oh, shit. She skirted around the wall until her knees hit the side of the bed. Now she was trapped and had nowhere to run.

"Diaz, I didn't mean that, really. I wasn't after Crush's dick. Or any other part of him for that matter. But you have to understand that when you pushed me away I—"

She never got to finish her sentence. Diaz jerked her against him, pulling her into his powerful body at the same time his lips crushed hers in a kiss she could only describe as breath-stealing. She'd gasped at the first contact and lost all ability to breathe after that.

Oh, God, he was kissing her. It was . . . sweet heaven . . . hot. There was such fury and passion in his kiss—she felt him boiling, the heat pouring off him and onto her. Yet he held her in a gentle embrace, not one of anger. His arm wrapped around her waist, the other holding on to her hand, lacing his fingers with hers in a way that made her heart melt.

Neurons were firing a million times a second, sending her senses haywire, and she still couldn't breathe. Not with the masterful way he slid his lips over hers, commanding her to part her lips so his tongue could snake inside to slide against hers.

Her heart jackhammered against her chest as he licked her tongue in slow, deliberate movements meant to coax her surrender.

Coax? There was nothing to entice out of her. She'd waved the white flag as soon as he touched her. Did he think she would fight him? No way. She was his for the plundering. When he pushed against her and they fell onto the bed together, she damn near cried out in victory, because this was what she had wanted all along. Her body against his, the two of them lying side by side, Diaz's warm, full lips possessing hers.

He rolled her onto her back and climbed over her, his mouth still on hers and doing delicious things to her senses. He was so big—everywhere, and yet so gentle as he held his weight off her and still pressed full-on against her. His cock rode against her hip, thick and hot, penetrating through her jeans, through her mind, the promise of what could be. She reached up, threading her fingers through his hair, overwhelmed that she was actually touching him, that this was real and finally happening when she had convinced herself it would never be. Maybe pushing him to his limits had been the key. She didn't know and didn't care. They were here now and nothing was going to stop it.

DIAZ FELT LIKE EXPLODING, BUT IT WASN'T FROM ANGER. NOT anymore. Any irritation he felt at Jessie evaporated as soon as he touched her, kissed her, put his hands on her.

All of which was wrong. Damn wrong. He shouldn't be doing this, shouldn't be lying in bed with his mouth on hers. But goddamn she felt good. Her mouth was sweet and spicy, just like the woman. And her body was all curves, soft and firm and making his dick rock hard.

The logical part of his brain told him he should get off this bed and explain to Jessie all the reasons they couldn't do this. Like they were practically family. They were on assignment, which made him her boss at the moment, and that screamed conflict of interest. And the other guys would kick his ass for compromising Jessie. It was his job to protect her, not fuck her.

Unfortunately, the only part of his body thinking at the moment was his dick, and it wasn't listening to reason.

To hell with it. She tasted like too much temptation to resist, and he wanted a little bit more. Then he'd stop, before things went too far. He had enough control for that.

He withdrew his lips from hers and stared down at her. Her eyes were half-lidded pools of dark green, filled with desire and something else—a touch of fear, maybe, or innocence?

If he read that expression right, he'd never be able to go on. Not Jessie. Not the way she'd thrown herself at him. She was experienced, knew exactly what she wanted and what she was getting herself into to. He refused to believe what he'd seen. And yet conscience wouldn't let him continue. Not until he was certain of her intent.

"Are you sure?"

"God, yes," she whispered, pulling his head down to her neck. No hesitation.

He buried his face against the soft column of her throat and inhaled the scent of her—a little wild and earthy, like the outdoors.

He licked her riotously beating pulse point and she whimpered, lifting her hips against him in a silent plea for more.

Yeah, he had a lot more to give her. His throbbing cock wanted inside her. Just lying next to her told him their bodies would fit together.

Wait. Not yet. Not . . . ever. Restrain. Just touch her, play a little. That's all he'd allow. Which meant whatever he did with her, her clothes were staying on. Otherwise he wouldn't be able to resist doing everything to her, with her.

Though he could well imagine what was going on underneath her clothes. He shifted, grasping her ass and sliding his thigh between her legs. She moaned, rocked her pelvis against him. He felt moisture through her jeans.

"Are your panties wet, Jessie?" he asked.

"*I'm* wet, Diaz," she replied, her voice hoarse against his neck. She rubbed against his thigh again. "Fix it."

Christ, it unraveled him that she was so outspoken with her needs. It made his dick pulse, his balls ache. He slid his hand over her hip, squeezing her flesh, content to just be able to touch her. But he knew that wouldn't be enough. Not when her shirt had ridden up, exposing a sexy expanse of tanned stomach. He rolled her onto her back, one of his arms pinned under her neck, and surveyed her body.

Her breasts were crushed against the tight shirt, enough that he could tell she didn't have a bra on. Her T-shirt was one of those spandex numbers that held everything in. He palmed her stomach, using his fingers to walk upward and lift the shirt up over her ribs, exposing the emerald piercing dangling at her navel. So sexy. He'd like to see her naked wearing nothing but that jewel at her belly.

"When did you have that done?" he asked.

She lifted her head, glanced down at the piercing. "When I turned eighteen."

"I like it."

Her lips curved, a devilish little smile. "I like your hands on me."

He slid his palm under her shirt. Her skin was buttery soft, like the finest worn leather. He smoothed his hand over her, higher, up to her ribs, letting his fingers rest just below her breasts. He could feel her rapidly thrumming heartbeat, watch her face as she licked her lips, kept her gaze focused on him.

"Touch me," she whispered. "I've wanted this for so long, Diaz."

Her honesty was going to tear him apart. If only he could be as honest with her. But there were too many doubts, too many things he couldn't say.

He shouldn't go any further. If he did, he wasn't sure he could stop. Just smoothing his hand over her skin was torture. His balls felt knotted up, his dick twisted and on fire.

But the decision was out of his hands when Jessie lifted her shirt over her breasts, revealing two perfect globes with round peach nipples that puckered right before his eyes, just begging for him. He groaned, inched forward, and covered one with his hand, the other with his lips. So much for leaving her fully dressed.

She tasted just as good as she looked—sweet and warm. She arched her back, sliding her nipple farther into his mouth, shoving the other breast into his palm. He toed off his boots and climbed onto the bed so he could lean over her, feast on her, lick and suck and tweak her nipples until she writhed against him. The more he lavished attention on her breasts, the more she arched into him, twining her fingers through his hair and holding on tight as if she'd never let go.

Don't let go. He liked her holding on to him, seeming to need what only he could give her. It was as if she was desperate for his touch, and he loved that, because he had so much more to give her than just this.

He tilted her up, long enough to lift the shirt over her head, then laid her head down on the bed again. Naked from the waist up . . . damn, she was so beautiful, her short hair framing her heart-shaped face, her eyes so wide open and beautiful as she studied his every move. He cupped her cheek, bent down to taste her lips again, slid his tongue between her teeth to lick at the velvety softness of hers—could he ever get enough of her sweet mouth?

As he explored her mouth, he reached for her belt buckle, undoing it and finding the button on her jeans, then drawing the zipper down. When he reached inside and laid his hand against her satin panties, she sighed softly against his lips. He pulled his mouth from hers, gazing down at her. Her panties were white, low cut, but he wanted to see more of them. He drew away from her, grabbed the denim, and pulled the jeans down her legs, drawing them off.

Jessie had the most beautiful legs, tanned, toned from her hard workouts in the gym. He worked his way back up by sliding his hands over the soft skin of her ankles, her calves, her thighs, moving to the edge of the bed to spread her legs apart, to inspect the tiny scrap of her panties, the only item of clothing she still wore.

"This isn't quite fair," she said, sounding a bit breathless.

"What isn't?"

"You still have all your clothes on."

Damn good thing, too, or he'd already be inside her. That little scrap of satin was no barrier to him. If he was naked, he'd rip it off and plunge his cock deep inside her in seconds. He was hard, aching, pulsing with a need to fuck her. Yeah, good thing he still had all his clothes on.

"I want to see you, touch you, Jessie."

"I want to see you, too."

"Later." *Never. Too much at stake.* This was enough . . . had to be enough. He held on to her knees, spread her legs apart, and came down between them, sitting on the bed so he could be close to her. He inhaled the musky sweet scent of her arousal. The smell of sex, the best aphrodisiac ever. It intoxicated his senses, made his balls knot up tight against his body, his cock quiver in anticipation.

It could anticipate all it wanted. All he was going to do with Jessie was play a little.

Or a lot. He laid his palm over the satin at the apex of her thighs. Steamy wet heat greeted him. She raised her hips, pressing her sweet pussy against his hand.

"Diaz."

The way she whispered his name—part praise, part plea—a man could only take so much torture.

"I'm going to make you come, Jessie."

Her lips parted and she let out a slight gasp of surprise, her eyes widening again in that way that spoke of innocence. He frowned, then dismissed it. Maybe it was pleasurable surprise, instead.

He pressed his palm against her mound, rubbed up, then down, enjoying the moist feel of her, the way she bucked up to meet his hand, tilted her head back, and let out a low moan. She gripped the bedspread, digging her heels into the mattress.

He needed more than this. This satin barrier annoyed him.

"Hang on, baby." He grasped the tiny straps at her hips and with a slight tug, the material gave way. Jessie's head shot up as he pulled the fabric from her body.

"Oh, God," she whispered.

And then she was bare.

And she *was* bare. Completely. Diaz swallowed, caught sight of the small silver ring piercing on the hood of her clit, and nearly dropped to his knees and cried.

"Jesus, Jessie. When did you have this one done?"

"On my twenty-first birthday."

He'd like to kill the son of a bitch who got to touch her there.

"It was a woman," she said in response to his frown. "A friend of mine who does tattoos and piercings."

Good thing. Not that he expected her to be a virgin or anything, but the thought of anyone being down here before him made him decidedly . . . damned irritated.

Which he had no right to be. She was twenty-three, not a kid.

"Do you like it?" he asked.

She cast him an arched brow and a half smile. "It's . . . fun to play with."

He could well imagine. "Let's just see how much fun it is." She was wet, glistening with her own juices. He dipped his fingers along her pussy lips, then trailed them upward, slow and easy, getting her used to his touch. She trembled, tensed, then nearly rocketed right off the bed when he used the pad of his thumb to circle the hood of her clit. He had to press one hand down on her lower belly to hold her in place.

"*Shh*, baby, it's okay," he murmured, coming up beside her to hold her steady. Good God she was sensitive.

"I'm not . . . that is I haven't . . . Shit."

Warning bells and chimes of *uh oh* sounded in his head. He pulled his hand away and sat up. "You haven't what?"

"Nothing. I haven't come in a while, that's all." She grabbed his wrist and moved it back to her sex. "Please, don't stop."

Diaz was no idiot. That's not what she meant. He pushed back, grabbing a pillow to shove against the headboard, and dragged Jessie with him. "Let's take a short break."

She gave him an incredulous stare. "Are you kidding me? You're stopping now?"

"Hell yes, we're stopping now. Tell me what you haven't, Jessie. What haven't you done?"

Her cheeks flamed pink. She looked down, then back up again through the fringes of her eyelashes, not quite meeting his probing gaze.

He didn't want to know the answer, did he?

But he had to know. He tilted her chin up, forcing her to look at him. He needed her to say it.

"Jess, tell me."

"I've never done this before."

He stilled, every muscle in his body tight. "You've never done what?"

"Um . . . anything."

Son of a bitch. Fuck, fuck, fuck. Instinctively, he'd already known. Something in her eyes had told him. That innocence he'd kept seeing wasn't an act. It was real.

He slid off the bed, dragged his hand through his hair, and paced the room.

"Goddammit, Jessie. How the hell could you be twenty-three years old and a virgin?"

She rolled her eyes. "Diaz, I've been with the Wild Riders since I was fifteen years old. From the time I got there Grange guarded me like a mother hen, never let me out of his sight. And if it wasn't him, it was one of you guys watching over me. I was homeschooled, and when I wasn't doing that I was trained. That took up all my time. It wasn't like I had a normal life. When would I have dated, when or where would I have met a guy? It wasn't like I'd go out to the mall and bring one home with me. And if I had, you all would have been all over him. No way would he have stood a chance."

She had a point. They would have never let a guy near Jessie back then. Diaz wasn't sure they'd let one near her now. No wonder she never brought guys around them.

"When you became of legal age and started riding and going out on your own?" All those times Jessie disappeared, out riding, by herself? He thought a taste of freedom would have given her the opportunity to meet a guy or two . . . gain some experience. Hell, they all thought that.

She shrugged. "I was . . . picky. By then I compared every man I met to you–to you guys." Her eyes swept down, then back up again. "No one measured up. It's not like I was going to jump the bones of the first available guy just because he had a dick. Hence my dilemma—twenty-three and still a virgin."

He still couldn't fathom this. Not the way she looked, the way she acted . . . so bold, direct, as if she knew exactly what she wanted. "What about those piercings?"

Her lips curled. "What about them? They're body art, they don't signify sexual experience."

"The clit ring?"

She rolled her eyes. "I masturbate, Diaz. I might be a virgin, technically, but it doesn't mean I lack experience. Masturbation is my only sexual outlet right now. And the clit ring heightens my sexual pleasure. Since no one is doing it for me, I do it for myself."

He shouldn't be having this conversation with her. He shouldn't be in this room with her. There were a lot of *shouldn't*s going on in his head, his body. His hard-on returned in an angry rush. The mental visual of Jessie, naked and spread-eagled on her bed, toying with that tiny little piercing on her clit, bringing herself to orgasm . . .

Despite what he knew, he still wanted to throw her down on the bed and eat her pussy until she screamed. Which was *so* the wrong thing to be thinking about. Now. Ever.

"I can't believe this." He walked the carpet from end to end, frustration eating away at him. How could they have not seen this? Well, hell. It's not like any of them ever discussed Jessie's sex life with her. She'd never had other females around. Not until Lily arrived on the scene, and that was just recently. Did Lily even know? Even if she did, it wasn't like she'd call a meeting with all the guys to discuss it.

Jessie crossed her arms under her breasts, seemingly unaware or at least unconcerned of her complete nudity. "I'm so sorry that I didn't unburden myself of my virginity sooner. How inconvenient for you tonight."

"You know that's not what I'm talking about." Or maybe it was. Dammit, it *was* inconvenient. He'd thought she was experienced.

Would that have eased his guilt over what they were going to do? Probably.

He turned to the window, easing back the curtain an inch to peer out, to turn his gaze toward anything but her luscious body. "If I'd known . . . I would have never touched you."

"I'm glad you didn't know, then."

He flipped back to gape at her. "You want this to happen?"

"I wouldn't be sitting here naked with you if I didn't."

He frowned. "I thought you were picky."

"I am."

"But you're here with me."

She rolled her eyes. "Duh."

"You're obviously not picky enough. You shouldn't be with me."

"Why not? You're the one I want. I'm an adult, Diaz. I get to choose the man I make love with."

Him? The man she'd give her virginity to? *Christ.* It would have been him. His thoughts about no one else having touched her . . . his cavemanlike behavior . . . it was accurate, wasn't it? And he had to admit there was a part of him screaming a *hell yeah!* at the thought of no man ever touching Jessie before.

What was wrong with him? He couldn't do this.

"I'm not going to be the one to take your virginity, Jessie."

She sighed. "Why not? It's more of a semantics thing than physical anyway. I've used vibrators."

He dropped his chin to his chest, closed his eyes, and there went the visuals again. Jessie with a dildo shoved into her pussy, rubbing her clit, lifting her ass off the bed as she pleasured herself. Her eyes closed tight, her breathing labored as she brought herself to orgasm.

Fuck. His dick was telling him one thing, his conscience another. And he was getting a headache.

He opened his eyes, looked at her. "Because you need to find a great guy, fall in love, have a relationship. And I'm not the kind of guy to do that with."

"You are a great guy, Diaz."

She knew so very little about him. If she did, she'd get dressed and run like hell. "No, I'm not. And I'm not going to argue with you about this. I'm flattered that you think you want to give it up to me, but I'm going to have to pass. I really think you should find a different guy."

She leaned back on the bed. "Someone like Crush?"

He shot her a glare. "Don't even think about it."

"You don't get to tell me who I fuck. If it isn't going to be you, then I'll choose someone else."

"For someone who claims to be picky, you've suddenly become rather indiscriminate."

She inhaled, let it out. "Okay, fine. I don't want to have sex with Crush. This is frustrating. You built me up, got me hot, and you're kind of leaving me hanging here, Diaz. That's not really fair."

His lips lifted. She had a point. "You're right about that. Sorry."

She laid back on the bed, planted her feet flat, and widened her legs, letting her fingers drift between them, resting on the top of her sex, oh so close to that tantalizing piercing. She tapped her fingers, drawing his attention to her smooth pussy lips, her still swollen clit. "So if you won't fuck me, how about releasing a little tension?"

The woman was going to be the death of him.

seven

Jessie had always considered herself brave, bold, and sexy.

She also knew what she wanted. And since she was already naked and had come this far with Diaz, she intended to go all the way. She'd push him if she had to—force him, even, though that thought caused her lips to curve. He was easily twice her size. She could hardly throw him down and force him to have sex with her.

The mental visual was appealing, though.

Unfortunately, she was tired of doing things mentally. Or by herself. She was naked, lying on the bed. Diaz was in the room with her, and from the look on his face, definitely interested. If she could find a way to break through his wall of chivalry or whatever misguided notion of honor that currently kept him across the room from her, she could have him on the bed with her.

And maybe, just maybe . . .

"Jessie."

His voice had gone hoarse, as if he struggled with indecision. He stood rooted to the spot, his fist clenched in the drapes, staring at her, at where her fingers rested just above her pussy. *Good.* At least this time he hadn't walked out on her. They were making progress.

"Come here, Diaz. I know you want this as much as I do."

"You don't know what I want. Or even what you want. Think about this, Jess. This is a mistake."

He was the one who didn't know what he wanted. Emboldened by the heated look in his eyes, the way he couldn't drag his gaze away from her, she slid her fingers down, parted her legs farther. Her clit trembled, knowing he watched. She was both embarrassed and aroused. She'd never done this in front of a man before. She'd never done *anything* in front of a man before. But when Diaz palmed his cock, rubbed it as he watched, her lips parted and she began to pant, her body melting from the inside out. She suddenly couldn't breathe, her throat had gone dry, no doubt because all the moisture in her body had rushed to her pussy. She felt the warm wetness there and ran her hand down, circled her pussy lips, and dipped inside just a bit to wet her fingers.

Diaz let out a strangled groan, and she knew then that he wasn't going to leave her. She let her fingers drift upward, wetting her vulva, circling around her clit, waving her fingers back and forth.

He moved forward. "How often do you do this?"

"Do what? Lie naked on a hotel room bed with a man watching me?"

"No. Touch yourself."

"Every day. Sometimes more than once a day."

"Christ, Jessie."

"I'm tired of touching myself. It's time I had a little education. I need you, Diaz."

He stripped off his T-shirt, and she dug her heels in so she could push her back up onto the pillows and watch.

His chest was smooth, dark, and muscled, a few scars the only thing marring its absolute chiseled perfection, though even those added to his masculine beauty. He looked like a warrior, from his broad shoulders to his wide chest, narrow waist, and his six-pack abs. She wanted to lick all the way down to the dark feathering of hair that disappeared into his pants. He released the belt buckle and Jessie swallowed, her gaze riveted to his zipper, to the straining erection pushing against the crotch of his jeans. She followed his fingers as he drew the zipper down, realizing he'd gone commando. She held her breath as he reached for the waistband of his pants and pushed them down over his thighs, then sighed in pure feminine appreciation.

Strong legs, and a thatch of dark hair centering his cock. She leaned forward on all fours and reached out, circling his cock with her hand. Diaz inhaled, the sound sharp and guttural, almost like a curse. She tilted her head back to meet his gaze. He looked angry, his eyes dark.

"Let me," she said.

"That's not what this is about."

"Let me anyway. I want to explore you."

"Christ, Jessie."

She took that as a *yes* and left her hand on his cock, maneuvering around to a sitting position and letting her legs dangle on the bed. Diaz moved closer, his knees bumping the mattress. He widened his stance, giving her free access to all his treasures.

God, he really was a treasure, especially here where he was so masculine. He felt all man, and smelled it, too. Like the outdoors, so crisp and musky and utterly primal. She breathed him in as she began to stroke his length with gentle movements, exploring what she had in her hand, mesmerized by the feel of soft skin surrounding a steely hard piece of flesh. Her pussy quivered as if by instinct, knowing the pleasure his cock could awaken in her.

Her virginity had long ago been technically disposed of by the vibrators she played with. But those were lifeless toys—without emotion, cold and impassionate. Diaz's cock was hot, thick, pulsing with a life beat. Responsive, too—it jerked in her hand as she grazed her thumb over the wide crest, spilling drops of pearly liquid in its wake. She captured those fluids against her thumb, brought them to her mouth, and licked, surprised at the tangy flavor. She stroked, bringing him closer, and licked the soft tip.

"Jessie."

Her name rolled off his tongue as a strangled whisper. She liked hearing that, so she licked him again, tasted more of his salty flavor, felt his cock jerking in response. He reached out to tangle his fingers in her hair, gripping a handful of it as he rocked against her tongue. She closed her lips around his hard flesh and brought him deeper into her mouth.

"That's it, babe, suck me."

Who knew sucking a man's cock could be such a turn-on? She'd seen movies, thought this was done only for the man's pleasure. She had no idea she could get so excited having Diaz at her mercy like this. But the more pleasure she gave him, the more it aroused her. And she seemed to be doing it right, since he gripped her hair hard and began pumping his cock between her lips, gently at first, then harder as she increased suction. She reached up and cradled his balls in one hand, gently massaging them, and he shuddered.

"You keep that up and I'm going to come in your mouth."

His voice was harsh, and as he said the words he thrust his cock deep into her throat. God, it was so exciting, feeling him lose control like this. She realized that's exactly what she wanted. To make him come, to feel him shatter.

Instead, he pulled his cock away from her lips, pressed her down on the bed, and covered her mouth with a deep kiss, penetrating with his tongue, licking and sucking hers. She wanted to protest that he hadn't finished, he hadn't come. But he'd pushed on top of her and to feel him naked against her like this was almost more than heaven, so her protest died on a shuddering moan. She'd wanted this for so long, and now it was happening. His cock, still wet from her mouth, rode along her clit, sending lightning shots of pleasure along her nerve endings. She lifted, needing more, wanting that sensation to continue, to drive her right over the edge.

But Diaz shifted, grasping her wrists and lifting them over her head, holding them there with one hand while he grazed her cheek, neck, and collarbone with the other. Was his mere touch on her skin supposed to drive her this crazy? He rested his fingertips along her jaw, using his thumb to caress her bottom lip. He looked down at her, his eyes so dark, hot, intense.

"You are so beautiful," he said. "And your mouth . . . damn, Jessie, you have an amazing mouth."

She smiled up at him, glad that she'd pleased him. "I wanted you to come in my mouth."

He slid his thumb just inside her lips, letting her lick and suck it. Her womb clenched, recalling the sensation of sucking his cock, of how it made him feel. She wanted that in her mouth again, to give him that kind of pleasure so she could be that turned on.

His gaze darkened. "You're killing me. I want that, too. But first, *you're* going to come."

She liked that idea, too. She felt strung out, needy, her body tense and on fire. She wanted a lot of things and she wanted them all right now. Was sex always like this, the running toward the finish line yet wanting it to last forever kind of thing? She needed, wanted so much, and yet she yearned for it to last forever.

All thought fled when Diaz hovered over her breast with his hand. Then, a light caress, teasing her nipple with the barest touch. She jerked, lifted in an attempt to drive her upright nipple against his calloused palm. He lowered his hand, circled his palm over her nipple in gentle motions. The sensation shot south, making her clasp her legs together in an attempt to create friction. She wanted her hands free so she could rub her own clit.

"No, babe. You wanted me to do it, so I'm in charge now."

She wasn't sure that was a good thing, since Diaz seemed determined to do things slow, and she was ready to come, to experience that explosive magic right now. Instead, he eased down her body and captured her tortured nipple between his teeth, then licked it, sucked it, nibbled some more until she went mad from the pleasure. He took her other breast in his hand, fit the nipple between two fingers and rolled it. She had no idea her nipples were so sensitive. She played with them a little bit by herself while she was masturbating, but hadn't lavished attention on them the way Diaz did now. And oh, were her nipples ever connected to her clit. Then again, maybe it was just Diaz's hands, his mouth, the way he did it. Every place he touched her seemed connected to her pussy, because she quivered and quaked there at his every kiss and caress.

But he wasn't content to stop at her breasts. He released her wrists, at last, but only because he snaked lower, kissing his way down her ribs, her belly, lingering at the piercing at her navel, flicking it with his tongue, dipping into her belly button until she giggled. And then he moved even farther down, spreading her legs apart to situate himself between them and draw them over his arms.

He was so dark, his head between her thighs, his hair brushing her skin. She tensed, waiting, barely able to breathe as his mouth moved toward her skin. He kissed and licked her inner thigh.

"You smell good, Jess."

She blushed, her skin went hot, knowing what was going to happen, anticipating it, wanting it, this first she'd never had before. At the warm, wet touch of his lips to her sex, she trembled, shifted the pillow under her head so she could watch his mouth cover her clit, shuddering when his tongue made contact with the piercing. He flicked the silver ring, licked around it, played with it, then laid his tongue over her clit and took her so close to the edge she gripped the sheets in a tight knot. But he pulled back, letting his tongue glide along her pussy lips, down, then back up again, avoiding her clit, then right on it again, taking her close and moving back, seeming to know how far to take her without letting her fly.

The man was maddening, and each time the sensations grew more and more intense, building her pleasure to a fevered pitch. Soon she was raising her butt off the bed, driving her pussy into his face. He held on to her and pushed her back down, but she was mindless now, didn't care, wanted only the orgasm he could bring her.

"Diaz, please."

She felt his fingers probing near her pussy, and oh was he going to?

He did, sliding one inside her as he continued to lick along the folds. Then two fingers, stretching her, pumping them in and out as he licked and sucked her clit, his mouth and tongue hot and wet, the dual sensations overwhelming. It was all she could take. She went off like the space shuttle in a burst of light and flames.

"I'm coming, Diaz, I'm coming!" she cried as she lifted off the bed, shuddering through one of the wildest orgasms she'd ever felt. He held on to her, his fingers continuing to fuck her with relentless strokes until she felt the contractions subside. He withdrew, kissed the top of her sex and made his way up her body, taking her mouth, letting her taste her own pussy juice on his lips. She licked at his mouth, sucking his tongue inside. He rolled her over on top of him and she kissed him deeply, pouring out her feelings with her mouth, cradling his face between her palms and then pushing up to stare down at him.

"Thank you," she said.

"You're welcome. And thank you. I enjoyed it, too."

She smiled down at him, then slid her now soaking wet pussy along the length of his cock. It would be so easy to fuck him right now, to ease it inside her and ride him. She quivered at the thought.

"No, Jess."

She frowned. "Why the hell not?"

He grasped her hips, lifted, and the sensation was incredible. "Because you need a relationship, a boyfriend. Not a fuck buddy."

"I want to fuck you." The thought of having him inside her gave her goose bumps.

He bucked her off of him and rolled them both to the side so they were facing each other. "No, you don't. You want someone who'll be there for you, all the time. You want the tenderness, the companionship, all the emotional stuff that goes with a relationship. That's not me."

"You're always around when I need you, just like the other guys."

"And that's exactly what I'm talking about, Jess. Me, the other guys." He dragged his hand through his hair. "We shouldn't even have done this much. This is wrong." He pushed up and sat on the edge of the bed.

Diaz had some seriously misguided notions about her, about the

two of them, about the Wild Riders and where she fit in the scheme
of their relationships. She really needed to set him straight.

She slid to the end of the bed with him, took his hand in hers.
So big, it nearly dwarfed her small hand. She laced her fingers
with his.

"Your problem is that you've known me since I was a kid, since
Grange and all of you sort of 'adopted' me. So you've all thought
of me as some little sister or something for all these years."

He turned his head and looked at her. "Yes. That's it exactly."

"That was fine back then. It isn't now. Well it is and it isn't. I
think of all the guys as family, and Grange, too. He was the father
I never had. He's been good to me. The guys have all been brothers. I came into the Wild Riders at a time in my life when I needed
family more than I needed anything."

"See? That's what makes this wrong."

She shook her head. "No, let me finish. It was wonderful then,
but I'm not a child anymore, and I haven't been for a long time. I
grew up, and when I did I started noticing men. Or rather, *a* man.
You, specifically."

He arched a brow. "Me? Why?"

She shrugged. "I don't know. Call it chemistry or whatever
you want, but I suddenly saw you as someone other than 'family.'
The other guys? Yeah, they're like brothers to me. Funny, silly,
they can grab me and hug me and I feel nothing at all but warmth
and connection and the feeling of belonging. You? You were different. I look at you and I feel something that's very unlike family. When I look at you I tingle inside, my toes curl, and I get hot.
You're a sexy, desirable man that I've wanted for many years. I've
just been waiting for you to wake up and notice me as a woman."

His eyes widened. "Honey, I've noticed you were a woman for
several years now. And that's been a huge problem for me."

"Really?" The thought pleased her.

"Quit smiling. I said it was a problem."

"Oh. Sorry. But really, it's not a problem." Why was he making this so difficult?

He heaved a sigh. "Yeah, it is. I'm not going to do this, Jess. We're not going to be a couple. I'm not going to fuck you and ruin your life."

She rolled her eyes. "You having sex with me isn't going to ruin my life, Diaz. I have no expectations that it'll be followed by a marriage proposal. I'm a big girl. I can handle it."

He kissed the tip of her nose. "But I can't, knowing I'd have taken something from you that you should give to someone special."

She laid her palm across his cheek. "I think you are special."

"You're making this very hard for me."

She reached between them, circling his semihard cock. "Not very hard, but I'll bet I could get it that way."

He laughed. "Damn, Jessie. I'm trying to be serious here."

"Me too. I'm damn serious about getting your cock in my mouth again. So don't stop me."

Before he could say anything, she shimmied down his body. This was her chance to explore, and she prayed he wouldn't stop her this time. Not when she had the opportunity to feel and kiss the hard planes of his chest and stomach, which rippled when she pressed light kisses against it and palmed it with both hands. With a gentle push she rolled him onto his back and she climbed onto his thighs, raking her fingernails down his sides to test his tickle response.

Nothing. The man was a rock. A solid tree trunk of muscle and iron will. It was her duty to break his will, to make him sweat, to test his limits and make him crumble.

She was going to enjoy this. How could she not, having free

rein to discover Diaz's body? He wasn't moving, just watching her with a guarded expression. She loved his eyes—dark, fathomless, she could drown in them. But not now. Now she was going on an expedition of skin. She leaned forward and kissed his shoulder, then sank her teeth into it, nibbling with the tiniest of bites. She felt the gooseflesh rise on his skin, but he didn't shiver. She moved across to his chest, doing to him what he'd done to her—waving her palms over his flat nipples, circling them until they hardened like pebbles under her touch.

Oh, she liked that, and used her thumb and forefinger to capture each one, tug them, pinch them, then bent down and took each in her mouth, dragging her tongue over one, then the other, rewarded when he sucked in a harsh breath. So . . . he liked his nipples played with, too. Knowing that made her pussy wet.

She licked along his rib cage, then lower, scooting down his thighs. Damn, he was so big underneath her, reminding her how small she was and how gently he treated her. He was so wrong about what she needed. He thought he couldn't be the kind of man she wanted? He was exactly what she wanted. His patience right now astounded her. If all he wanted was a pussy to fuck, he'd never let her explore like this.

His hard cock jutted against her belly, then her breasts as she snaked her tongue along his hip bone, loving the way he tasted, the differences in the way their bodies were made. She buried her nose in the wiry thatch of hair at his sex, inhaling his musky fragrance, realizing the primal scent excited her. She ran her tongue along his inner thigh, then lower, where his ball sac lay nestled against his ass. She licked there too, toyed with the seam separating his balls, and he groaned, his thigh muscles clenching as she captured one of his balls in her mouth and licked his flesh, only to release it and play with the other.

There wasn't a part of him she didn't want to touch, to taste, to play with. She grasped his cock with one hand and licked the underside from the base to the tip, following the seam like a road map leading to the soft crest. Now she met his eyes, which were smoldering like a barely banked flame. When she looked at him and captured his cockhead in her mouth, covering it while flicking her tongue over it, that flame burst into an inferno. He rocketed onto his elbows, pumped his hips upward and thrust his cock between her greedy lips, feeding her.

She grasped his cock with both hands, playing with him, squeezing and stroking while sucking him, watching the way he undulated under her hands, the way his eyes nearly rolled back into his head when she swirled her tongue over the tip, then brought him fully into her mouth. Then she gave up control and let him sink deep, all the way to her throat, content to let him thrust and withdraw.

Instinct drove her, and she began to stroke him in earnest as she felt his muscles tense under her, knew he was getting close when he grasped the back of her head to direct her movements. She felt the dampness of perspiration on his legs, knew that driving force of impending climax, when nothing else mattered but reaching the pinnacle.

She wanted to take him there. She squeezed with her lips, sucked with her mouth, and a low groan tore from his throat at the same time Diaz erupted, gifting her with sweet come. She held on to his cock and to him as he shuddered violently, pumping furiously into her mouth. She swallowed, holding on to him as he emptied, swallowed until he had nothing left to give her and collapsed onto his back, his muscles relaxing.

Content to lay with her head on his thigh, she stroked his leg, licked her lips, and smiled. Diaz caressed her hair and she listened to him breathe, first raspy and hard, then finally normal again. Her pulse had been racing, too. She'd been as turned on as he was, her nipples tingling, her pussy quivering and wet. Giving pleasure was as thrilling as getting it. She had so much to learn about sex. And such a wonderful teacher.

She lifted her head. "Thank you, again."

He lifted his. "For what?"

"For another lesson. That was fun. I had no idea making you come would excite me so much."

He shuddered a breath and shook his head, then disengaged himself, sliding off the bed and heading into the bathroom to turn on the shower. She followed.

"There's really no point in cleaning up. Yet," she said, hoping her meaning was clear.

"Yeah, there is, because we're finished here."

"No, we're not. We just started."

He opened the shower door and stepped inside. Undaunted, she followed him in and closed the door behind her. "Diaz, don't do this."

He stuck his head in the shower spray, shaking his head so water droplets flew everywhere, then turned to face her. "I think I've already done enough."

"Not enough."

"Too much. No more, Jess. I already told you I'm not fucking you." He stepped out of the spray and reached for the soap, giving her room to move into the warm water.

She did, wetting her hair and body down, and taking the soap from his outstretched hand. "Don't you think we already crossed the threshold? What's holding you back?"

As he soaped himself, he said, "You don't want me. I don't know how much clearer I can make it."

She was getting irritated with being told what she did and didn't want. "I think I can choose for myself."

"Not without knowing me better. You only know what you've seen. Not the rest of it."

She ducked under the spray to rinse her body, then moved so Diaz could do the same. "What rest of it?"

He stepped out of the shower, and she turned it off, grabbing for the towel he held for her as she walked out.

"My father beat my mother every day, Jess. His temper was monstrous. Do you know how angry I get? That kind of temper can only run in my family. I have it. I've seen it. Hell, everyone in the Wild Riders has seen it."

She wrapped the towel around herself, moving toward him, needing to touch him. She put her arms around him, held him for a moment before pulling away to look at him. At least he let her hold him. "I'm sorry for your mother, what she had to go through, Diaz. That must have been awful for her."

"It was. But that's not my point."

"What is?"

"I'm not the kind of guy you need. I'm like a ticking time bomb."

"Because of your father?"

He nodded.

She smiled, shook her head. "That's not who you are."

"You don't even know me." He walked out of the bathroom.

She followed. Again.

It was time she explained a few things about herself. She sat on the bed.

"I never knew who my father was. My mother probably didn't know, either. One of her johns, I would imagine."

Diaz stilled, turned to her. "I didn't know. Grange didn't—"

"Of course he didn't. He wouldn't, because he protected me. None of you know anything about me. My mother was a whore and a crack addict. She tried to sell me, to turn me out into the streets in order to make money to get her next fix. When her looks became so bad she couldn't make money lying on her back anymore, she tried to get me to do it for her so she could get her drugs. Her drugs were more important than I was, Diaz. She would have sold my virginity for a fix."

Diaz's eyes narrowed, his jaw clenched, shock and fury evident on his face. "Son of a bitch. Wasn't there anyone to help you?"

She shrugged. "Not really. It wasn't like she had family who cared. And she only thought of the drugs. As soon as she figured out I was young and pretty and the guys were giving me the eye, she saw dollar signs."

"Christ, Jessie. Did any of them—"

She shook her head. "No. I was faster, and I was sober. I knew when to get out of the way and I had great hiding places."

He leaned his head against the wall. "What you had to go through . . ."

She shrugged. "I'm over it. It took a while, but I got past it. As soon as she tried to use me like that I was history."

"Goddammit, Jessie. I'm sorry." He came toward her, but she rose and backed away, crossed her arms, hating that she had to dredge up the past.

She narrowed her gaze at him. "Don't feel sorry for me. Don't pity me. I never did. I survived. So did you. None of us are products of our past, Diaz. We're survivors. We're tough. That's why Grange chose us. I did fine after Mac pulled me off the streets and brought me to the Wild Riders. So did you. So don't give me that bullshit about you being who your father was. That's a flimsy excuse for you not wanting to make love to me, and I won't accept it."

He stared at her for the longest time, and Jessie couldn't decide if he wanted to turn tail and run or grab her and hold her. She waited. Then he grabbed clothes, jammed his legs into his pants, and pulled on a T-shirt, then socks and boots, keeping his back to her until he was dressed.

Dressed. Like armor, she thought, crossing her arms over her chest. If he had his clothes on, he could be protected against big, bad Jessie. She'd laugh if it wasn't so sad.

When he finally turned to her, he had his jacket and his keys in his hand.

"It's the only excuse I have, Jess. I'm sorry."

This time when he walked out, she didn't even try to stop him.

EIGHT

DIAZ WAS DETERMINED TO KEEP HIS HEAD IN THE JOB TODAY, and not on Jessie. He'd made a critical error last night, one he didn't intend to repeat. He couldn't blame Jessie for it, either. She might be putting the full press on him, but it was up to him to say *no*, to back away before things got out of hand. Though how much more out of hand could they get?

This morning he sat and nursed a cup of black coffee while he waited for Spence and Jessie to join him in the hotel restaurant. He'd buzzed Jessie's cell this morning and notified her they'd have a meeting over breakfast. She seemed fine enough, not angry, said she'd be down shortly.

He hoped like hell Jessie would someday forgive him for what he'd done to her, for leading her on. It could have been worse. He could have fucked her. Granted, her virginity might not be an actual physical thing any longer, but it meant something to him. And obviously, to her. She hadn't given it to anyone else, and he sure as

hell wasn't going to be the one to take it from her. That had catas-
trophe written all over it. Thankfully he'd come to his senses last
night before he'd taken that step, though it had been a close call.

He'd wanted her. To be honest, he still wanted her. Spending
the night in Spence's room hadn't changed that.

When he'd called Spence's cell and said he was bunking in his
room for the night, Spence told him he was insane. Spence was probably right. But at least Spence had the decency not to ask questions.
Diaz wasn't sure he had good enough answers to explain this mess.

He glanced up at the swoosh of the elevator doors opening.
Hotel guests spilled out, lugging their suitcases or laptops. Jessie
was at the back of the crowd, dressed in skintight jeans, another
body-hugging shirt cut low in front and revealing an ample amount
of cleavage. She didn't smile, her full lips pressed together as she
approached. Still, she took his breath away. His cock tightened as
he remembered what it was like to touch her, to taste her. He'd
only had a sample, and it wasn't enough. Not nearly enough.

Tough. It was going to have to be, because he'd had all he was
going to.

She laid her bag down on the chair. "I'm going for breakfast.
Be right back," she said.

He nodded, taking another long swallow of his coffee and
watching her as she filled her tray.

"Can't take your eyes off her, can you?" Spence asked as he slid
into the chair next to Diaz.

"Don't know what you're talking about."

"Jessie. You. Watching her ass. Practically drooling. I'll need a
raincoat just to eat next to you."

Diaz turned to Spence and frowned. "Asshole. I am not
drooling."

Spence leaned back in the chair and grinned. "You're so obvious. It's really kind of pathetic. You have this lost puppy dog look about you. Does she have a cock ring on you yet, one she can tie the leash to?"

Diaz narrowed his gaze, and lowered his voice. "You really don't want me beating the shit out of you at this crowded restaurant, Spencer."

Spencer's only reply was to snort, then kick back the chair and stand. "Yeah, right. You're too preoccupied sniffing after pussy to kick anything. I'm going for coffee and something to eat. Why don't you crawl under the table and look for your balls while I'm gone?"

Diaz would be pissed if he didn't know Spence so well. It was Spence's way of teasing him about Jessie, about the two of them having a thing together.

Spence was wrong. *Dead wrong.* There was nothing going on between them.

Not anymore.

He watched Spence come up behind Jessie and poke her in the ribs. She jumped, jabbed her elbow in Spence's stomach, then laughed. Spence threw an arm around Jessie and kissed her cheek. The exchange was warm and affectionate. Like brother and sister. Diaz didn't sense any tension between the two of them.

Nothing at all like when he and Jessie were together. Then there was lots of tension, and it was all sexual.

Just as she'd told him last night, Jessie definitely acted differently with him than she did with the other guys.

His lips curled. He couldn't help it. Despite knowing it was wrong, the all-male part of him liked the fact that he was special . . . different . . . to her.

She and Spence returned with their food and ate. Diaz had been up for hours so he'd already eaten. He refilled his coffee and listened to the two of them chatter, mainly about Spence and the woman he'd hooked up with, Stephanie.

"Does she know anything?" Diaz asked.

Spence shrugged. "She knew Rex, who's numero uno tight with Crush. But right now she's wary. I think Rex dumping her stung a bit. I'm trying not to push her too hard for information. I don't want to make her suspicious. I'm approaching it as the new guy who's interested in the girl and not wanting to step on the toes of the ex-boyfriend thing."

"That's a good idea," Jessie suggested. "It's best if you get to know her gradually, let her think you're only interested in some fun, not trying to pry secrets out of her."

"We're all walking the tightrope with Crush and his gang," Diaz reminded them. "We can't be too careful about what we do or say. The last thing we want to do is blow this."

"I'm just letting her think I'm after her body," Spence said with a grin.

Jessie rolled her eyes. "That shouldn't be too much of a stretch for you, should it?"

"Just like normal."

"While you're out there being yourself with Stephanie, see if you can get some information. We are on assignment here."

Spence nodded at him. "Yeah. I'll do that. See if you and Jessie can take your eyes off each other long enough to remember that, too."

Jessie went crimson and stared down at her plate. Diaz glared at Spence, who cracked an innocent smile. Diaz would like nothing more right now than to wipe the floor with him.

As soon as this assignment was over . . . it would be payback time. Diaz and Spence would be working out together in the gym. The boxing ring. And then he'd get his revenge.

Spence knew what was coming, too, because his smile turned into a wide grin and he nodded. "Anytime, pal."

Good thing they were friends or they might possibly kill each other.

"There's way too much testosterone at the table this morning," Jessie said, grabbing her tray. "I need to go upstairs, grab my gear for the day. I'll meet you two down here in a few."

Diaz nodded and watched her leave. As soon as the elevators closed, he turned to Spence. "Knock it off."

"Knock what off?"

"The teasing about Jessie."

"Why? It doesn't seem to bother her. Only you. And why is that?"

Diaz clammed up.

"You're tense, man," Spence said. "You and I have done this before, this verbal sparring. It's never gotten to you like this."

Diaz inhaled, let it out, trying to relax the knots of tension in his shoulders. "You're right. Sorry."

"Hey, it's no big deal to me. I can handle it just fine. But there's obviously something going on between you and Jessie."

Diaz dragged his fingers through his hair. "Shit. No, there isn't. There can't be."

Spence drained his coffee and placed the cup on the tray. "Why the hell not?"

"For the obvious reasons."

Spence laughed. "She's an adult now, Diaz. She's beautiful, smart, the kind of woman any guy would be lucky to have, and the great thing is, she wants you. Unless you're stupid and blind you have to be able to see that."

"Yeah, I see it."

"So what's the problem?" Spence asked with a shrug. "You're two consenting adults. Go for it."

If only it were that easy. "We're supposed to protect her."

"And we will, just like we always have." Spence stood and grabbed his tray. "I couldn't think of a better guy for her to be with."

Diaz studied his friend, stunned speechless by his words.

"But if you hurt her, I'll have to kill you."

Diaz watched Spence walked away, realizing he'd stepped into a no-win situation with Jessie. He wanted her so badly he couldn't think straight. Typically the solution to that kind of problem with a woman was simple—fuck her, then forget her.

But this was Jess, and she was special. She wasn't just another fuck.

Which meant he'd have to screw his head on straight and forget about Jessie as a woman, do this assignment, then stay the hell away from her after that. He'd convince Grange not to assign the two of them together again, that there was a conflict. It would work out, if he could get them through this case.

He and Spence headed outside, met Jessie out there.

"I think we should try and get into that wooded area we rode past yesterday," he suggested. "I could have sworn I saw an encampment there."

"Shouldn't we meet up with Crush's gang?" Jessie asked.

"Not necessarily. I don't want us to appear too eager, following him around like we have nothing better to do. We do want an invite to initiation, but I'd like him interested in us as independent riders, not hangers-on. Let him wonder where we are today."

Jessie nodded. "Oh, good point. So where are we supposed to be today when he asks?"

"Since we're heading east, we'll tell him we went north. Once we check out the area, we'll take one of the roads that jogged up north so we can report back and answer any questions. Remember, this is his backyard so we don't want to be caught in a lie."

Jessie climbed on her bike, looked to Diaz. "You're a pretty smart guy."

Diaz leaned over, smiled, and tipped her nose with his finger. "That's why I'm in charge."

They fired up their bikes and rode out of town, heading east toward the back roads they'd traveled yesterday. Diaz remembered clearly the mile marker where he'd spotted the smoke and glimpsed the flag. When they came around the curve toward it again, he searched for the smoke but didn't see anything. At the lead, he slowed, pulled off at the side of the road and stopped.

"Is this the spot?" Spence asked.

"Yeah. I don't want to call attention to ourselves in case someone's watching." Diaz bent over to look at his bike as if there was a mechanical issue. "But over my left shoulder at about eight o'clock there was smoke, and I thought I saw a white flag with a red mark on it deep within the wooded area."

"You decoy bike maintenance," Spence said. "I'll walk across the road and into the woods to take a leak and check it out."

"Then I'll stay here," Jessie said, doing a quick about-face to join Diaz. She squatted down underneath him and looked up. "What will we do if we spot something?"

"You mean like a camp?"

"Yeah."

He grabbed a wrench out of his saddlebag. "Hold this nut for me. Might as well tighten it so I look like I'm actually doing something. As far as a camp, if we investigate and see something, we'll do . . . nothing for the moment. We don't have the manpower or adequate firepower to combat an entire survivalist camp. And we wouldn't be certain that's even the right one."

"There's more than one?"

"Honey, there could be hundreds of survivalists in different encampments in this state alone. No way of knowing. They pack up here in the hills like ant colonies, hiding out from organized government."

She wrinkled her nose. "Don't like anyone telling them what to do, do they?"

Diaz frowned. "Or how to do it. They make their own laws, have their own way of doing things. They resent government interference in any form. That's only minor compared to their other . . . thought processes."

"Running guns is still illegal."

"And if we find them, we'll work with the government in taking them down. That's what we're here for."

Spence came up behind them. "There's a road. Camouflaged pretty well, but it's there. Didn't see smoke or any flags, but thought I heard a twig snap so it's possible we're being watched. I think we should make some noise about seeing it, then let's go off-road riding, see what happens."

Jessie met Diaz's gaze. "Dangerous?"

He nodded. "Stay with me and get ready to hightail it out of there in a hurry if there's trouble. No arguing, understand?"

"Got it."

"Keep your eyes and ears open at all times. Right now we're just biker tourists doing a little off-road exploring, and that's it."

Diaz tossed the wrench in his saddlebag.

"Bike okay now?" Spence asked, loud enough to be heard across the road.

"Good as new."

"Great. Because I think I might have found a trail over there," Spence said, motioning with his head and keeping his voice normal, but making sure anyone listening could hear him.

"Yeah? Let's go check it out."

They fired up the bikes and turned around, easing down the barely discernible path. Spence had been right. The road was covered with brush and leaves, deliberately hidden from regular traffic's view, but fairly easy to follow once they were on it. The wind from Diaz's bike in the front blew the leaves out of the way, clearing the road in his wake. The road twisted and turned around a dense crop of trees and bushes.

Jesus. How easy it would be to hide up here in the hills. One turn and you could get lost. The road snaked out tendrils in multiple directions. They should have probably left a bread-crumb trail so they could find their way out.

A flash of movement to Diaz's left caught his eye. He cut his engine. Spence and Jessie did the same, bringing their bikes up level next to his.

"What's up?" Spence asked.

"Movement on the left," he said. "I wanted to cut the engines to listen."

They climbed off the bikes and looked around. The quiet was incredible. Birds, the rustle of limbs and leaves in the wind whipping through the trees. The sound of water somewhere far off in the distance. No footsteps, though.

Until the crack of a branch on the ground caught their attention. Diaz swiveled, reaching around to palm the gun tucked into his pants. He didn't want to pull it out unless necessary, though, didn't want to cause suspicion. So he waited, trying to maintain a relaxed posture while positioning himself in front of Jessie just in case someone came at them or, even worse, fired at them.

"Someone's behind a tree," Spence whispered, coming up beside Diaz.

"Where?"

"About ten o'clock. They're not very good at this. I see weaving movement. Just watch."

Diaz saw it, too. Whoever was there kept low to the ground. "Okay, stay alert and ready for anything, including jumping on the bikes and getting the hell out of here if we find ourselves outnumbered."

"Is someone there?" Jessie finally asked, loud enough to be heard.

A little boy around eight to ten years old came out from behind the tree, followed by a woman. Not at all who he expected to see, but then again, it didn't surprise him that they'd use a woman and a kid as fronts. Scary-looking woman, too, wearing a ball cap, brown pants, a sweatshirt, all baggy. And not a friendly expression on her face. Her entire outfit was designed to disguise her appearance. He'd never be able to describe her, from hair color to build to eye color.

"We fooled you," the little boy said with a wide grin. His face was dirty, his hair wild and uncombed. The mother didn't look much more put together, either.

"Sorry to scare y'all," the woman said. "My boy wanted to play hide-and-seek."

Bullshit, Diaz thought. These two were decoys. He could tell from the suspicious and wary look on the woman's face. It wasn't that she was worried for the kid. She was protecting something, or someone. Instinct told him these two weren't the only ones out here. He could feel other eyes on them.

"So you were out playing?" Jessie asked, crouching down as the boy came up to her.

"Yeah. Hide-and-go-seek."

"That's a fun game."

While Jessie interacted with the little boy, Diaz checked out the surrounding area.

Yeah, they weren't alone. He couldn't see anyone, but there were others nearby. Well hidden, but close, watching. And he'd bet his bike they had guns trained on them. He kept his hand on his hip, within reach of his gun. He took a quick glance at Spence, noticed he did the same thing, his body language showing he was ready for anything.

Diaz searched, but didn't see even the slightest movement through the trees or beyond.

These people were good.

"Is this your property?" Diaz asked.

The woman shook her head. "We're camping."

Diaz nodded.

"So, is this your mom?" Jessie asked the little boy.

The kid jerked his head up to the woman, who nodded.

"Uh, yeah. It's my mom."

Another lie.

"How's the camping out here?" Diaz asked.

"Good," the woman said. "Our whole family's here. Got a spot a ways back in the deep woods. We like our privacy, like to be alone. And your bikes are loud and scarin' away the fish."

That message was clear: Don't come any closer.

"Sorry to intrude," Spence said. "We found a road and went exploring."

"Nice bikes," the boy said. "They yours?"

"They sure are," Jessie said. "Do you ride?"

"Nuh uh. We don't even have a car."

"Bobby."

One terse word from the woman and the little boy took a step back.

"Of course we have a car," the woman said, laying her hands on the boy's shoulders. "It's just my brother's. Ours is being repaired so we came in his motor home. Ya know, back there where we're campin'."

"Yes ma'am," Diaz said. "We'll let you two get back to your game and we'll head out. Sorry to disturb you."

The woman nodded and stepped away, motioning to the boy, who moved with her. Diaz noticed neither of them turned their backs as they retreated, but walked backward, keeping watch over Diaz and Jessie and Spence as they climbed back on their bikes and rode away. He didn't pull over again until they'd reached a gas station about twenty miles away from the area where they'd stopped.

"That was interesting," Spence said. "What do you make of it?"

"Gotta be a survivalist camp back there. Those people had something to hide, and they sure as hell didn't want us to come any closer."

"Did you see anyone else?" Jessie asked.

"No, but they were around. That woman and boy weren't up there on their own. They were decoys, sent to . . . discourage us from traveling any farther."

"And if we'd gone on anyway?" she asked.

"We'd have been stopped. That isn't a group the three of us could take on our own."

"Hence the retreat," Spence added.

Diaz nodded. "It's enough to know the encampment is there. I'm going to alert Grange, see if he can get us some satellite and infrared intel on that area to determine what and who and how many are in there. Maybe he'll be able to confirm an encampment."

"Then what?" Jessie asked.

"Then we'll know. It may or may not be one affiliated with Crush and his gang, but we can keep an eye on the location. At least it's a start. We can watch who comes out to this area, see if Crush rides out here again, especially if we get through initiation."

Jessie's face went pale at that.

"Something wrong?"

She shook her head. "No."

She was lying. Something bothered her. He'd have to ask her again later. "Okay, let's head back to town and see what's going on."

A couple of hours later they roared into town and mingled with the other bikers on the main drag. Crush's gang was already there, most of them hanging out at one of the bars lining the main street. Diaz pulled around and stopped to talk to Crush, who was walking out of the bar just as they drove past.

"Hey, where have you all been today?" Crush asked.

"Great day for a ride, so we decided to bag the festivities and cruise for a while," Diaz said.

"Oh yeah?" Where'd you go?"

"Up north a bit, rode around toward Beaver Lake."

Crush nodded. "Pretty up there. Nice ride."

"Anything going on around here today?"

"Half-naked women in chaps, lots of beer and food, and riding. Same as always," Crush said with a grin.

Diaz laughed.

"We're going to a bonfire tonight outside of town. You want to come?"

"Sure." Diaz knew if they didn't seem too eager, Crush might be more interested in them. No bike leader wanted hangers-on, but would respect those who were more independent. Diaz's intent was to get them invited to initiation when the rally was over.

Only then would they get closer to the Devil's Skulls' inner workings and figure out what, if any, involvement Crush and his gang had in the illegal arms dealings in this part of the country.

And in order to do that, he had to know how to play the game.

"You're quiet today, Jessie," Crush said, looking over Diaz's shoulder.

"Just soaking it all in. Plus, I had a late night last night," she said, her gaze flitting to Diaz.

Crush's brows raised, then he grinned. "I see." He nodded at Diaz, then said, "You are one lucky son of a bitch."

Diaz looked to Jessie, then back at Crush. "I know." Too bad it was just a game, that his and Jessie's "relationship" was only a front for this mission. His stomach tightened remembering what it felt like to hold her in his arms, to touch and taste her. Being preoccupied with the mission today had helped, but thoughts of Jessie were never far from his mind. They still had so much left unfinished.

He'd walked out on her last night. Again. For someone so strong, he sure as hell was a coward where she was concerned. But he had to protect her.

From himself.

They hung out on the streets for a while and at the bar visiting with the other Devil's Skulls, until dusk shadowed the main drag in filtered sunlight.

"I'm going to gather everyone up," Crush said, then gave Diaz directions to where the bonfire was going to be. "I'll see you all there about ten."

Diaz nodded. Spence left with Stephanie and said he'd meet up with them later. Once they were alone, Diaz and Jessie hopped on their bikes and headed back to the hotel, mainly because Diaz wanted some privacy to report to Grange on what they'd found this afternoon and ask for a satellite feed on that location. They grabbed a bite to eat on the way, then went up to the room. Diaz got on the phone to Grange first thing, filling him in on what they'd found.

"I'll get right on it and report back to you by morning with intel on the area," Grange said.

"Great."

"How's Jessie doing?"

"Fine."

"That's not a very detailed report."

Considering Jess was standing right next to him in their room, that was all Grange was getting. "All you can have at the moment."

"Is she competent?"

"Yes."

"Not getting in the way?"

"Not at all."

"She's good, Diaz. Give her a chance."

"That's what I'm doing, Grange."

"Okay, I'll get back with you in the morning."

Diaz hung up and turned to Jessie. "He'll run a satellite feed on the area, see what they find."

"Good." Jessie turned away and headed toward the closet, sliding open the door and staring into it.

"Jess, what's wrong? You've been quiet ever since I mentioned initiation."

"Nothing. I'm fine."

"You wanna talk about last night?" He owed her an apology for walking out on her again, or at least some sort of explanation.

"No, I definitely don't walk to talk about last night." She grabbed some clothes. "I'm going to change before the bonfire." She slid into the bathroom and shut the door.

Something wasn't right, and Diaz was determined to find out what. Maybe it had to do with what happened between them last night, but he had an idea it was more than that. They hadn't exchanged more than a few sentences all day, and those had been mainly about the mission. Nothing of a personal nature at all.

Great. Wasn't that what he'd wanted? To keep their relationship all business? So why was it bothering him?

Can't have it both ways, dickhead.

After the bonfire tonight, he'd make her talk to him. He needed to know what she was thinking for the good of their mission.

Or at least that's what he told himself.

nine

IT WAS THE LAST NIGHT BEFORE INITIATION, THE LAST NIGHT OF THE
bike rally. Jessie knew this was her last chance, too. *Now or never.*

Maybe it should be never—maybe she should give up.

Oh hell no. She wasn't a quitter, never had been and wasn't
about to start now. Though after last night's defeat, it was difficult
mustering up any kind of enthusiasm to try again with Diaz.

How many times could a girl throw herself at a guy, get rejected, and try again, before she got the message that he didn't
want her?

She stripped and faced the mirror, thinking about last night,
remembering the look on his face as he touched her, put his
mouth on her.

Okay, so it wasn't true. He *did* want her. That much had been
quite clear last night. He hadn't put a stop to their play. They'd
both had amazing orgasms. Her pussy clenched remembering the
way he'd taken her over the edge. She closed her eyes, cupped her

breasts, sliding her thumbs over her painfully sensitive nipples, wishing it was Diaz standing behind her, stroking her nipples with his fingers, watching her reaction in the mirror. She could picture his big body behind her, his erection stiff and hot and pumping against her hip as he leaned into her, grasping her nipples and plucking them, forcing her to watch as he grazed the tiny pebbles until she couldn't stand it anymore. Then he'd move one hand over her belly, play with the piercing at her navel, but only for a few seconds, because he wouldn't be able to resist going lower, just as she did now with her hand, sliding into her panties.

Dampness greeted her, the spill of her arousal, hot and wet. She palmed her sex, shivered at the sensation as she teased her clit, then went lower, tucking two fingers into her pussy. She hissed as her walls contracted around the invasion, couldn't hold back the moan as she began to finger fuck herself, imagining it was Diaz's oversized fingers inside her.

Here in the bathroom in front of the mirror she'd be able to watch it all, see his fingers disappear inside her as he fucked her with one hand and rubbed her clit with the other.

She wasn't going to last long, needed this orgasm, a bursting release from the pent-up tension she'd held inside all day.

"Please," she whispered, rocking her pelvis against her hand, feeling the tight squeeze as orgasm rushed ever closer. "Yes, yes, make me come."

She felt dizziness as she climaxed, shoved her fingers all the way inside, imagined Diaz's dark, encouraging words as she sailed over the edge with a blindsiding orgasm. She whimpered her release, riding it, enjoying it, wishing he were here to do this for her.

Spent, perspiring, she opened her eyes, studied the heated desire in them, and shuddered, palming the bathroom counter.

God, she wanted more from him. So much more. Why couldn't

he see that making love wasn't going to change anything between them?

She needed him, needed him to make love to her, for more reasons than she could explain. Though she was going to have to come clean, tell him one of those reasons. And it was going to have to be tonight.

She really had to get a decent sex life. One that didn't involve doing it herself.

After freshening up, she got dressed, fixed her hair and makeup, and sucked in a cleansing breath, preparing for the night ahead. There was a lot to accomplish tonight. When she opened the door, she was stunned to find Diaz leaning against the wall right outside the bathroom, his arms crossed.

He made her mouth water. He had his leather chaps on and a black long-sleeved shirt that stretched tight across his chest. She shuddered a breath.

"Have fun in there?"

Faking nonchalance, she shrugged and brushed past him. "Not as much fun as I would have if you'd been in there with me."

Clearly he'd heard her, knew what she'd been doing. *Good.* She hoped he'd get worked up thinking about it, visualizing it. She grabbed her bag and her keys and turned around. Her nipples hardened at the way he looked at her, his gaze dark, penetrating. She refused to look anywhere but his eyes, knowing his cock was hard. Moisture dampened her panties.

"Ready?" she asked.

He paused for a few seconds, then gave her a short nod. "Yeah. Let's do it."

They rode east out of town, using Crush's directions, following the road signs until they came to an unpaved road to the left with one of the Devil's Skulls' helmets slung on top of a fence post. That was their signal to head into the woods. They had to slow down on the gravel road for several miles until they came to a clearing, a two-story farmhouse on a huge patch of land. Out in the pasture everyone was gathered by bales of hay and what seemed like a mile-high pile of wood.

The Skulls were all present, loud and rowdy and seemingly having a great time. There was already a fire blazing, and the smell of meat cooking. They parked and headed over that way until they found Crush, Rex, and a few others. Crush reached into a cooler and tossed them a couple of beers.

"Enjoy the party," he said. "Tomorrow's initiation, you know."

"We know," Diaz said.

Jessie realized Diaz wouldn't ask if they were going to be invited. That would be too . . . desperate. But she had a feeling from Crush's secretive smile that they had a pretty good chance of garnering an invite tomorrow.

Which brought about its own set of unique problems. Ones she refused to ponder until the time came.

Jessie was glad she'd worn her leather jacket. The night had a crisp chill. The lack of breeze was good, too, otherwise in this treeless clearing she'd be freezing. She stood closer to Diaz to ward off the chill as they talked with the guys. Surprisingly, he must have noticed her shivering, because he slung his arm around her and drew her close to the heat of his body. Maybe he was doing it for the mission, to cement the two of them as a couple. No way was she going to argue with whatever his reasons were. It felt good to be held by him, both from a comfort and an emotional standpoint. She needed his support.

Spence and Stephanie came over and they all grabbed spots on bales of hay. A couple of guys had guitars and started playing music. The night was clear, a million stars putting on a show overhead. Jessie leaned her head on Diaz's shoulder, content to listen to the music and the deep reverberation of Diaz's voice as he and Crush and Spence talked bikes and road trips they'd taken over the years.

"What about you?" Stephanie asked. "How long have you been riding?"

Jessie smiled. "Since I was sixteen and my . . . my brothers taught me."

Stephanie nodded, tossing her red curls over her shoulders. "I had a boyfriend who loved bikes. I rode with him for a couple of years, but man, I hated riding behind him. I wanted my own bike. After we broke up, I gravitated toward bikers, and Crush hooked me up. I eventually found a guy who got me a bike of my own and I've been riding ever since."

"It does get in your blood, doesn't it?"

"Yeah, I guess so. Or maybe it's the men who ride them. And ride us, too," she said with a laugh, trailing a bloodred fingernail down Spence's leather jacket.

Spence grinned down at Stephanie, who batted her lashes at him. Jessie rolled her eyes. Could the woman be more obvious?

Spence didn't seem to mind the attention, though. As Stephanie laid her head against him and hugged her full breasts against his arm, Spence winked at Jessie. She shook her head and fought back a laugh.

"So how do you handle multiple . . . uh . . . boyfriends in the same gang?" Jessie asked.

Stephanie sat up and turned to Jessie. "Oh the guys don't mind sharing. Sometimes things work out, sometimes they don't, ya know? I mean, take Rex, for instance. He and I had fun, and then we didn't anymore. He's always so busy riding, especially late at night, going off who knows where. He likes his alone time, which so didn't work for me. I need a stud warming my bed, you know what I mean? I don't want a guy I can't keep tabs on. So we ended things. No hard feelings, right Rex?"

Rex, sitting nearby, shrugged. "Uh huh."

Jessie smothered a laugh. "I see. Well, that works out nicely for you, doesn't it?"

Stephanie shrugged. "I'm a free spirit. Just ask any of the guys around here."

So, she was a slut. Jessie fervently hoped Spence was using condoms, because *ick*.

Crush had long ago lit the bonfire, which warmed the area considerably. The flame shot high into the air and there was plenty of wood for it to burn the entire night. Jessie was content to watch the dancing orange and yellow flames reaching toward the sky. Guitar playing was still going strong, beer was still flowing, and people were even dancing, some close and sensually, some quite comically. Other couples were huddled under blankets or curled up on hay bales, making out or simply passed out.

Jessie occupied herself by watching the ones making out or doing who-knew-what under those blankets. She heard moans and whimpers and lots of movement under the covers, even caught glimpses of leathers being pulled down to the knees. There was definitely sex going on. Her body heated, and it wasn't from the bonfire, but she couldn't tear her gaze away from the raw, un-apologetic sensuality of watching couples get it on right in front of everyone.

"Voyeur," Diaz whispered in her ear, drawing her back tighter against his body.

She smiled, but didn't reply. Instead, she watched a man's rear end lift up, slide down, then the look of utter rapture on his partner's face in response. They danced as beautifully together in sex as the flames danced under the moonlit sky. It was a picture-perfect moment. She'd love to be that free, to be half naked under the covers with Diaz, making love and not caring about the world around them.

She sighed, shuddered at the sudden longing. Diaz wrapped his arm around her chest, and she closed her eyes, fighting the tears that pooled there.

"What's wrong, baby?"

They were alone now. Spence and Stephanie had moved off to a dark corner somewhere. Crush and Rex were nowhere around. It was just the two of them on a stack of hay bales.

She shifted, half turned so she could see his face. Bonfire flames flickered in his dark eyes, giving him a devilish look.

"I need you," she whispered, sliding her palm across his cheek, loving the feel of a day's growth of beard scraping her hand. It gave her goose bumps.

He lifted her hand, kissed her open palm, then drew her onto his lap. "I'm here."

"I want more."

"I know." He slipped his arm around her back, pulling her against his body, then trailed a finger along her jaw, capturing it in his hands. Inches from his face, she refused to initiate, wanted him to take.

He did, palming the back of her neck and drawing her the last few inches that separated them. When his lips touched hers, she ignited like the first flames of the bonfire, an explosion of heat, melting her instantly. And then he took it deeper, using his tongue to drive her crazy with soft, velvet strokes.

She was lost in sensation, in Diaz, but still cognizant of other people around, possibly watching them as she'd been doing with the other couples. She didn't care. She pulled back, sat up, then wrapped her legs around him and held on to his shoulders so she faced him. His cock, hard and hot, nudged her thigh. She shuddered. So close, yet miles apart. "Do you know what happens during initiation into a gang like the Devil's Skulls?"

"Yeah."

She motioned her head toward the couple going at it under the covers nearby. "I don't want my first time to be in public, Diaz. Please help me."

He looked over her shoulder, watching for a few minutes, then looked at her again. "Shit. I hadn't thought of that."

She had. Countless times since given this assignment. A silly thing, probably, but it meant something to her.

"I've spent a lot of years imagining my first time, what it would be like. I don't expect candlelight and romance or other girlish fantasies, but I sure don't want it in front of an audience, either."

"We'll send you home, Jess. You don't have to do this."

Her eyes widened. "Are you serious?"

"Hell yes. No assignment is worth compromising your virginity."

She shook her head. "You don't understand."

"What don't I understand?"

"It's not just the job. I mean, it is and it isn't."

"Explain it to me, then."

"It's in my way, this whole virginity thing. It's like a cement block around my neck—always there. Yes, this particular assignment requires someone with more experience, something I definitely don't have. But I can do the job, Diaz. Besides, it's more than that. More than just this assignment and what it entails." She laid her palms on his chest, felt the mad rhythm of his heart.

"I want you. I want this. I always have. I don't want anyone else to make love to me but you. And that has nothing to do with our jobs or this assignment."

His gaze shot toward the couple moaning under the covers, then back at her, his expression unfathomable. "We need to get going."

She sighed, then climbed off his lap, refusing to say a word as they rode back to the hotel. What would be the point? She'd asked, and once again he'd slammed the door in her face.

She was out of options.

Jessie felt like a rock was sitting on her chest. She refused to cry. That was childish. She was going to have to accept the inevitable, and that was that. She couldn't force Diaz to compromise his principles.

Diaz opened the door to their room and held it while she walked in. She'd barely stepped fully into the room before he grabbed her, kicked the door shut, and slammed her against it, taking her mouth in a kiss that left her breathless.

Whoa. Unprepared for his assault, she palmed his chest, then his upper arms, holding on for dear life as he pressed up against her—fully against her—his body lining up oh so perfectly, his cock already hard and insistent against her pussy.

Her senses went haywire as he jerked her leather jacket off, then his own, his lips still latched on to hers, his tongue sliding inside to ravage her mouth. She had no idea what was going on with him, but she wasn't about to interrupt this bliss to ask. Not when he slid his hands along her waist and began to lift her shirt, his hands warm and searching upward, lifting the material as he did.

He rested his hand just under her breast. Her heart slammed against it. She tore her lips from his, panting, trying to catch her breath. As she did, she inhaled his scent. Outdoors, sweat, man—Diaz. Her knees felt weak. This was all so overwhelming, so incredible.

Could this really be happening? She had to know, had to be certain that this time . . .

"Diaz, what are you doing?"

"Shh," he breathed against her ear. "Let me."

Oh, God. She'd let him do anything. Her clit pulsed, her pussy quivered, her breasts swelled against her bra, waiting for his hands. So close. He laid his forehead against hers, his breath rough and rasping like hers.

He snaked an arm around her waist and lifted her, carried her into the room, deposited her on the bed. He moved away, bent down to remove her boots and socks, then stood again, going for her pants.

She wanted to ask, but didn't dare, in case he changed his mind. If, in fact, he was going to—

He flipped the button open, drew the zipper down on her jeans, and began to pull. She lifted, helping him, watching him, the intense look of concentration on his face, as if this were the most important task of his life. Her jeans discarded, he kneeled over her, crawling up her body. His clothes were still on, and she was half undressed—why was it always that way? She reached for him, for his shirt, and this time, he paused to lift it over his head and toss it on the floor before proceeding on to her shirt, which he drew upward over her ribs, bending down to press his lips there. She closed her eyes and let out a whimper, loving the feel of his mouth touching her—anywhere.

When he drew up, his eyes were dark, glassy, filled with desire. He grasped the hem of her top and lifted it over her head, then undid the clasp of her bra, opening it, pulling it off, tossing her clothes around the room as he did. And with each revelation he captured her flesh in his mouth.

Her nipples stood erect, waiting for his mouth. He didn't disappoint, bending over and dragging his tongue across them. She moaned at the exquisite contact, cried out when he took one nipple between his teeth, holding it there while he tortured it with flicks of his tongue until she couldn't think straight anymore. Then he did the same thing to the other while kneading her breasts with his hands. It was torment feeling his hands and mouth on her. The pressure, his tongue, and his touch, it was all such sweet heaven. She lifted her butt off the bed, trying to grind her pussy against his hard cock. Maybe she appeared desperate, but she didn't care. She knew what she wanted, and tonight she wouldn't be denied.

But Diaz pushed her down, held her hips, continuing his slow and thorough torment of her nipples with his magical mouth.

"Please," she cried, unable to stand it any longer. She was turned on, goddammit. She didn't need any more foreplay.

He lifted, sat back on his heels, studying her, his face all harsh lines and incredibly sexy. How could he be so desirable when he wasn't smiling? "What do you want, baby?"

"I want you to fuck me."

He dragged his palm between her breasts, down her rib cage, letting it rest above her panties. "Relax, Jess. I *am* going to fuck you tonight, and nothing is going to stop that now."

She caught her breath at the sensual promise in his voice, the commanding way he'd taken charge. Diaz was a man on a mission, all right. *She* was his mission now.

Pulling his gaze from her face, he reached for her panties and dragged them over her hips, down her legs, discarded them onto the floor along with the rest of her clothes. Still on his knees, he undid his pants and drew the zipper down, revealing that dark line of hair leading to his cock. As he pulled his jeans aside she saw his cockhead, swollen and pressed tight against his belly. She licked her lips, swallowed, watched as he eased off the bed to shuck his boots and pants until he was naked, too. His cock sprang out, thick and pointing at her. All hers.

She was dizzy with anticipation, had awaited this moment for so long. She was almost afraid to move, to speak, to do anything that might cause him to stop, to change his mind. Especially since he seemed so content on taking control, on touching her body. She really liked the way he touched her, this almost reverent caressing of every inch of her skin.

"Soft," he murmured as he smoothed his hands over her thighs, spreading her legs, circling her skin with his thumb. He drew closer to her pussy, caressing her, teasing her by drawing near, then moving away. Her nerve endings were on fire waiting for his touch there, her clit swollen and throbbing. And the way he looked at her . . . his jaw set tight, his gaze devouring her as if he wanted to eat her alive.

She saw the hunger there, reflecting what she felt inside. She shuddered a ragged breath, leaned up, reaching for him, needing his mouth. He met her halfway, his lips brushing hers in an achingly tender kiss that was all too brief but filled with passionate promise. He pushed her back down onto the bed, held her there with his palm pressed to her belly, then laid between her thighs, cupping her buttocks to raise her sex to his mouth.

The visual was erotic, his mouth wavering temptingly close to her pussy. He looked at her and dipped, licked along each side, the heat of his tongue sending a wildfire of sensation along her nerve endings. Diaz covered her sex with his mouth, his tongue like liquid velvet along her clit, then pressing and dipping into her pussy to lap up her cream. His tongue was everywhere, licking upward to tease her clit, flick and play with the piercing, and slide back down around her pussy lips again.

She felt everything, including his fingers as he tucked one, then two inside her, pumping with a slow, steady rhythm as she'd done to herself earlier. This was so much better. His fingers were bigger, hotter, filling her, stretching her, making her long for his cock inside her. He hummed against her clit, licked her with relentless strokes until she came up off the bed, shooting into a blinding orgasm. Her pussy gripped his fingers as she spiraled out of control, trembling as the waves of her orgasm crashed over and over. He held on to her, pumping into her, then slowing, withdrawing. He climbed up her body, pausing to lick his fingers before sliding them into her mouth.

"Taste."

She sucked his fingers, watched his eyes darken as she did. He replaced his fingers with his hungry mouth, ravaging her with a demanding kiss that left her panting.

He pushed off the bed, grabbed the foil packet from the pocket of his jeans and tore it open, slid the condom on, and nudged her legs apart. When he pressed down on top of her he grabbed a handful of her hair and turned her head to the side. Did he have any idea how much it aroused her to feel the tight grip of his hand in her hair, to sense his primal need to possess her? She couldn't even explain it to herself, other than it excited her beyond the ability to think coherently.

He took a long, slow lick of her neck at the same time he slid his other hand between their bodies and cupped her sex, rocking his palm over her clit until she saw sparks. She shivered at the drugging sensuality of his every movement, one part caveman, the other part sensitive lover. She never knew what to expect from Diaz, in or out of bed. Maybe that's what she found so compelling about him.

"Tell me you're sure," he whispered against her ear. "Are you ready for this?"

"Yes." She avoided saying "please," but she was damn close to saying it if he didn't get to it and soon.

He moved his hands, sliding them underneath to cup her butt, tilt her up.

"Look at me, Jessie."

He let go of her hair to free her head so she could turn it and meet his gaze. His eyes were so raw and intense.

"Just you and me, Jess. This is for us and for no other reason, you understand?"

ten

He wasn't doing this for the mission. He wanted her. Jessie lost focus through the tears that welled. She threaded her fingers through his hair, nodded. "Yes. Just for us, Diaz."

She felt the hot tip of his cock at the entrance to her pussy, then the slow, sweet slide as he pushed through. He was so much bigger than any vibrator she'd ever used. He took his time, entering her with gentle ease, letting her grow accustomed to his thickness. Then he pushed and was in her, and her pussy gripped him. The most intense contractions she'd ever felt surrounded his cock, swelled inside her as he began to move, withdrawing and going slowly at first, but as she raised her hips to meet each thrust he plunged harder, his fingers digging into her ass cheeks.

She'd never felt anything like this. He was hot, actual flesh and not an object or machine manufactured to simulate pleasure. He moved, flexed inside her, growing impossibly bigger with every stroke.

He held her so tenderly, one arm wrapped tight underneath her so that not even air separated them. He stroked her neck, her breasts, not once stopping as he continued to rock inside her. He mastered her body with every movement, withdrawing partway only to thrust oh so firmly against her that she felt his touch deeper than she'd felt anything before. He'd dip down, take her mouth in a light brush, then press his lips hard against hers, tangle his tongue with hers, and meld them together in a tight, mesmerizing kiss.

But what really got her, what was so different about this experience, was the eye contact—the intimacy of the way he looked at her. She hadn't thought about sex this way, that a man like Diaz would make such soul-deep contact with his eyes while he moved inside her. It went beyond a physical joining. She felt it in her heart and it shattered her. She wasn't prepared for it, and the tears rolled down her eyes.

Diaz stilled. "Am I hurting you?"

She cupped his cheek. "Oh, no. It's perfect. Too damn perfect. Please, don't stop." She couldn't bear it if he did.

He stared at her for the longest time and she was afraid he would stop, that he'd quit before this magic finished. He swept his hand over her face, bent down to brush his lips against hers. Then he moved again, forward, his pelvis rubbing her clit, and she was close, tightening around him. He clenched his jaw, holding back for her, waiting until she went over the edge. She gripped his arms, wrapped her legs around him, and lifted, wanting him buried deep, as far inside her as he could get.

She pulsed around him, quivered, and when he came down against her this time, she felt the splinters of orgasm driving all the way through her, in every part of her body, curling her toes and tingling her scalp.

"Diaz!" Some part of her realized she dug her nails into his arms, but she couldn't stop. It was fierce, uncontrollable, having this man inside her when she came, feeling him tighten, draw her close, and let out a loud groan against her as he, too, shattered in orgasm, sent her shuddering into aftershocks nearly as strong as the climax itself.

He took her mouth, kissed her hard, held her tight and rocked against her until the spasms subsided. And even then he didn't let her go.

She stroked his damp hair, his back, loving the feel and scent of him surrounding her.

So this was what it was like. She'd missed so much holding out for so long, and yet she had no regrets, would have never wanted this experience with anyone but Diaz. Admittedly, he'd surprised her. She really didn't know what she'd expected from him, but Diaz was street tough. Maybe she'd expected him to be . . . coarse and unrefined in bed. Rough with her. He hadn't been like that at all. Instead, he'd been gentle, loving, taking time and care, making this not at all about himself, and all about her. He'd made it perfect for her, had cherished her through the process. She'd needed the maturity of her years to truly understand how important this was, what sex really meant beyond just fun and physical release.

Of course it helped that she'd been half in love with Diaz for a few years now, but she shouldn't think about that. Not now, not when all this was so new, so magical, so perfect.

He rolled off her, stepped into the bathroom for a few seconds, and returned, gathering her close so they faced each other, side by side.

"You okay?" he asked.

She smiled, nodded. She might have even purred a little, unable to help herself.

"You look like a cat who just ate a whole bird."

She laughed. "Something like that."

"You're beautiful when you come."

Embarrassment colored her face. She shivered at the memory of how it felt to come apart under him. "Thank you for doing this for me."

"It wasn't just for you." He kissed her.

Her stomach fluttered. She'd never tire of the feel of his lips on hers. She rubbed her finger across his bottom lip. So soft, about the only thing on his entire body that wasn't hard as steel.

"I still appreciate it. I didn't want my first experience with a man to be in front of a group."

"You mean initiation."

"Yes."

"You still don't have to do it, Jess. It's above and beyond what's necessary for this assignment. I can send you back to head-quarters."

"Why? You'll have to do it. I'm pretty sure public sex is part of initiation for everyone—male and female."

His lips curled. "I've had sex before. Lots of times."

She didn't want to think of those "lots of times," who he'd been with, who he'd touched and made love to. It made her stomach tighten in uncomfortable ways. Of course he had a past. The man was gorgeous, and a fantastic lover. He probably had a waiting list. She had no rights to him.

But he was here now with her, for as long as it lasted. That would have to be good enough.

"I wanted this assignment, Diaz. I knew going in that the idea was to get into Crush's gang and what that meant."

He traced her hip with his fingers. "Do you really know what it means, Jess? Do you understand that biker gang initiations are tough as hell? Fights, public sex? Hell, sometimes there are orgies."

Jessie knew exactly what would happen. She also had her limits. Even a gang leader would have to understand that. "I'm not fucking anyone but you. The rest of it I can handle."

DIAZ WAS STUNNED BY JESSIE'S STATEMENT.

He liked the idea of her wanting only him. He liked it more than he should. Because he sure as hell wasn't sharing her with any other guy. Not for the gang initiation, anyway. The thought of watching her have sex with another man made his blood churn hot, even though he had no right to claim her as his own. He had nothing to offer her.

She really didn't know him, not enough to have gifted him with as much as she'd done tonight, with as much as she continued to give him. He'd walked away from her countless times, treated her badly, just as he knew he would. And yet she kept coming back for more. All he did was take, when he knew he shouldn't, when he couldn't offer her anything. There was no future for them. He'd vowed to never have a relationship with a woman—nothing long lasting, nothing that spelled commitment. Not when he knew where he'd come from. Whose blood was in his veins.

Shit. Wasn't this just fucked up? He couldn't have her, but he didn't want to see her with anyone else. What the hell was he going to do with all this . . . feeling? He knew he shouldn't have touched her.

"You've gone quiet on me," she said, tracing his bottom lip with her fingertip.

"Thinking about the mission."

"You have a naked woman lying next to you and you're thinking about work?" She frowned, but her lips quirked.

"If it helps any, you're included in that thought process."

"It helps . . . a little. But still, shouldn't you be wholly focused on sex . . . with me?"

"That is part of the 'work' I was thinking about."

"I see. So now having sex with me is work."

Diaz laughed, grabbed a handful of her hair and tugged. "Hell yes, it's work. I have to please you, don't I?"

"All you have to do is look at me and I'm pleased."

Damn. Sometimes Jessie made it so easy. And so hard at the same time. "You should get some sleep."

"I don't want to sleep." She splayed her hands across his chest, began to move them down, over his stomach, pushing him so he lay on his back. He let her have her way. She climbed on top of him, sitting astride him. His dick paid attention, growing, with a mind of its own.

So much for thinking about work, for telling himself sex with Jessie was a onetime thing.

"There's so much you can teach me," she said, rocking her pussy against his now fully-hard cock.

He grabbed her hips and dragged her along his length. "Oh yeah? And what would you like to learn?"

Her eyes went all liquidy soft, pools he could get lost in if he let himself, a constant reminder to keep this physical only, not to get involved.

"All kinds of things. Your body, for instance."

"I think you've had plenty of body play."

"Oh not nearly enough. I want to touch you all over, Diaz. Taste every inch of you. See what you like and what you don't like. Do you know some men like to have a finger slid in their ass during sex?"

"Jesus, Jessie! Where the hell did you learn stuff like that?"

She grinned. "I used to lift the guys' porn movies and sneak them into my room. That's how I learned about sex."

He rolled his eyes. "Great. Just great."

She shrugged. "It's not like I had girlfriends to discuss sex with. And sure as hell Grange or any of you guys weren't going to talk to me about it."

She had that right. The thought of sitting a teenaged Jessie down and having a conversation about sex made him cringe. But porn movies? Good God. What the hell had she learned watching those?

"So I figured some of it out on my own. And watched movies. Very educational."

"Hardly. Sex isn't like what you see in porn movies, Jess."

She slid her palms over his nipples. They hardened in a rush, making his cock lurch against her pussy. "Sure it is. You get hard. I get wet. It's basic biology after that. I mean the movies were pretty much bad acting, but I got the idea of how it was done."

"No, you got all the wrong ideas."

"This is where you tell me about porn being bad, how it victimizes women, right?"

He snorted. "Women in that industry are typically paid way more than men, so . . . no. But it doesn't show the true side of relationships, the emotional part of lovemaking between a man and a woman who care about each other. There are big gaps in reality with those movies. Sure, they're fun to watch as sexual enhancement, but that's not what sex is about."

She stilled, sat back, and looked down at him, confusion evident on her face. "Then tell me what I'm missing."

Someone to care about her. Someone to love her.

That someone could never be him.

And he didn't know how to respond to Jessie's question.

What was she missing? She'd gotten her sexual education from watching porn movies. She was missing everything. A part of him

wanted to be her teacher . . . to show her all that she was misin-
formed about. The fun stuff. Dating, emotions, holding hands,
getting to know someone first. Talking, laughing, all the fun times
you could have with someone. Those breathless, anticipatory moments leading up to making love. The waiting until you couldn't
wait anymore.

The way it *should* have been for her. Hell, the way it should
have been for him, too. All the things he'd never had either, because he hadn't allowed it.

But hell. What did he know about that other than what he'd
read about? He didn't know how to teach her. He didn't have relationships. He sure as hell couldn't base it on what he'd seen
growing up. That had been disastrous, ugly, nothing he'd want to
pass on to anyone he cared about . . . to any woman at all. That's
why he'd always kept sex simple, uncomplicated, unattached. He'd
purposely chosen women who were content with occasional sex
and nothing more.

Until Jess. She wanted way more than he'd ever be able to give
her. He owed her honesty, if nothing else.

"I can't give you what you need, Jessie."

"What is it you think I need?"

"Romance. Relationship."

Her brows raised. "I thought we were talking about sex."

"It's all part of the deal. Or should be for someone like you."

She climbed off and kneeled next to him. "Why do you always
presume to know what's best for me? What if I just want sex with
no strings?"

He grinned. "I know you better than that."

"I don't think you really know me at all. I could be perfectly
content with you teaching me the ropes, sexually."

"I don't think so."

"Let me ask you a question. If you hadn't known me for all these years, if you'd just met me at this rally and had the opportunity to be with me here in this room . . . would you?"

"It doesn't work that way."

"Just answer the question, Diaz. Are you attracted to me?"

He didn't understand what kind of game she was playing, but he shrugged and said, "I think you already know the answer to that question."

"You'd want me."

"Hell yes."

He caught the hint of a smile.

"Because?"

"Huh?"

"Why would you want me?"

"Come on, Jessie."

"Just tell me. Why would you pick me out of, let's say, all the other women in Crush's gang?"

"Well first off, because I know you."

She rolled her eyes. "You're not playing the game right. Pretend you didn't already know me. There are, let me think . . . twenty or so women in his gang? Line them up mentally and tell me why you'd choose me."

He sighed, closed his eyes, and thought about all the women he'd seen who were members of the Devil's Skulls. A variety of women to choose from in every shape, color, and size, but in his mind's eye, Jessie stood out as the one woman he'd want. And he knew why.

He opened his eyes and turned to face her. She stared down at him expectantly. "Because you have a smile that screams sex."

She pursed her lips, frowned. "That's it?"

"Yes."

"You'd want to fuck me because of my smile?"

"Yeah."

"There's got to be more than that."

"Well . . . you also have great tits."

She snorted and punched his arm. "Dickhead."

"You asked."

She looked down at him, studied him. "My smile, huh?"

"Yeah. You smile in this slightly off-kilter way. One side of your mouth curls up just a tiny bit more than the other."

"It does?"

"Yup."

"I never noticed that before. So I'm lopsided?"

"No. It's very sexy, makes you look secretive. It's like you . . . know things."

"No doubt about porn movies."

He laughed. "No doubt." She really was damned irresistible, and it had nothing to do with her breasts. Yeah, she was beautiful, but it was more than that. He just liked being in the same room with her—her being gorgeous and utterly hot was a bonus. And she did it all naturally. She didn't affect a pose or attitude to turn a guy on. She was just . . . Jessie, proving it by giving him that lopsided smile right now, and she had no idea she was doing it.

Danger bells clanged loud and clear in his head as he looked up at her, as he reached for her, palming the nape of her neck to draw her down to him.

Don't do this. Once was bad enough. To continue would be disaster, like drawing too close to the fire. He was in too deep with Jessie, and taking her down with him. He could pull up, knowing this was going nowhere. But Jessie? She was falling. Would she understand that they couldn't be anything more than this moment, than right now?

Her lips brushed light and easy across his, her breath warm and inviting. Her tongue rimmed his teeth as she explored, then slid inside, searching for his.

He should be the strong one here. But how many times was he going to walk away? That was the coward's way out. It was time to face it—he wanted her and he was damn well going to have her for as long as he could.

She was a big girl. She understood: he'd made it clear enough that he wasn't interested in a relationship. He'd never turn Jessie over to the monster that lived inside him. He didn't trust himself enough to love someone. He cared too much about her to unleash that on her.

Her skin was so soft as she leaned forward, draping herself over him to lean farther into the kiss. He roamed her body, memorizing every lush curve, determined to enjoy these moments while they had them, because this was all going to end once this assignment was over.

But he had her now, right where he wanted her—on top, her body writhing over his while she explored and kissed him, letting her hands roam freely over his chest and shoulders. His dick clamored for attention, rising up between her legs to spear her pussy lips. The wet heat of her body singed him.

"I want inside you."

"I wanted to play," she protested, but she rocked against his shaft, shuddering as she did.

She was in no more mood to linger than he was, and he knew it.

"No play. Let's fuck."

She gave him that smile again, and leaned over to pull out the drawer next to the bed.

Box of condoms. Thank God she was well prepared.

"Thought I was a sure thing, did you?" he teased.

She snorted as she tore the wrapper and slid the condom over him. "I was hoping."

He grabbed her hips, lifted her into position, and held his cock so she could mount him. Damn, it was hot as hell seeing his dick disappear into her inch by inch, to watch the way her pussy swallowed him up like that. He felt every heated squeeze of her body as she welcomed him.

Jessie closed her eyes, tilted her head back as she seated herself fully on top of him. Her face bore the most beautiful expression, her body arched perfectly in a bow. She looked almost pained, yet as if she enjoyed an exquisite torture.

He pulsed inside her as her walls contracted around him, and still she hadn't moved.

"Am I hurting you?" She was so tight, and wasn't used to having a dick inside her yet.

"I'm fine. Just . . . feeling you." She tilted her head forward, opened her eyes, and looked at him, her eyes, laden with desire. "It's an incredible sensation having you inside me, Diaz."

He'd never known a woman as honest as her, as forthcoming with her emotions. She unraveled him, in both good ways and bad.

"The way you grip my dick makes me want to fuck you hard until I come."

Her lips tilted. "Is that a bad thing?"

"You don't want a minuteman for a lover, darlin'."

She leaned forward, raising her butt as she slid her breasts along his chest. When she lowered onto his shaft again, she quivered, inside and out. The sensation was shattering. "I have every confidence you'll last as long as I need you to."

He would, too, because he wanted her to come apart around him again, wanted to feel her pussy grip his dick as if it would squeeze the very life out of him. Only then would he let go and come inside her. He reached for her hips, lifting her up and down as she nuzzled against his chest, licking and biting at his nipples.

She made his hair stand on end as she wriggled against him, pumping her pussy up and down on his dick, running her hands over his body in a way that could only be described as . . . possessive.

He loved it. He could never tire of her touch, the way she seemed to enjoy every moment of the experience. She wasn't the least bit passive. Instead, she'd thrown herself headlong into sex as if she knew they had a limited time together and she wanted to feel everything she could.

So did he. He snaked an arm around her waist and flipped her over onto her back, then slid his arm down to grab on to her ass, pulling her hard and tight against his body.

Jessie gasped, her eyes widening as Diaz drove hard into her, not once, not twice, but over and over again, refusing to stop even to let her catch her breath. She held on to his arms, her nails digging grooves into his skin as he pumped thrust after thrust into her body. She whimpered, moaned, then lifted into him, urging him deeper.

"More," she cried, her voice no more than a throaty whisper as her pussy began to tighten around his shaft.

He reared back, powered deeper, grinding against her clit until she shattered, convulsing around him in wave after wave of climax. She let go with a loud scream, arching against him, crying out his name and raking her nails against his skin. Watching her, feeling her, was too much and he couldn't hold back, catapulting with a loud groan, grasping her hair to tip her head back so he could take her mouth, meld with her while they shared this orgasm and fell together.

Spent, sweating, he lightened the kiss, sipping from her mouth while she caught her breath. Her heart still pounded against his chest with fierce, ramming beats. She was wheezing, every inhalation a struggle.

He'd been too rough, too violent. He rolled off her, started to move away, but she caught hold of his arms and pulled him toward her.

"Where are you going?"

Her voice sounded raw, no doubt from all the panting and screaming. How could he be both proud and appalled by that?

"I hurt you."

"You did not. It was . . . oh my God, Diaz, I didn't know I could come like that. No, you didn't hurt me at all. Now get back here."

He slid back onto the bed and pulled her against him, stroking her hair, listening to the sounds she made.

Contented sounds. She ran her hand down his arm.

"I hurt *you*," she said, smoothing her hand over his arm, the marks she'd made with her nails.

"I didn't even feel it. I was concentrating on your pussy."

She shuddered, sighed, and eventually her breathing returned to normal. Calm, even, until her eyes closed and he realized she'd fallen asleep. Still he continued to stroke her body, surprising even himself when his cock began to harden again.

Christ, he was a goddamn beast. Insatiable, wanting her again even though he knew she had to be worn out.

He was capable of hurting Jessie because he was mindless when it came to her. She brought out violent emotions in him, including passion—a passion that wasn't at all restrained.

He looked down at her, her lips swollen from his kisses, her face red and raw from his beard. Her pussy was probably sore from the pounding it had taken. So much for his desire to be gentle. Wanting and doing were two different things, weren't they?

He'd completely lost it with her, had thought only of himself. He'd been so into fucking her, he hadn't stopped to think about the possibility of hurting her. Yeah, who did that remind him of?

This thing between them was a nightmare, was never going to work.

Of course he already knew that.

But was Jess clear on it?

eleven

Jessie inhaled the crisp night air, ready for anything tonight.

She was charged, energized after last night with Diaz.

He'd stayed with her, held her all night long. First thing this morning he'd run a bath for her, put her in the tub, and ordered her to soak while he went downstairs and brought them both a cup of coffee.

Apparently he was convinced she'd be so sore she wouldn't be able to walk.

She couldn't help it—she'd actually laughed when he said that.

A real-life dick was different than her vibrators or her fingers. Wow, was it ever different. He'd fucked her good. Her body heated in a flash of desire remembering how it had felt to have him inside her. Pulsing, swelling, filling her. And when he moved against her, she'd connected with him in ways she'd never imagined possible.

Even now, everything sexual inside her quivered in anticipation of doing it again.

Any soreness she'd felt was welcome. She'd do it again in a heartbeat.

She wasn't sore. She told him the bath was heaven, but she'd sure wanted to have sex with him this morning.

He'd looked at her like she'd asked him to boil small kittens on her behalf. He'd told her she should take it easy today. It was really sweet how he was so tender with her, and so unlike the normally gruff Diaz.

They spent the day taking in the sights, hanging out with Crush and the gang, and taking some time alone to talk about the case and figure out different scenarios, like what would happen if they didn't get asked to go through initiation. Which Jessie didn't think was an option. Crush would ask them, she knew he would. But if he didn't, they intended to follow him and his gang, at a discreet distance, and see where they were going. Not the best plan, but Jessie felt it was unnecessary anyway. They were going to be asked. She was 100 percent confident. Diaz wasn't, so he wanted to make sure they had another option.

Shaking her head, she placed her hands on her hips and searched among the main drag crowds for Spence, who'd made himself scarce all day long. Darkness swallowed the crowds, making everything a blur of nothing more than motorcycle lights and people milling about the sidewalks, crowded so close together you couldn't differentiate one body from another. Diaz was down the street talking with Crush. Jessie had come out of the dense crowd to use the bathroom and get some air, and she'd told Diaz she'd see if she could spot Spence while she was walking around.

Not that she figured she'd have much luck finding him. When he'd called Diaz's cell phone this morning, Spence had said he was busy with Stephanie and a few of the Devil's Skulls. He'd explained he heard a few things from Stephanie last night that had made him curious, and he'd report in later.

They hadn't seen him all day, and tonight was the initiation. Which they hadn't yet been invited to, though they had run into Crush this morning, who'd asked them to ride with the gang today. Jessie took that as a sign of things to come. Crush seemed to be comfortable with the three of them. God knows Spence had ingratiated himself with Stephanie, who stood at the upper echelon of the group and was also a relative of Crush's, so that at least gave Spence an in. And Jessie knew Crush liked her. He didn't seem to have a problem with Diaz, either, so things looked promising for initiation.

And initiation meant gaining access into the inner workings of the Devil's Skulls, which meant hopefully finding out how deeply Crush and his gang were involved with selling guns to the survivalists. If at all.

She kind of liked Crush. It was really too bad that a guy who seemed nice on the outside might be the leader of a tax-evading, gunrunning, God-only-knew-what-else kind of gang.

Appearances could be deceiving. She had to remember that. Still, she'd always let her instinct guide her, and she was rarely wrong about people. Her gut told her that Crush wasn't a bad guy.

Then again, she was the novice in the Wild Riders, so she wasn't about to go off half-cocked and try to save the day, insisting that Crush was the good guy. She could be dead wrong. But she still intended to reserve judgment until there was solid proof.

Either way, she was prepared for initiation and everything it entailed, as long as she had Diaz by her side.

DIAZ WAS ACTING WEIRD AS HELL, WHICH WAS NOTHING UNUSUAL for him, especially lately. He either treated her with kid gloves, loomed over her yelling at her like she was a ten-year-old, or threw her against the wall and fucked her brains out.

Ideally, she preferred the last option.

Giving up her attempts at finding Spence, she skirted through the ever-thickening crowd, taking her life in her hands by crossing the zooming, bike-heavy street, and made her way back to Diaz. He was in the beer tent, still engaged in heavy conversation with Crush, Rex, and a few of the other guys.

Rex was the only one who glanced up when he saw her. He looked her up and down, smiled, and nodded. She shivered and moved to Diaz's side. He snaked his arm around her waist and pulled her down next to him, stopping only long enough to plant a quick kiss on her lips.

His public show of affection surprised her. He'd done it in such a distracted manner, she wondered if he was even aware of it. Him kissing her so naturally, without thinking about it, warmed her.

She sat quietly next to him and listened in.

"I was cornered by no less than ten guys," Crush said. "My ass was on the line. It was fight or die."

Diaz nodded. "Sucks to be in a situation like that, but not much you can do. You either fight and maybe get your ass kicked, or cry like a baby, beg for your life, and get branded a pussy."

"Exactly. And no way was I going to beg, so I threw myself into the middle of it."

Diaz grinned. "Got your ass kicked anyway, didn't you?"

Crush laughed. "Yeah, but I kicked a few of theirs, too. And gained their respect."

Jessie shook her head. Guy talk about battles fought and won. It figured. These types of conversations cropped up a lot at Wild Riders' headquarters, too. She often had to sit through talks about fist or knife fights, speed races on deserted streets, gang initiations and the like. It was a show of bravado, a game to see which one was the bravest of the bunch.

Too much testosterone in action.

"So, tonight's initiation," Crush said.

That got her attention. She turned from scanning the crowd and focused on him.

"The Devil's Skulls would like the two of you and Spence to come to the initiation tonight."

Diaz nodded and lifted his lips in a half smile. "Thanks."

"We'd love to," Jessie said. "Thank you for the invite."

Crush laughed. "You might not thank me after it's over."

Diaz leaned a forearm on the table, taking a lazy position. "Oh, I think all of us can handle it."

"Good," Crush said with a nod, then stood. "I've gotta go. Meet us back at the farmhouse where we had the bonfire last night. We'll party for a while, drink a few beers, and start at midnight."

"We'll be there," Diaz said.

After Crush left, Jessie turned to him. "We need to find Spence."

"Agreed." Diaz pulled his cell phone and tried Spence's number. "You rang?"

Jessie tilted her head back at the sound of Spence's voice.

"Yes. We've been trying to get hold of you."

"Where've you been?" Diaz asked.

Spence slid into one of the seats and leaned forward. "With

Stephanie and a few of the others. I wasn't in a place where I could talk."

"Find out anything?"

"Yeah. The Devil's Skulls aren't one big happy family, I know that much. Rex isn't content with Crush as their leader. There's been talk of making some changes."

Jessie's eyes widened. "Did they say why?"

Spence shrugged. "I'm hearing all this secondhand, through Stephanie, which means it may or may not be reliable. She says Crush is untrustworthy as a leader—or at least that's what she heard from Rex and a few of the other guys—that he goes off on his own a lot, that he doesn't have the best interests of the gang in mind."

"I wonder what that means?" Jessie asked.

"No clue," Spence said. "But it's interesting. I'm trying to get in closer with Rex, which is kind of hard since he and Stephanie used to have a thing."

"I think Stephanie used to have a thing with just about everyone except Crush, and that's only because they're related."

Spence snorted at Jessie's comment. "Yeah, so I've heard. The girl gets around."

"I hope you have a lot of condoms." Jessie wrinkled her nose.

"I do, honey. I do."

"We were invited to initiate," Diaz said, changing the topic.

Spence nodded. "Great. More ass kicking and fucking then."

Diaz shook his head. "I guess. But if we get in, that should bring us closer to the action."

"*When* we get in," Jessie said.

"You stick close to Spence and me tonight."

Jessie knew Diaz was worried about her, but honestly, she had no fear about tonight. "I don't think initiation works that way. I'll be on my own for part of it." She laid her hand on his shoulder.

"I really can take care of myself, Diaz. I've been doing it for a very long time."

"You're ready, then?" Spence asked.

Jessie looked at Diaz, then back at Spencer. "Yes."

"You're like my baby sister, Jessie," Spencer said, stroking her hair. "You get into trouble, you just holler and I'll be there for you, assignment or not. You know I'd compromise a mission for you."

She beamed a smile up at him, grateful that he cared that much for her. "I love you, too, Spence. But I think I'll be just fine."

"Okay, let's ride," Diaz said, his brows knit in a tight frown.

Jessie was more worried about him than herself. She knew he was concerned about her, about tonight. She'd just have to prove to him she could handle anything that came up. Then maybe he'd relax a little and stop treating her with kid gloves. She really wanted to be a valued member of the team, not someone Diaz felt he had to babysit.

On the long ride out of town Jessie wondered if one of the Devil's Skulls owned the farmhouse and land surrounding it. Considering the bonfire the night before, and what would be going on tonight, the rowdiness and partying, it would almost have to be Skulls property. It was very private, located over a mile down a gravel road from the two lane they'd traveled to get there. Out here, you could do pretty much whatever you wanted and no one would bother you.

It was the perfect place to host initiation. The secluded area afforded the Skulls the privacy they wanted for . . . whatever was going to happen. Because she had some idea of what that could be, yet really didn't know for sure, maybe she should be nervous. But she wasn't. Diaz would be there and so would Spence. She was going to be perfectly safe. Besides, she was an adult now.

A woman. A real woman now, thanks to Diaz.

Before, she'd felt lacking and unsure of herself. Not anymore.

Yeah, right. One night of great sex and she was worldly. She snorted, climbed off her bike, and took a deep breath of the night air. It was tinged with a slight chill and she wrapped her arms around herself. Someone had started another bonfire in the center of the bales of hay.

Funny though, she couldn't stop shivering.

"You cold?" Diaz asked.

"A little."

"Let's get closer to the fire."

She nodded and Diaz wrapped his arm around her, drawing her close to his side. She zipped her jacket up and walked with him to one of the bales of hay in the circle around the bonfire. Yes, it was definitely warmer here, especially when Diaz pulled her between his outstretched legs, letting her lean back against his chest, then closed his arms around her.

Perfect now. She was plenty warm cocooned within his embrace. Spence had gone off to find Stephanie, leaving Diaz and her alone.

"Who looks like initiates besides us?" she asked.

"*Hmmm.* Probably those guys huddled over there against that building," he said.

She followed where he pointed. Sure enough, about ten guys leaned against one of the farm sheds, smoking cigarettes and drinking beer. None of them wore the Skulls' jacket or anything else identifying them as members.

"I wonder if they all know each other."

He shrugged. "Hard to tell."

"You think you can take them?"

"Hell yes."

She smiled.

"Okay, so let me see if I can pick out the women." She scanned the area, spotted one or two, pointed them out to Diaz.

"That one looks scary."

He was right. Tall, broad, a woman built like she'd done some wrestling in her past. She was at least twice Jessie's size.

"That's okay," Jessie said, sizing up her competition. "I know a few tricks."

He skimmed his hands up and down her arms. "I'll just bet you do."

More bikes arrived, the crowd of Skulls and initiates thicker tonight than last night. Obviously a big event for the gang and worth a sizeable turnout.

Great. Just what Jessie wanted—a huge audience. *Oh well.* She said she could handle it, and she could. But as Crush moved behind the hay bales and signaled for everyone's attention, she saw how big that crowd was, and what might be required of her tonight in front of all these people. She realized she might be just a tiny bit . . . nervous.

Not that she'd admit that to anyone—especially Diaz.

"Okay everyone, settle down," Crush said, raising his hands. "It's time for the Devil's Skulls favorite time of the year—initiation."

His statement was followed by whoops, hollers, and whistles.

"Pipe down. I know you're all excited. This is the fun stuff. This is where we test candidates to see if they have what it takes to become a Skull. You either make it through tonight or you're out. If you survive the night, then we'll let you know whether you've passed or not. If you pass, you'll be a Devil's Skull and a part of our gang.

"We'll start with the guys and the physical part of the test. I need our initiates to come forward and stand next to me."

"That's my cue," Diaz said.

"Good luck." She squeezed his hand, then scooted out of the way as Diaz pushed off the hay bale and moved toward the front of the crowd. Spence met him there and they stood together—like brothers, both wearing the same confident smirk on their faces.

They looked dark and menacing. Compared to the other ten guys standing up there, Jessie liked their chances. Both were strong, in great shape, and could kick some serious ass.

"Okay guys, here's the deal," Crush said. "Fist fights, one-on-one. I'll select your partners. And it won't be with one of the other initiates, it'll be with one of the members."

Oh. Well that wasn't what she thought would happen. Crush brought up twelve of his own guys. Big, powerful, with broad chests, massive legs, and a hell of a lot of muscle. Even these guys' knuckles looked powerful. Obviously Crush knew what he was doing. Spence seemed evenly matched with his guy. The one Crush matched Diaz up with was taller than Diaz, and more muscular, which seemed unfathomable since Diaz was pretty damn big. But Diaz didn't blink, just nodded and got into position.

"Bare fists, no weapons," Crush said. "Those are the only rules. Otherwise, you fight until one of you goes down or until I stop you. Ready? Go."

Jessie dug her fingers into the hay and held tight as action exploded around her. Diaz's opponent reared back and threw a punch, which Diaz ducked, before pivoting and rising to land a good round right in the guy's stomach. The guy doubled over, giving Diaz a perfect opportunity for an uppercut to the chin. Unfortunately, the dude was so strong he rebounded right away, and oh, man was he pissed. He went after Diaz like an angry freight train, pushing Diaz back at least ten feet before throwing a punch that leveled him to the ground. Adjusting his jaw, Diaz shoved a boot in the guy's knee and he howled in pain.

Jessie grimaced at the fierceness of the fighting. Spence seemed to be about fifty-fifty on his, giving as good as he got, but his left eye was already swelling. Then again, the other guy looked about the same, so Spence was holding his own. She turned her attention back to Diaz, ignoring all the other guys, especially since several were already lying flat on the ground, no doubt out cold. She didn't even know which were initiates and which were Skulls. All she cared about was Diaz.

In the short period of time she'd pulled her attention away from him, Diaz had grabbed the upper hand. She had no idea what had happened, but the Skulls guy's face was a bruised, bloody mess, and Diaz was pummeling him without mercy. Punch after punch, he went after him. Jessie sucked in her lip, cringing as she watched the way Diaz beat the man. If it wasn't for Crush coming in between them and putting a stop to it, she wasn't certain what would happen.

"Enough," Crush said, turning to Diaz. "Go sit down."

Diaz nodded and found his way back to Jessie. He had a few cuts on his face and his knuckles were in pretty bad shape, but other than that he seemed okay. He was breathing pretty heavy when he sat, so Jessie went and got him a bottle of water. He unscrewed the top and guzzled the entire thing down in a few swallows.

"Thanks."

"Are you all right?"

"Fine." He tossed the bottle in the nearby trash can and kept his head turned toward the other guys still standing.

Spence had knocked his guy to his knees with a well-delivered punch and Crush had ended his fight, too, so Spence came and sat with them.

"That guy do something to piss you off, Diaz?"

"No."

"It sure looked like you wanted to beat him to death."

Diaz shot Spence a venomous glare. "I did what I was asked to do, what we were all asked to do. Is that a problem?"

Spence held up both his hands. "Not at all." But Spence looked at her with a question in his eyes.

A question Jessie had no answers for. Diaz was obviously upset by what had happened out there. And this wasn't the time or place to talk to him about it. It was clear he wanted distance.

The melee was over. The initiates who hadn't stood up to the fight were escorted out. Spence and Diaz stayed.

After several minutes to break and regain order, Crush came back to the center.

"Now it's the ladies' turn," Crush said with a wicked grin. "Initiates, come on up."

Jessie leaped off the hay and moved to the front, along with six other women.

"Our women have to be just as tough as our men, to be able to defend the Skulls. Can you handle it?"

She nodded, hands on her hips.

Crush motioned to the crowd and six women wearing Skulls shirts came forward. All the tough-looking ones, too. Not surprisingly, fluffy Stephanie wasn't one of them. Probably wouldn't want to mess up her makeup. How did a little thing like Stephanie ever pass initiation?

Maybe she got in because she was Crush's cousin, and she'd never had to fight. Jessie couldn't imagine Stephanie doing this. She might break a nail. Jessie grinned.

"Confident, are you?" Crush asked.

"You could say that." Jessie had been challenged her entire life. This was nothing to the kind of people she'd had to fight off when she was just a kid. He couldn't scare her.

"Same rules as before," Crush said.

One of the taller, broader women lined up in front of Jessie. Mean-looking thing, too, with a determined expression on her hard, lined face. She had about ten years on Jessie, and a lot more muscle and weight.

But Jessie had fought off men, and she'd been trained well by the Wild Riders. She could take this woman.

"Ready? Go," Crush said.

Jessie waited for the attack. The woman lunged and Jessie side-stepped, using her feet to keep moving. She wanted to see what this woman had, wanted to go on the defensive first. The woman balled her hand into a fist and took a swing. She might have some strength but she was wild and inaccurate, no doubt used to brawling in groups. Jessie was used to one-on-one defense, so she ducked the punch, grabbed the woman's wrist, and pivoted, shoving an elbow into her midsection. Momentarily out of breath, the woman bent over, giving Jessie the advantage she needed. She used her fist and clipped her on the chin. Her head went back and Jessie kicked her in the stomach.

The Skulls woman might be built hard like an oak tree, but she fell hard, too, hitting the ground and sending up a cloud of dust around her.

Almost too easy.

"I guess there was a reason for your confidence," Crush said, laughing and shaking his head. "Go sit down."

She grinned and couldn't help sauntering back to the hay bale, her gaze focused on Diaz and Spence.

"You fucking rocked that, Jessie," Spence said, smacking her on the back as she sat.

"Thanks."

She waited. Turned to Diaz.

"You did good," Diaz said with a nod.

The rest of the women didn't take long either. About half of the initiates won their fights. The others were escorted off the premises after their butts had been soundly kicked by the Skulls women.

The fighting was over.

"Those who remain, you did a fine job," Crush said. "We need good fighters in our group. You passed the first test. You have guts. Grab something to drink, and we'll get on to the second part in a few minutes."

Spence grabbed several beers, tossing one to Diaz and the other to Jessie. She popped open the can and took several long, courage-inducing swallows.

"Are you sure you can handle this?" Diaz asked.

She shrugged. "Sure."

"You don't sound convincing."

"I've never done it before. I guess we'll see, won't we?"

He frowned. "I still don't like it."

"It's not for you to like or not like. We're here for a reason." She didn't want to think beyond right now, this moment. What would happen later would happen. She was just going to let it unfold.

Someone turned on music, tossed more kindling on the bonfire. Flames licked higher in the air, turning their circle into a veritable sauna.

Crush returned to the center, a bottle of whiskey in his hand. He unscrewed the top, took a long pull, then wiped his mouth with the back of his hand. Two of the women came up next to him, one a petite brunette with her hair in braided pigtails, the other a tall blonde, her hair loose and flowing down to her waist. The brunette grasped the bottle from his hand, took a drink, and handed it to the blonde, who took a drink. Crush wrapped his arms around both the women.

"The Devil's Skulls are a tight group," he said. "We share everything. We live together, fight together, love together. There are no secrets. If you can't bare it all in this gang, then you don't belong here. We expect our initiates to prove it. Pick a partner, or two, or three, and show you want to be with us."

He turned to the brunette and kissed her. Jessie's breath caught at the savagery of the kiss, the way his tongue tangled with hers. Then he pulled away from the brunette and turned to the blonde, taking her mouth with equal passion.

Jessie's pulse begin to race as she watched the women move their hands over Crush's body. He seemed oblivious to the gazes of everyone on him as the women cupped his crotch, palming his now rigid cock through his leathers.

Mesmerized, Jessie couldn't move. But others did. All around the circle couples began to touch each other. And those who hadn't yet coupled up began to find someone. Women walked up to men—did they even know them? Did it matter? Men approached women, who offered up knowing smiles and welcomed them with open arms. Some weren't even initiates, but already established members of the group, apparently deciding to partake of tonight's party atmosphere.

Wow. A hedonistic pleasure circle. And she had a front row seat, a voyeur's paradise. Between the bonfire and her body heating up from the activity around her, she was ready to strip off her leathers and lie naked on the bales of hay, touching her pussy and getting herself off as she watched the action.

Until a set of strong arms wrapped around her, sliding her off the hay bales and jerking her to her feet.

"We're not here to watch, darlin'. We're participants in this."

A lightning jolt of desire shot low, pooling heat between her legs as Diaz drew her jacket off and bent down to kiss the nape of her neck. She shivered, but she wasn't cold. All doubts about what would be happening tonight fled. Arousal had taken its place. No one was focused only on her—at least not at the moment—there was way too much activity going on around them, too much to look at to concentrate on only one person. Gazes wandered around the area, just as hers did.

Even Spence had found Stephanie, pulled her into his arms for a deep kiss. She'd never seen Spence . . . intimate before. Watching him kiss the woman—touch her—it was shocking, yet exciting.

There were going to be a lot of things tonight she'd never seen before.

Diaz turned her around to face him, his hands on her shoulders, then across her back, rubbing her skin through the thin shirt she wore. "This is just about the two of us. Don't pay attention to anyone else, to anything else going on around us. I'll keep you safe and as hidden as I can."

He had no idea, did he? She palmed his chest, loving the rock solid feel of him against her hands. "I want to watch."

One dark brow arched, then his lips curled. "You're a naughty girl, you know that?"

She smiled. "Yes."

He spun her around and pulled her back against his chest, smoothing his hands along the side of her ribs. He leaned in to whisper against her ear, "I like to watch, too."

His warm breath caressed her neck at the same time his hands swept under her breasts, causing her nipples to harden and press against her shirt. Could others see? Who was watching her? She searched the crowd, her gaze capturing Spence's, who stood behind Stephanie in a similar position to theirs. Spence had lifted Stephanie's shirt, detached her bra, and grasped a handful of Stephanie's breasts in his hands.

But Spence was watching Jessie, and not at all in a brotherly way.

Then again, none of the Wild Riders were her brothers—never had been. They kept telling themselves she was like a sister to them, but she'd always figured it was bullshit. It was to her. They were men. She was a woman. That had never become more evident than on this mission.

Between what she saw and what she felt, she was overwhelmed—in a good way. She'd worried about this moment? She shouldn't have. It was hot as hell. Her gaze flitted to Crush. The two women were on their knees now, unzipping his pants and reaching inside to pull out his cock. While she watched, Diaz was behind her, his hard cock pressed against her. He rocked, insistently, making sure she understood clearly who she was here with.

As if there was any doubt. She reached behind her and placed her palm over his erection. He hissed.

"Do you know how much I want to fuck you?"

"What are you waiting for?" she asked, pushing back against his hard-on. Her panties were damp, clinging to her pussy. She could already imagine him pounding into her as they watched other couples go at it. Some of them were already undressed, others were halfway there. Moans and whimpers, a few unintelligible murmurs could be heard above the crackles and pops of the bonfire.

This was so much more than the movies she used to watch. It was up close, personal sex really happening in front of her. It wasn't staged, wasn't fake, it was actual people having actual sex. No prettified stars in weird positions showcasing body parts for the best camera angle. It was tall people, short people, some older, some younger, a few couples were gorgeous, and a few were ugly. Some had killer bodies, some didn't.

It didn't matter. Every bit of it was exciting. She was watching other people have sex, and it made her pussy wet. A woman, completely naked, fell onto a bale of hay right in front of her. The guy with her fumbled with a condom, then plunged his sizeable cock between her pussy lips. The woman screamed, lifted her hips while the man pumped into her and buried his head between her breasts.

Jessie shuddered, tempted to reach out and touch them, as if she couldn't quite believe this was real. There was too much to see. She didn't know where to look next but couldn't wait to turn her head, afraid she'd miss something exciting.

She heard Diaz's dark laugh behind her. He cupped her breasts, his thumbs brushing across her nipples, making her knees weak.

"I think you're ignoring me in favor of watching."

She laid her head against his chest, panting with excitement. "I could never ignore you. You have a great dick. Now fuck with me with it."

"I love a woman who knows what she wants." He jerked the button of her pants open, pulled her zipper down, slid his hand inside to cup her sex. She sucked in a breath as he caressed her, wished her pants were off so he could have free movement to play with her clit and pussy. Why wasn't he undressing her? Other people were naked, some women spread-eagled and enjoying oral sex. Her clit quivered as she watched, her pussy spilling more moisture onto Diaz's questing fingers.

"Fuck me," she demanded.

He maneuvered his fingers along her vulva, then drove two into her. She stilled, shuddered, gripping his forearm while he finger fucked her with hard, short strokes.

"Like that?" he asked.

"Yes." She clenched her jaw, could barely force the word out. Her gaze drifted to Crush, his pants around his ankles as the two women took turns devouring his cock with their mouths, their lips and tongues lapping at each side of his swollen shaft, then taking his angry purple cockhead between their lips. They cupped his balls, then one licked and sucked them into her mouth while the other swallowed his cock. He held on to the blonde's hair as she took his shaft deep into her mouth. Then he looked over at Jessie and smiled at her, nodded, while Diaz continued to pump his fingers furiously inside her.

But she needed more.

"Diaz, please." She lifted against his hand, holding on to his wrist to shove it farther inside her pants. But he grabbed her wrist, lifted his hands out of her pants.

She could have cried. Until he began pulling at her jeans, drawing them over her butt. She felt cool air on her pussy.

"Bend forward."

He pushed her over so she palmed a stack of hay, half bent, her jeans down around her knees. She heard his belt buckle, his zipper, the tearing of a foil packet.

Hurry.

And then he was probing, his cockhead parting her pussy lips to plunge inside her with one violent push. Her pussy tightened around him in welcome, her orgasm fast approaching.

"Oh. Oh, God, Diaz."

He didn't speak, just half pulled out before harshly penetrating her again. Was he watching the sex going on around them? Did he see Spencer fucking Stephanie's widespread thighs as she stood against one of the buildings? Did he see Crush being sucked by those two gorgeous women, or any of the other people fucking around them? Or was he concentrating on her ass, on the view of his cock disappearing between her pussy lips?

Her answer came when he leaned over and reached between her legs, finding her clit and rubbing it with deliberate strokes.

"I want you to come on my dick, Jessie. Watch all these people fuck and come for me."

She couldn't focus now; she was too lost in the sensations of his cock, his fingers, and the magic they created. She whimpered, cried out when he hit that spot, and lost it completely when her climax roared through her.

"Yes! Fuck me, harder, I'm coming!" Her pussy gripped his dick and waves of ecstasy washed over her. She grabbed on to the hay bale and bucked back against Diaz.

She heard his guttural groans as he came, his body pressed tight against her in powerful shudders that nearly equaled those she'd experienced. She held tight to the hay bales as he nearly fucked her off her legs until he finally spent all he had and slowed his movements, his bare legs pressed against hers. He kissed her neck, caressed her breasts, then withdrew, lifting her up and pulling her clothes in place before he'd fixed his own. After he'd taken care of himself, he pulled her around to face him, locking gazes with her. He kissed her, a deep but soft and tender kiss that left her with more questions than answers. When he pulled back, his gaze was dark but warm.

"You have a black eye," she said, tracing the bruises on his face, the cuts that would need tending to.

He pulled her hand away, kissed her palm. "I'm fine."

"You always are," she said, smiling up at him.

He sat on one of the hay bales and drew her against his chest. "Enjoy that?"

She shuddered at the memory of the way he'd loved her. "Yes. Very much."

"I never figured you for a voyeur or an exhibitionist, Jessie."

"Me either. There's a lot about me that even I haven't explored yet. Won't it be fun to figure me out?"

He laughed and kissed her. "I'm not sure anyone could figure you out."

He turned her around and wrapped his arms around her. Could she be more contented? Granted, this had been for show. They'd had to do it. Still, Diaz had protected her, had minimized her exposure to everyone else while still allowing her to fully enjoy the experience.

He never failed to surprise her.

Eventually, the sex play began to die down. Everyone was finished, cleaning up, and Crush had gotten himself put back together again.

"Okay, everyone," Crush said. "I need the initiates to come up here."

Jessie, Spence, and Diaz lined up with the remaining initiates. They'd lost about half of them during the fighting portion of the night.

Crush reached into a box that Rex handed to him. "These are insignias indicating you belong to the Devil's Skulls." Crush handed one to each of them. "Welcome to the gang."

Jessie grinned as Crush gave her the insignia. She slipped it in her pocket.

"There are also T-shirts in the other boxes. Go find one in your size. Tomorrow morning, we're riding east to spend a few days camping out at the Buffalo River. If you want to come, let me know. If not, leave your contact information with Stephanie and we'll be in touch about the next ride. You all did good tonight. We're proud to have you as part of the gang."

The crowd began to disperse. Diaz told Crush they'd ride to

the river with the gang tomorrow. They grabbed shirts, then headed out on their bikes back to the hotel. They had a lot of work to do. They needed to figure out the next part of their plan.

They had passed the test and were now Devil's Skulls.

Jessie had a feeling the real action was about to begin.

TWELVE

DIAZ GAVE THE FULL REPORT TO GRANGE ONCE THEY GOT BACK to their room. Okay, not the full report—he left the sex parts out. There were some things Grange didn't need details on. He and Jessie having repeated hot sex was one of those.

Grange also let them know about the satellite information from the campsite they'd discovered. It definitely appeared to be an encampment. Satellite infrared counted about twenty people. Maybe survivalists, maybe not, but Grange didn't feel that group was big enough to be the one they were hunting for.

So they were back to square one.

At least they were now in with the Skulls and taking off with them tomorrow for the river, an area deep in survivalist country. They should make some serious headway and soon. Which meant Diaz had to become Crush's best friend.

"So we're in. Now what?" Spence asked, sitting on the window ledge in Diaz and Jessie's room.

"Now we embed, get as close to as many of the members as we can, and hopefully find out something. Keep your eyes and your ears open."

"Stephanie knows everyone," Spence said. "I'll make sure she takes me around and introduces me. I'll get close."

Diaz nodded. "Jessie's already tight with Crush. I need to get tighter, get him to start trusting me. The best way to get in on the secrets of this gang is to get front and center in their organization."

"That isn't going to happen overnight," Jessie said, toeing off her boots and pulling her legs onto the bed. She scooted backward and fluffed the pillows so she rested against the headboard.

"No, it isn't. But the more he trusts us, the more he'll give us in the way of information. He already knows you from before," Diaz said, nodding his head toward Jess. "And the three of us didn't hesitate when it came to the bar fight. Plus, tonight we were all in. Every step we take ingrains us further into their core group. I can already tell Crush trusts us more each day."

"And if there's friction between him and Rex, that means Crush is looking for allies," Spence reminded them.

Diaz nodded. "Exactly. Which means we need to be there for him. He needs people he can trust."

"He told me once he isn't close to a lot of people," Jessie said.

"And that can work to our advantage." It was about time things went their way. Diaz needed some action, needed this case to move forward.

"I'll head on out," Spence said, pushing off the window ledge. "I'm beat."

"See you in the morning," Diaz said, closing and locking the door behind Spence.

It was already three in the morning. They weren't going to get a lot of sleep. When he walked back into the room, Jessie was yawning.

Still, his cock twitched to life. Just seeing her kicked back on the bed, being alone with her, drove his urge to be inside her. Hadn't he had enough? When would he be satisfied?

Never.

Her lips lifted in that lopsided smile as he approached the bed.

"I need a shower," he said. "I have battle dirt on me."

"You're bloody, too. You probably need some gentle nursing care."

He let out a short laugh. "Is that right?"

She slid off the bed and raised her T-shirt over her head. "That's right."

He went into the bathroom, Jessie on his heels. As he flipped on the light, she was unzipping her pants. "I suppose you're going to nurse me back to health?"

"Something like that," she said, kicking her jeans off as he turned the shower on.

He stepped into the shower first, holding his hand out and helping her inside before closing the door and letting the steam envelop them.

It felt damn good. Hot water and Jessie. He pulled her toward him, her full breasts meeting his chest. He backed her under the water spray and she lifted her hands to smooth her hair back.

"God, I need this."

His cock rose as he watched her, her nipples tilted upward, pebbling under the pelting water.

She kept her eyes closed, washed and rinsed her hair, then directed him to wet his. He did, and she poured shampoo onto her hand and scrubbed his hair, using her fingertips to massage his scalp. He had to bend over so she could reach his head, of course, but still, it felt damn good to have her hands on him, even if it was just his hair.

He rinsed and grabbed the soap, lathering his hands.

"Turn around."

She gave him her back and he soaped her up, lingering over the smooth skin of her shoulder blades before trailing the soap bubbles on their way south. He dipped his finger in the crack of her ass and she shivered, turned her head, and gave him a look that made his balls ache.

Oh, yeah.

He slid an arm around her waist and drew her against him, loving the slippery soap feel of their bodies gliding together. He rocked against her, his cock slipping between her legs.

"I need to fuck you," he said, letting his shaft slide back and forth across her pussy lips.

She bent from the waist, giving him the same view he'd had earlier tonight. Only this time, she was wet, slick, her legs widespread.

"Do it," she said, reaching behind her to grasp his shaft in her hand. He paused, then drove against her, the water and her tight grip reminding him of her hot pussy. He could let her do this all night. But he wanted more, wanted to feel the grip of her cunt, listen to the sounds she made while he fucked her.

He opened the shower door long enough to grab a condom. He didn't think he'd ever put one on in such a hurry. He felt like a kid having his first sex, that desperate, I-need-to-get-inside-this-woman sense of urgency that he always felt whenever he was near her. He didn't recall ever feeling this way about another woman.

Then again, didn't he already know Jessie was something special?

He kneed her legs apart again, then moved between them, using his palm to push her forward so her butt rose up in the air. He took a moment to step back and admire the view of her ass, to spread apart her beautiful buttocks and slide his finger over the puckered hole.

She shuddered, but didn't pull away.

He liked that. Using his fingers, he coated them with the juices from her pussy, spread her apart and speared her with his dick. Her gasp of pleasure was his favorite music and he reared back and gave her more, wanting to hear those sounds she made when she really liked it. He made sure he'd hear them by reaching around to play with her clit, to strum the piercing until she cried out. She tightened, jerking against him while lifting herself on and off his cock.

He grasped her hips and began to pump inside her with long, measured strokes. Jessie slid one hand between her legs and began to play with her clit.

"That's it, baby," he said, thrusting deep. "Touch yourself. Make yourself come."

Her cream was hotter than the shower water, spilling over his balls. With every stroke she gripped him tighter, making more friction, bringing him closer to getting off.

He spread her butt cheeks apart, using his finger to tease there.

"Oh, God, Diaz!"

"You like it?"

"Yes. Yes!"

He slid the tip of his finger inside her anus, feeling the muscles there resist, then give as he pushed a little farther.

"You're going to make me come."

"That's the idea."

He continued to tease her ass while giving her long, even strokes with his shaft. Jessie rubbed her clit with frenzied motions, and he used her responses to tune in to her pleasure. He thrust deeper, faster, with both his cock and his finger until she stilled, shuddered, and let go, her walls convulsing around his dick, her asshole gripping his finger.

That was all he could take. His orgasm ripped through his spine, jerking him upright and forcing him to hold on to the top of the shower door for support as he was hit by lightning strokes of pleasure—her pussy squeezing him with relentless pulses, pulling everything he had until there was nothing left to give.

He withdrew, soaped and rinsed them both, then turned off the shower, handing her a towel when she stepped out.

"It has to be almost dawn," she said when she hung the towel up.

She looked exhausted. Faint shadows were starting to appear under her eyes.

He scooped her up in his arms.

"What are you doing?" she asked.

"Putting us to bed."

"I can walk from the bathroom to the bed."

"This is more fun."

She laughed and twined her arms around his neck. "Then be my guest."

He laid her on the bed, turned out the lights, then slid in beside her, drawing her next to him. She sighed and snuggled closer, wiggling her butt against his crotch.

"Keep that up and we'll never get any sleep."

"Sleeping's overrated," she said with a loud yawn.

Within a few minutes, she was sound asleep.

And he was really damned content having her in his arms.

There were a million reasons why that was a bad thing, but he was too tired to think about them. All he cared about was having Jess in his arms and needing at least a few hours sleep.

He could brood tomorrow.

THANKFULLY, CRUSH HADN'T WANTED TO TAKE OFF UNTIL NOON. Jessie felt like there were lead weights pressing on her eyes. Lead weights coated with sand.

They'd managed a few hours of sleep before having to get up, eat, check out, and find Spence, then head over to meet Crush and the others.

She craved a nap like nobody's business. She'd bet it was going to be a really long day. Once they met up with the Skulls, Crush informed them they were going to ride east toward the Buffalo River, then stay at a lodge for a few days and ride the trails.

Jessie loved roughing it—typically. But right now she could use a day in her room with the covers over her head. The past couple of days had been monumental, to say the least. She needed some time to absorb it all.

Unfortunately there was no time to think about her and Diaz, about sex, about anything but the mission. They were too busy. She was pretty impressed by Crush's gang. She'd thought it was just bikers, but it wasn't. When they met on the outskirts of town, there were the typical bikes, but also a few RVs and trucks towing enclosed trailers, too.

"It appears the Skulls have an entourage," Jessie said to Crush.

Crush shrugged. "Some of our people like to travel in comfort, some don't care for hotels so they use the campsites. Then we have a few folks who come in from far enough away that they trailer their bikes and drive in. Plus we pack tools, parts, and equipment in the trucks and trailers."

"But not you," Diaz said.

Crush patted his side saddlebags. "Everything I need is on my bike."

After Crush took off to head the motorcade, Diaz exchanged looks with Spence and Jessie. "I didn't know about the RVs and trailers."

"You think they could be housing weapons?" Spence asked.

"It's a possibility. I'd like to get inside and see."

"We'll have to figure out who's driving them," Jessie said. "Maybe we'll get a chance to sneak in, or if we're friendly enough, get an invite into the RVs."

"Don't need an invite." Spence looked at Diaz and raised his brows, his meaning clear.

They were, after all, thieves.

"Damn straight. It's all about opportunity. We'll have to keep close watch on those RVs and trailers, see where they go."

Jessie nodded. "If we're all going to the same place, that should be easy enough."

"Let's hope that's the case," Diaz said.

Crush fired up his bike, signaling all of them it was time to go. The bikers led the way, the RVs and trucks bringing up the rear.

They rode for several hours and for a while Jessie forgot all about the mission because the day was gorgeous—a hint of fall in the crisp, biting air, the wind swirling around them as they took the narrow, curving, two-lane roads heading east. On one stop Crush explained the RVs and trucks would have to take the highway because the narrow switchbacks and steep hills were too tough for them to navigate. In other words—bikes only. The others would meet them at the river in a few hours.

The ride was an absolute blast. Over fifty bikers lined up in single file maneuvering over one hell of a fun road—and the view was incredible. The higher the elevation became, the closer they got to the national forest and river, the denser the trees became. Even the smells became more prominent. Earthier, more woodsy and primitive—cleaner. Jessie could feel herself growing closer to nature up here. Maybe it was the utter quiet; despite the roar of all the bike engines, she still felt at peace here. And there were no houses, no businesses, just sky, trees, and birds flying along with them as they soared through the hills.

DIAZ HAD TOLD HER THAT'S WHY THE EXTREME SURVIVALISTS liked it up here. They wanted to isolate themselves from government interference, from anyone who didn't meet their religious, political, and racial standards.

She disagreed with everything these types of radical groups stood for. Anarchy. Violence. White supremacy. None of it agreed with her belief system. Stockpiling illegal weapons for their deluded plans was a frightening prospect. With any luck, she, Diaz, and Spence would be able to stop them. She wanted to protect innocent people and prevent unnecessary bloodshed.

They finally veered off the main road and headed south, entering a small town. It didn't have much, just a tiny independent grocery store and a few other shops that seemed to cater to seasonal campers. They stopped for a quick refuel, then followed Crush into the campgrounds. The roads were well paved, which helped a lot. Maneuvering a bike across a gravel road could be treacherous. Crush pulled into what looked like a country resort, with a main lodge that had a connected restaurant and several group and individual cabins.

They stopped at the lodge to check in and get cabin assignments. Diaz opted for one of the remote cabins for the two of them.

"It'll give us some privacy, allow us to sneak out if we need to and to keep an eye on the others," he said to her.

She nodded.

Spence was going to bunk at the main lodge with Stephanie, because that's where Crush would stay, as well as Rex and some of the other top Skulls. In this way, they had the front and back end of the group covered. It was perfect.

Rural didn't begin to describe the place. Set back a mile or so from the road, it was nestled among thick, towering trees, on a hill overlooking miles of sloping green valley and flowing river. It was breathtaking. The cabin she and Diaz would be staying in was cute. A single room containing one bed, it had wood floors and knotty pine walls, a trestle table and small kitchenette and even a tattered sofa. No television. Jessie supposed the entertainment was outside, not inside. That's why the room had all those windows, with little apple- and pear-decorated curtains. Very homey and adorable.

"Great, isn't it?" Jessie asked Diaz as he tossed their bags on the bed.

He moved behind her as she stood in front of the picture window. The view was of the slope leading down to the river.

"It'll work. No one can exit this way. The incline is too steep. Can't transport arms in this direction. There's nothing down that way but the river. There'd be no way to set up an encampment or even a meeting point."

"I meant the view."

"Yeah. It's nice." He turned away from her and unzipped his bag to unpack.

Jessie shook her head, realizing the beauty of the scenery was lost on him. Clearly he was singularly focused on the mission now. With a sigh, she unpacked, too, and while Diaz was on the phone with Grange, she wandered around the kitchen, imagining this was her and Diaz's place. An apartment, maybe, since they'd be on the go a lot. They wouldn't need much space. A couple of bedrooms—one could be used as an office. Maybe they'd get a cat. Did Diaz like cats? They'd need a king-sized bed because he was so big. She'd enjoy rolling around in a huge bed with him.

She fell forward across the bed and watched as he paced the confines of their small domain, thinking what it would be like to share a place with him. She could cook, they'd watch sports together—they both liked football and auto racing. They really did have a lot in common. Did he already have a place of his own? She'd never even asked him that. She lived at Wild Riders' headquarters, but he only came in when there was an assignment or if he wanted to use the gym. Though lately he'd been there a lot, staying for weeks at a time. All of the guys were welcome to live there—Grange didn't care. It was up to the guys.

He hung up the phone. "Okay, report given to Grange."

"Where do you live?" she asked.

He tilted his head and frowned. "Huh?"

"When you're not at headquarters. Where do you live?"

"Oh." He shrugged. "Right now, nowhere. I bunked with AJ for a while, but his lease was up and he wanted to do a little traveling, so I've been moving around and staying with friends or at Wild Riders."

"I see." So, maybe he was looking for a new place.

Foolish dreams, of course, but she could play house if she wanted to. At least in her mind. Diaz would never even consider it. He'd already made it abundantly clear there was no future for the two of them.

"Why did you ask?"

She looked down at the quilt on the bed, picking at the loose pieces of thread. "No reason. Just curious where you hang out during your off time." When she glanced up at him again, he was staring at her with a curious expression. He probably thought she was nosy as hell, which she was. Time for a topic change.

"So now what?" she asked.

He looked at his cell phone. "Time to find Spence, meet up with the others, have something to eat, and see if the RVs and trucks have arrived. I want to know where they've parked so we can establish their location and figure out a strategy to see what's in them."

"Okay." She swung around off the bed, determined to keep her mind on the mission.

They decided to take a walk to the lodge, since it would give them a chance to figure out who was situated where. In addition to the cabins there were also tents erected in a cleared area just off from the main lodge up ahead. It was a fairly steep climb up the hill, and since their cabin was at the bottom it took a while to get there. They made a slow stroll of it, stopping along the way to visit with other Skulls. Diaz either held her hand or wrapped his arm around her waist while they hung out visiting. It might be for show, but she still enjoyed it and leaned into him, liking the way he smelled and the warmth of his body. With the sun beginning to set and the higher elevation, it was cooler. In fact, by the time they had made their way to the lodge, she was shivering.

"Are you cold?" Diaz asked as he opened the door for her to step inside.

She rubbed her hands together. "Yes. Temps are cooler up here."

"I guess I'll have to find a way to keep you warm tonight."

He'd even said it with a straight face. She smiled up at him.

"I guess you will." Now she had something delicious to look forward to besides dinner. She knew he wasn't implying that he would toss extra blankets on their bed.

Long wood tables were set up in the dining hall. Crush said one of his friends owned this lodge, which was why he selected it. Plus it was remote, gave them plenty of privacy, and they didn't have to cook over an open campfire.

"Sure beats beans and weenies, doesn't it?" Diaz asked as they sat at the table.

"Hey, I like roughing it as much as the rest of you. But John and Beth make the best damn meatloaf I've ever tasted," Crush said.

Jessie couldn't argue with home cooking and eating indoors, warmed by the fire in the stone hearth. The place was homey, with polished dark wood floors, floor to ceiling windows offering views of the nightscape and rising moon, and plenty of food to go around. Crush was right. John, Beth, and their staff were friendly and great cooks. The food was wonderful. After dinner, Diaz and Jessie found a minute alone with Spence, who'd signaled them over as soon as he managed to break free of clingy Stephanie.

"A few of the guys mentioned they're going out tonight for a late ride," Spence said, keeping an ever watchful eye out for whoever might be listening in. "It sounded a little suspicious to me."

Diaz arched a brow. "In what way?"

"They were keeping it low key, like they didn't want anyone to know about it. I just happened to overhear."

"Okay. Who's going?"

"Rex and a half dozen others."

Diaz nodded. "What's your plan?"

"I'm going to get into a fight with Steph and take off on my own right after these guys leave. It's a good excuse for a solitary ride."

"And you're going to follow them."

Spence nodded. "Discreetly, but yeah, that's my plan."

Diaz nodded. "You got a good reason to suspect them?"

Spence shrugged. "Right now I suspect everyone."

"Agreed. Want me to go with you?"

Spence shook his head. "It's better if I go off alone. It'll just look like I'm letting off steam. I'll make the fight with her pretty public."

"Be careful. Take your phone and holler if you need backup."

Jessie worried about Spence tracking the group by himself. But she had to trust that he'd be able to take care of himself if the need arose.

They hung out at the lodge for a bit after eating. Diaz nudged Jessie when Rex and a few others slipped out the door. Within a minute or so, she heard their bikes roaring to life. Diaz searched the crowd for Spence, who was already working on Stephanie. She was frowning, shaking her head, and the timbre of her voice rose with every sentence. It didn't take long for their argument to grab everyone's attention.

"I don't need this shit. I'm out of here." Spence threw his hands up in the air in disgust and turned, walking away.

Stephanie stomped after him. "Where the hell do you think you're going?"

He stopped, pivoted, and even Jessie was taken aback at the venomous look on his face. "I don't answer to you, Stephanie. Or to anyone else. I need a ride to clear my head so just back the fuck off."

Spence stormed out, the door slamming behind him. *Whoa. That was good.* Jessie wanted to applaud his performance, because from the look of shock and utter fury on her face, Stephanie was pissed. She sniffed and turned on her heel, walking away.

Jessie turned to Diaz. "I'm worried about him."

Diaz cupped her cheek and leaned in for a kiss, surprising her. "He'll be fine. Spence knows how to take care of himself. In the meantime, we have our own reconnaissance to do, and the best way to do it is to split up and start asking questions about the RVs and trucks. I'm going to hit up Crush about the RVs—tell him you and I are looking for a new place and are thinking of buying an RV. Maybe he'll hook me into the owners of the two that are parked outside."

"Sounds good. I'll go hunt down who owns those trailers."

They went their separate ways to do some sleuthing. Jessie joined a group of women having a few drinks in one of the corners, figuring the best way to get information was to ask the ladies—typically, they would know everything about an organization like the Skulls.

She was right. Within an hour she knew the names of the owners of the four trailers and in fact had been talking to the wives of two of them. Of course then she'd had to endure open versus closed trailer discussions before the two women dragged their husbands over to meet Jessie. She asked them questions about trailer ownership, managing to tamp down her squealing excitement when they both invited Jessie and Diaz to visit their trailers tonight.

She nearly jumped out of her skin, her gaze searching the room for signs of Diaz. No time like the present to get their hands on two of the trailers for an impromptu inspection. But Diaz was nowhere in sight. Neither was Crush. Which is what she told the men, so they and their wives offered to show Jessie the trailers. She agreed and walked down the hill with them, chatting pleasantly about biking and road trips and which truck or SUV was well equipped to tow which trailers.

Not that what they talked about mattered. What was important was getting inside both trailers, even if it was just a cursory look. Pretty much empty except for bike, luggage, and tool storage. Her inspection didn't turn up anything that looked like it could contain weapons storage, so she crossed both trailers off her list.

Partial mission accomplished. Two trailers down, two to go. She thanked the couples, who offered to show off the trailers to Diaz whenever he wanted to see them. Then she made her way back to the lodge to find Diaz.

Fortunately she only had to trek halfway up, because he was on his way toward their cabin.

"Where were you?" he asked.

She looked around to see if anyone was about. It appeared they were alone, but she wasn't going to take any chances. She told him about seeing the two trailers, hoping he'd play along with the game of wanting to "buy" them. He nodded as they walked back to their cabin. Once inside with the door shut, she told him what she'd found.

"No false bottoms or walls?"

She shook her head. "Nothing that I could see. Both were solidly constructed and not expandable. There didn't appear to be anyplace within either one where weapons could be stashed, at least not in the quantity that we're talking about for this mission."

"Okay. So that rules both of those trailers out."

"What about the RVs?"

He slid out of his jacket and tossed it in a nearby chair. "I hung out with Crush for a while, talked to him about them. He took me over to one of the guys who owns the brown RV."

Excitement rushed through her. She sat on the bed next to him, slipping off her jacket and tossing it over his. "Did you get inside?"

He nodded. "Yeah. Got the whole tour, inside and out."

"And?"

Shrugging, he said, "Nothing that I could see, at least on the surface. It's not like I could do a thorough inspection with Crush and Nate standing there. But nothing appeared out of the ordinary."

"Too bad." That was disappointing. Finding a cache of weapons would end this mission on a high note, meaning they could wrap up before they got involved in anything dangerous. Then again, maybe there weren't any weapons. As she unzipped her boots, her gaze flitted to Diaz. "Are you sure we're on the right track here?"

He frowned. "What do you mean?"

"Are we certain that the Skulls are the ones providing illegal arms to the survivalist group?"

"Yes."

No hesitation. Okay, then. "And are we sure that they have the weapons on them right now?"

"You mean at the lodge here? No. That we're not sure of. They could have a stash somewhere else that they plan to dig up before they make contact. That's why it was important for us to get in with this gang. Now it's our job to stay tight with them and watch their every move."

"We're not exactly watching from in here, are we?" she asked.

"Not yet. But we will be."

"Really. And how are you going to manage that?"

"Grab a blanket and come with me."

This was work related? *Cool.* If it required a blanket and Diaz, she was game.

He led her out the back door and around the wraparound porch. There was a two-person rocking chair situated in a perfect spot, tucked in the corner of the side of the cabin, with a great view both coming and going from the road. You could see all the way up to the lodge, and farther down the road past their cabin. Since no one could get anywhere behind them, this was the best vantage point for simply sitting and . . . watching.

In other words, excellent surveillance location.

"Come on," he said, taking a seat and holding the blanket out for her.

Now that it was dark, it was really getting cold outside. She grabbed the other seat and snuggled up close to Diaz. He pulled the thick blanket over both of them, tucking it in around her shoulders. Between the cover and his body heat, she was more than comfortable.

No one was wandering about down by their cabin, but there were several gang members hanging around outside the lodge at the top of the hill. A few lights were on at some of the cabins, others had gone dark.

They rocked together in silence for a while, both of them keeping watch on the bikers, the road, anything that looked suspicious. Jessie laid her head on Diaz's shoulder and he wrapped an arm around her, playing with her hair.

It was comfortable, warm, and the way he touched her made her feel safe. She wanted this to last forever.

Why couldn't it last forever? Why did relationships have to be so complicated? What was it about Diaz that made him hold back?

"Diaz . . ."

"*Shhh*. Don't talk." He turned, tipped her chin back with his fingers, and pressed his mouth to hers. His lips were soft as they brushed back and forth, and she lost her train of thought, lost everything but the desire for this moment to hang suspended forever. That cold chill she'd felt earlier dissolved into liquid warmth as he gathered her into his arms, pulling her across his lap and sliding his arms tightly around her. She moaned, her mouth opened, and he slid his tongue inside, claiming possession of hers with soft, velvet strokes that made her quiver inside.

He tugged at the zipper of her jacket, drew it down, slid his hand inside to cup her breast. Her heart pounded against his palm as he gently squeezed and cupped her, teased her already-distended nipple with his thumb.

"I thought we were doing surveillance." Her words were breathless, her thoughts scattered like the leaves tossed by the wind.

"I'm watching. You focus on what I'm doing."

"That's my problem," she said, gasping when he rolled her nipple between his fingers. "It's all I'm focusing on."

"Ah, Jess, I need to fuck you."

His words conjured up wicked things in her mind. She drew closer to him, kissed the corner of his mouth. Didn't he know she'd give him anything, anytime? "Yes."

He sucked in a harsh breath, lifted her off his lap, and stood her up. "Hold the blanket in front of you."

She stood between his legs, her back to him. He reached around and slid the button open on her jeans, then drew the zipper down. Her legs felt wobbly as he tugged her pants down her hips, then over her thighs, bringing her panties with them until they rested at her knees. Moisture spilled between her legs, her clit quivering with anticipation.

Hurry. This was so naughty, so exciting, right out here where someone could see. Did she care? *Oh, hell no.*

She felt him lift against her, heard his zipper, the tearing of the condom packet.

"Come here, baby."

Then warm hands on the bare skin of her hips, pulling her down onto his lap.

It wasn't the easiest position, but she didn't mind. She wanted his cock inside her, felt the tip nestling against her pussy lips. He guided her because she couldn't see, drawing her down over his cock, lifting his hips to impale her. She bit down on her lip to keep from crying out as the thick heat of his shaft thrust inside her until she was sitting on his thighs, his cock embedded deep within her.

It felt so damn good she wanted to cry. She pulsed around him and started to rock, back and forth, her clit rubbing his legs.

"That's it, fuck me just like that," he whispered, wrapping an arm around her to pull her back against him. The other hand slid up under her shirt and found her breasts, teasing her nipples until she couldn't hold back the moans of delight that escaped.

"Yes. Fuck me, Diaz, fuck me." Now she didn't care who heard her or who knew what they were doing. She wanted only the orgasm she craved, the one that hovered so close as he thrust upward, then retreated, only to bury his cock deep within her again. Every time he moved, her clit dragged against him, doubling the sweet pleasure until she had to hold on to the chair for support.

"Do you like fucking outside where someone can see you?" he asked, his whisper a warm caress against her cheek.

"Yes." She rocked forward, her pussy tightening.

"Someone could be watching us right now, Jess. They'd know we're fucking. Does that make you wet?"

"Yes."

"Yeah. I can feel your pussy getting wetter." He drove harder, lifting his hips to give her more of his delicious cock. She was getting closer, her fingers drifting down to cover her clit.

"That's it. Rub your clit and make yourself come for me."

He gave her nipple a light pinch, rolled it, and she shattered, feeling like a million pieces of her were scattering all over. She wanted to tilt her head back and scream but didn't dare. Instead, she shuddered against him, gripping his arm, the chair, while she climaxed repeatedly, panting through this intense orgasm that rolled in waves. Diaz buried his face against her, whispering her name in the softest way as he came, grasping her hand and holding it tight for the longest time until he finally relaxed.

When she had some sanity again, when she'd righted her clothes and he had, too, she shifted onto the seat and leaned her head against his shoulder.

"Is it always like this?"

"What?" he asked, caressing her arm.

"Sex."

It took him a few minutes to answer.

"No, Jessie. It isn't always like this."

She smiled. That's what she thought.

THIRTEEN

EVERY TIME DIAZ HELD JESSIE IN HIS ARMS, HE REALIZED HOW
hard it was going to be to let her go. He'd gotten used to having
her around, having her close. He'd started to think of her as his.

He was in deep shit.

But he *was* going to let her go.

She had nestled in close, her nose pressed to his chest, eyes
closed, lashes resting against her cheek. God, she was beautiful,
and still so innocent. He'd never mar that innocence by forcing
her to live with him. He'd ruin her. Maybe not today, tomorrow,
this month, this year or next, but eventually his true colors would
show. He already had a hard time reining in his temper. What
would happen when she really pissed him off? Would he go after
her like his old man had done with his mom?

The thought of hurting Jessie caused him physical pain inside.
He'd like to think he'd never do something like that, but he
couldn't take that chance.

It would be better to start distancing himself from her now, but he supposed he was weak, because he just couldn't do it.

The more time he spent with her, the more he craved. There never seemed to be enough, especially knowing that what they had could only be temporary. Every day the clock ticked louder, signaling time running out. Maybe if he just strung her along for a while, then abruptly cut her out of his life when they finished the mission, it would be easier. She'd hate him, but she'd get over him faster.

Yeah, he was a fucking saint, wasn't he? He wasn't thinking of Jessie. He was thinking of himself. If he'd been thinking of Jess he'd never have started anything up with her. He'd been weak. Instead of walking away like he should have, he'd fallen right into bed with her.

There were a lot of women he could have fucked, plenty of willing females to scratch the itch with.

But he wasn't interested in just scratching the itch, was he? With Jess, it was more than that. She'd knocked repeatedly. Hell, she'd pounded. The girl was relentless when she wanted something. What she'd wanted was him. Instead of barring the door, he'd flung it wide open and let her in, so he had no one to blame but himself for this mess. How to get out of it was the problem.

"Something's been bothering you."

He looked down at her, not even realizing she'd woken. "Just thinkin'."

"I know. You do that a lot. But you don't tell me what you're thinking about."

"This and that. Mostly the mission," he lied.

She pushed up so they were face-to-face, her eyes a clear emerald that even the darkness couldn't hide. He stopped breathing whenever he searched her face. Damn, he was in deep.

"It's more than the mission. It's us, isn't it?"

"Us? No."

"Diaz, you can talk to me. I'm an adult. I can handle a frank discussion if there's something on your mind."

Not this discussion. This one she wouldn't want to have. It would lead to tears and emotions he wasn't equipped to handle. "Trust me, Jessie. There are a lot of things on my mind about this case. That's what's keeping me busy."

She studied him carefully. He knew she wasn't buying his excuses. She could read him too well. Sooner or later, they'd have to talk about their relationship. He just didn't want it to be now.

The roar of motorcycles saved him. They both turned their attention to the lodge. Rex and the other bikers who'd ridden off earlier had returned and were dispersing to their designated sleeping spots.

"Did Spence ride back in yet?" she asked.

"No."

"That's not good."

"No, it's not." Diaz dragged out his cell phone and punched in Spence's number. He waited while it rang several times, then went to voice mail. "He's not answering."

"He might be on his bike and headed back. He won't hear it if he's riding."

"Could be." Diaz leaned back in the rocker. Something didn't feel right. It was unusual for Spence not to check in.

An hour later Diaz was convinced something had happened. Spence should have checked in or been back by now. "Let's go search for Spencer."

Jessie threw the blanket off. "I was hoping you'd say that."

They grabbed their gear and hopped on their bikes. As soon as they reached the lodge area, Crush strolled into the middle of the road.

Shit. Diaz stopped.

"Kinda late for a ride, isn't it?" Crush asked with a tilt of his brow.

"Yeah."

"Where are you headed?"

"Spence and Stephanie had a fight earlier tonight."

"So we all noticed," Crush said with a slight smile. "It happens."

"He went out for a ride to clear his head. That was four hours ago."

Crush frowned. "He's not back yet?"

"No."

"And he went out on his own?"

"Yeah." Diaz hoped Crush wasn't going to keep them sitting here asking questions. They needed to get on the road to look for Spence.

"Hang on. I'll go with you."

Double shit. That's the last thing Diaz wanted. "It's okay. We'll handle it."

"Yeah, I'm sure you can, but I've been to this area a hundred times. I know every trail. You don't. Let me help you."

No way could Diaz refuse an offer of assistance. They had no choice. "Okay. Thanks."

Diaz looked at Jessie, who shook her head while they waited for Crush to get his gear.

If Crush was involved with whatever Rex and the others were doing out there, and if it had something to do with the arms deal with the survivalists, then Diaz and Jess might be walking into a trap.

Diaz didn't like having Jessie along for this ride.

"You can go back to the cabin," he said to her.

She frowned. "And you can kiss my ass. I'm going with you."

He thought she'd say that. He hated that his gun was in his saddlebag and not tucked into the back of his pants, but at least he had one with him. Hopefully, he wouldn't have to use it tonight.

Crush came out and climbed onto his bike. "We'll start on the closest trails, figuring maybe he took a short ride. Then we'll work out from there."

"Lead the way," Diaz said.

They started up the bikes and headed out. Pitch-black and narrow roads weren't the best conditions for biking. At least there was a decent-sized moon overhead to light the way.

The first trail took about a half hour to maneuver, mostly downhill and dead-ending at the river bank. No sign of Spence on that one, so Crush turned them around and headed up the way they came, went a short way down the road and took the next trail, with the same results. As they rode, Diaz kept his eyes open for any other bikers or signs of a survivalist camp. The last thing he intended to do was to ride into a trap. He'd grab Jessie and they'd hightail it out of there in a hurry if it looked like Crush was setting them up.

Crush made an abrupt right turn down what didn't even look like a road. In fact, if he hadn't been leading them Diaz wouldn't have seen it at all. It wasn't marked and was difficult to maneuver because of trees and other vegetation in the way, all hazards for bikers. They took it slow. Damn good thing, too, because about ten minutes into the ride, Jessie hollered, honked, and grabbed their attention. Diaz and Crush stopped and turned around. Jess had turned her bike sideways so her headlights shined on a downed bike.

Spence's bike. They raced over to it, climbed off the bikes, and grabbed flashlights, shining them onto the surrounding areas.

"There!" Jessie said, already running toward a prone Spence.

He was half covered in fallen leaves. The three of them converged on him. Diaz held his breath while Jess checked him out.

"He's alive," she said, her fingers on his pulse. "Spence, can you hear me?"

He moaned.

"Shine the light down his body while I check him," Jessie said.

Diaz and Crush held their flashlights over Spence and Jessie inspected him, shoving the leaves out of the way.

"His leg is bleeding," she said.

"I've got a first aid kit," Crush said, already heading toward his bike.

Jessie turned her worried gaze to Diaz.

What the hell happened out here?

Crush brought back the kit and Jessie went to work on Spence, who was already starting to stir.

"Lie still. We're here."

"My goddamn leg is throbbing."

"Don't move it. I'm checking it out now." She grabbed the scissors and started to cut away the spot on his pants where he was bleeding.

Diaz bent over him. "Do you know what happened?"

"Yeah. I was fucking shot."

"What?" Crush's eyes widened. "Who shot you?"

"Hell if I know."

"Why didn't you call for help?" Diaz asked.

"I guess I was too busy being shot and tossed off my bike and getting knocked unconscious. Fuck, I don't even know where my cell is." He patted his pants pocket. "Where's my bike?"

"It's on its side about fifteen yards over. You must have gone flying."

Spence winced. "Great."

Jessie had a thick pad of gauze pressed to his wound. "Okay, the bleeding has stopped. I'm going to wrap this but we've got to get him out of here and have someone see to his wound."

"One of the Skulls is an MD," Crush said.

"No shit?" Spence asked, lifting his head.

"No shit," Crush said.

Then they needed to get Spence into the hands of that doc immediately. "Can you ride?" Diaz asked.

"Hell yeah. Just get me up."

Crush and Diaz lifted him, put his arms over their shoulders, and Spence limped over to Diaz's bike.

"You'll have to ride on the back of my bike," Diaz said.

"Like a fucking girl. No offense, Jessie."

She rolled her eyes. "I'm not kicking your butt only because you're injured and because I'm so grateful you're not dead. Otherwise . . ."

Spence laughed. That was a good sign. He and Crush managed to get Spence onto the bike with a minimal amount of wincing on Spence's part.

"I'll get my guys to come back for your bike," Crush said.

Spence gave a curt nod, exchanged looks with Diaz, and they started up, Crush leading the way. They took it deliberately slow on Spence's behalf, not wanting to jar his wound into bleeding any more than it already was.

By the time they got back into camp, there was a handful of people already waiting at the lodge. Crush must have gotten on his cell while he was riding to alert folks that they were on the way. Good. That meant plenty of hands to help pull Spence off the bike and carry him inside the lodge.

They took him into one of the bedrooms and laid him on a twin bed. Some guy named Mark who appeared to be in his late forties came in with a black bag in his hand. Diaz supposed he was the doc since he dug in and started cutting away the rest of Spence's pants while asking him a million questions.

"Cut the Q and A, Mark, and just stick to the medical, okay?" Crush said.

So Crush didn't want an interrogation of Spence any more than Diaz did. *Good.* The last thing they needed was someone calling the cops or asking a lot of questions Spence wasn't prepared to answer. This was a critical time and they couldn't handle having their cover blown.

Mark asked everyone to leave except for Crush, Diaz, Jessie, and a woman named Laura who was also a nurse. Nothing like bikers who made a living doing other things. Laura positioned herself on the other side of Spence, assisting Mark with cleaning the wound and numbing it so they could probe for the bullet.

"Bullet's lodged in the meaty part of his thigh, just on the surface," Mark said.

Diaz watched Mark drag the slug out with forceps and drop it into a bowl. They'd have to keep the bullet just in case they'd need it later for evidence.

"I'll take that for a souvenir, doc," Spence said.

"Sure. I'll bag it for you."

Good job, Spence.

"You're lucky it didn't go in any deeper and sever some arteries."

"Yeah, I feel real lucky," Spence said, rolling his eyes.

"So that's it? It's out now?" Jessie asked, peering around Diaz.

"Yeah. That was it. I'm going to stitch him up. He lost some blood and he'll be weak. I'll shoot him up with an antibiotic to ward off infection. Otherwise, he should heal up just fine."

"Thanks, Mark." Diaz blew out a relieved breath. It could have been a lot worse. He was glad Spence wasn't severely injured, and doubly glad they wouldn't have to blow their cover by taking Spence to a hospital. The guy was tough—he'd mend fast.

Once Mark finished up, he and Laura left the room with strict orders that Spence not move at all. Stephanie hovered near the doorway, but Diaz said she could come in later, after they talked to him. Then he closed the door. Unfortunately, Crush insisted on staying, and since this was his gang and they were allegedly part of it, there was no way Diaz could object.

"Okay, what the hell happened out there?" Crush said, his face twisted in an angry frown.

Spence looked to Diaz, then shrugged. "I was out riding by myself after Steph and I had that blowup. I heard bikes, so I thought it was Rex and the others who'd ridden out before me. I figured I'd catch up and ride with them. I was getting close, heading down that trail, when a shot rang out. I flew off the damn bike and that's the last thing I remember until you all showed up."

"Did you see anyone else around?"

"There wasn't anyone else on that trail, Crush," Spence said. "No one I could see, anyway."

Spence's statement hung in the air, his meaning clear. Had someone in Rex's group shot him?

"Crush, how did you know to take that road?" Diaz asked. "That path could easily have been missed. You had to know it was there."

"I've been to this area lots of times, taken that road before. We all have. I saw bike tracks so figured maybe Spence had gone that way."

Plausible enough, Diaz supposed.

"Rex could have taken that road with his friends, too," Diaz said, his meaning clear. He wanted to throw down the gauntlet and see what Crush did with it.

Crush dragged his hand through his hair. "That can't be. It had to be hunters or something."

"It's not hunting season," Diaz said.

"Fuck." Crush paced the small bedroom. "I need to go find Rex."

He left the room without another word to them.

Jessie sat on the cushioned chair in the room. "That was interesting. Crush seemed surprised. Upset. Like he had no idea what was going on."

Diaz shook his head. "I'm not buying it. He's covering up by pretending to be unaware of all this."

"Maybe he was surprised I was shot," Spence said, shifting up on the pillow.

"That might be. He sure as hell wouldn't want attention drawn to that area if there's an arms deal about to go down. But I'll bet he knows something."

"Why would he have taken us down that road at all if Rex and the others were dealing with the survivalists there?" Jessie countered.

"Good point. He'd have led us away from there," Diaz said. "None of this makes any sense. Who's the bad guy here?"

"I don't know, Diaz," Spence said. "I didn't see signs of anyone, but I thought I heard Rex and the others and couldn't get close enough to find out. They could have been out riding and nothing more. They might not have anything to do with the arms deal. Then again, maybe they do, and Crush isn't involved."

"And it could be just Crush involved in this. Or Crush and someone else," Diaz suggested.

"Or it could actually be Rex and that group, and Crush knows nothing about it," Jessie argued.

"I don't think so."

Jessie turned to him. "Why not, Diaz? Why are you so convinced Crush is the guilty one?"

"Because he's been our focus since day one. He's who we targeted and he's who we've been assigned to watch over. He leads this group."

"Which doesn't mean that someone else within his gang couldn't be selling those arms."

"She has a point, Diaz. It's worth considering," Spence said.

Could he be wrong? Had he been targeting Crush, singling him out instead of looking at someone else? "I'll check it out, start keeping an eye on Rex. If he goes riding with his buddies again, it's my turn."

"And I'll go with you," Jessie said.

That was the last thing he needed. He couldn't handle the case and worry about someone taking a shot at Jessie. "I don't think so."

"Why not?"

Diaz pointed to Spencer.

Jessie shrugged. "I'll be careful, and I'll be with you. Plus, forewarned is forearmed, right?"

"No, Jess. You won't be going, and that's final."

"Bullshit." Her gaze narrowing on him, Jessie said, "I don't think I need to remind you that we're on assignment. Look what happened to Spence. First, we should ride as a couple, and second, it's not safe for any of us to go off alone, including you. Quit trying to act as my protector. I'm a Wild Rider, too. Start treating me like one."

Spence snorted. Diaz shot him a look.

"Sorry, but she has a point."

Diaz felt his control unraveling. He couldn't do this—couldn't be Jessie's lover *and* her boss. His blood boiled with the need to lash out. He had to get out of here. He turned to Jessie, his hands clenched into fists.

"This situation is exactly why this . . . we . . . are not going to work."

He turned and walked out of the room before he did something incredibly stupid, like admitting how much he cared for her.

JESSIE STARED OPENMOUTHED AT THE DOOR DIAZ HAD JUST exited. She walked over to it, watching him stride with purposeful anger through the lodge and out the front door. She shut the bedroom door and went back to Spence's bedside.

Spencer wore a cockeyed grin on his face.

"What the hell are you smiling about? Did you just see that?"

"Yeah." Spence laced his fingers behind his head. "Damned entertaining, too."

Jess fell into the chair and shook her head. "I don't get it. He was pissed. Really angry. At me."

"Yeah."

She glanced at up at Spence. "Why?"

"Because he's in love with you, dork."

"In love . . ." She rocketed out of the chair. "Are you insane? He is not!"

Spence's grin widened. "Yeah, he is. And he has no fucking idea how to handle it, so he's dealing with it in typical Diaz fashion. He's angry, confused, and fucking it up."

She looked at the door, back at Spence, then sat again. Her heart did a little flip. Diaz was in love with her? Could that be true?

No. Spence was way off base. "He's been telling me in a hundred different ways why the two of us could never work."

Spence gave her a lopsided grin. "Honey, he's trying to convince himself, not you. He's scared."

"Of what?"

"Of you. Of commitment. Of a relationship. Mainly, he's afraid of loving someone and ending up hurting them."

"Like his father did to his mother."

"Yeah. A few of us came from abusive families, so we know the drill. It's hard to step out of that circle of violence untainted, hard to feel like that evil doesn't follow you. Diaz thinks he's going to end up like his dad, just because he has a temper, too."

"He would never hurt me. He doesn't have it in him. I push his buttons all the time. Aggravate him, irritate him, drive him right to the edge. I've never seen any signs of him lashing out at me. He's been amazingly patient with me."

"I don't think he's anything like his dad. But try and tell him that and he'll disagree."

"So what do I do?"

Spence shrugged. "I'm the last guy to give love advice, sweet pea. It's not really my thing. But I say if you care about him, you'll just have to convince him that the two of you belong together."

Wasn't that what she'd been trying to do all this time? She cared about him. She always had. But this time they'd spent together, having the chance to get to know him—really get to know the person he was, the way he treated her—she knew she wanted him in her life.

But Diaz was one hardheaded male. Trying to talk him into having an honest to God relationship with her—actually staying together beyond this assignment—was going to be tougher than the mission.

Apparently he'd decided sex was just fine between them, at least as long as the mission lasted. She had a feeling as soon as this case was over, he was going to give her "the talk." The one about how they worked together and couldn't have a relationship. Or how his past tainted him somehow, and he didn't want to hurt her.

She was going to have to be prepared for that conversation, because she was just as stubborn as he was, and she'd already decided that Diaz wasn't going to get rid of her.

She was going to keep him, whether he liked it or not.

And she might as well start right now, by tracking him down and figuring out what bug crawled up his ass, then doing her best to calm him down.

"Are you going to be okay?" she asked Spence.

"Yeah." He yawned. "I'm beat. I need to sleep this all off and I'll be ready to go tomorrow."

"Yeah, right. You'll be going nowhere tomorrow."

"We'll see, won't we?" He winked.

She shook her head, kissed his forehead, and turned out the light, closing the door behind her. She asked Mark to keep everyone out of his room—meaning Stephanie, who Jessie was certain would keep Spence up all night either talking his ear off or wanting to have sex. Mark said he'd make sure no one got in.

She headed out of the lodge and down the road toward the cabin, hoping she'd find Diaz there. He was sitting on the chair they'd occupied earlier tonight. Her body pulsed with heat as she recalled the two of them together on that chair.

How could a man filled with so much warmth, so much passion, ever worry about hurting her? Didn't he recognize his own feelings toward her?

Probably not. Sometimes men needed a good slap upside the head.

She didn't sit next to him, instead opting to lean against the railing across from him.

"Finished having your tantrum?" she asked, folding her arms across her chest.

He arched one beautiful dark brow. "Excuse me?"

"You heard me. What was that about up there?"

He looked past her toward the lodge. "Nothing. Forget about it."

"Well, that's communicative."

"Sometimes I don't want to talk, Jess."

"That's right. Sometimes you want to avoid topics. Especially if the topic is you and me."

His gaze shot to hers. "There is no you and me. Don't you understand that?"

"Oh, quit being so noble and playing the Beauty and the Beast card. It's bullshit, Diaz." She walked past him and opened the back door into the house.

As she suspected, he followed.

"Beauty and the Beast?"

"Yeah. You're the poor misunderstood beast, all mean and feisty. And I'm the tender beauty who sees past the monster in you, but you're still afraid to care for me." She rolled her eyes. "Please. It's an old tale and it doesn't apply to you. You're human, not a beast. You'll make mistakes, I'll make mistakes. But I never figured you for a coward."

"I'm no coward."

His voice had gone low. That meant he was angry, trying to maintain his control. *Good.* At least she had his attention now.

She turned to face him. "Aren't you? You're too afraid to even attempt to have a relationship with me. If that isn't cowardice, then what is it? And if you tell me one more time that you're try-ing to protect me, I'm going to kick you straight in the balls."

He opened his mouth, closed it, then damn if the corners didn't lift into the hint of a smile. "Maybe I should be afraid of you. Christ, woman, you're feisty when you're angry."

"Yes, maybe you *should* be afraid of me, Diaz, because I don't like being told how I should and shouldn't feel. And I don't need protecting. I haven't needed protecting since I was fifteen years old. In case you haven't noticed, I'm an adult now. A woman. And I have feelings, goddammit. Why don't you try noticing how I feel about you?"

"How do you feel about me, Jess?"

"I love you! Are you some kind of idiot that you can't figure that out on your own?"

Okay, so that had come out in a fit of anger. Probably not her best declaration of love, but she'd said it. It was out there. Ball was in his court now. What was he going to do with it?

He stared up at her with a shocked expression on his face.

She'd laugh if this entire situation wasn't so utterly pathetic. "You had no idea, did you?" *How could he not know?* Wasn't it ob-vious? Wasn't *she* obvious?

He wavered there on his feet for a few seconds, his hands jammed in his pockets. She started toward him.

"Don't," he said.

She stopped.

"Don't love me, Jess."

Her chest tightened. "It doesn't work that way, Diaz. You can't tell someone not to care about you."

"I can't give you what you need."

"Yes, you can."

He shook his head. "It won't work. I'm not the kind of guy you want."

"Why don't you let me be the judge of that?" Maybe he just needed a little push, a little convincing . . .

"I don't . . . I don't have the same feelings for you."

And just like that, the squeezing in her chest exploded. She'd heard the words he'd said but didn't want to believe them. And yet they echoed over and over in her thick skull, finally tearing through.

Tears welled in her eyes. She blinked them back, refusing to cry, refusing to fall apart like a child. She'd told him she was an adult, a woman, that she was tough.

Well, she was. She was going to stand there and take his rejection, even though she was shattering inside. Because there was nothing she could say in response to that.

He didn't love her. Spence had been wrong. She had been wrong.

Now she understood. Diaz had enjoyed the sex between them, but that had been it. Maybe he did care about her, but he didn't love her. Nothing was going to make him change his mind.

She inhaled and nodded. "Okay, then."

"I'm sorry, Jess."

She shook her head. "No, I'm sorry." Her voice cracked. She was going to lose it. "It's cold out here. I'm going to bed."

"Wait."

"No. I'm through waiting." She brushed past him and walked into the house, shutting the door, swiping at the tears running down her cheeks.

She barely made it to the bathroom, closing and locking the door before the waterworks started in a rush. She turned the faucet on full force so Diaz wouldn't be able to hear her sobs.

FOURTEEN

No sleep. Diaz hadn't gotten even a minute of it last night.

Between his own guilt and the crying Jessie had tried to hide from him, he couldn't even think about sleeping. He'd heard her through the walls, and it was like a knife tearing into his gut. He'd caused her pain, the one thing he swore he didn't want to do.

So he'd stayed outside, huddled up in the chair, the blanket his only warmth.

Why? Because he was an A number one asshole, and the biggest liar.

Jessie had bared her soul to him last night. What had it taken for her to share her feelings like she had? God, she was so brave. And what he had done when faced with the truth? He'd lied to her. He'd acted like an utter pussy, had turned tail and run like hell.

What he'd done to her was unforgivable. Because he did love

her. Everything inside him had screamed to tell her. The words hovered on his lips as soon as she'd said them to him. It would have been so easy.

And so wrong.

So he'd lied, told her he didn't love her back. And he'd destroyed her. He'd seen it on her crestfallen face, could almost feel her crushing pain. He felt it all night long.

He should never have touched her, should have stayed aloof and away from her from the start. That would have been the best way to handle the situation. She was young. He was older, more experienced. He could have let her down easily, told her that he wasn't interested, before things had ever gotten started between them. Instead, he'd touched her, loved her, gotten inside her physically as well as emotionally.

And he'd fallen in love with her. Hell, he'd already been in love with her before they'd ever made love. Touching her had only cemented what he already felt.

She knew it, and he knew it. He was the only one denying it.

But wasn't that better—to hurt her now rather than later on? Because he *would* hurt her, only later would be worse. Much worse. He knew it as sure as he knew his own name.

She'd feel some pain now, but she'd get over it—get over him. She'd move on, find another guy. A nice guy. And then she'd laugh again, be her old self again. She'd forget about him.

The thought of it made his insides twist. The thought of another man kissing her sweet mouth, laying his hands on her full breasts, sliding inside her warmth and taking what was—

No. She wasn't his. Not anymore. The sooner they both got used to the idea, the better.

Fog snaked along the river at the bottom of the hill, and the sun had begun its slow rise through the trees. He cursed the light, preferring the darkness that equaled his black mood. He rose, tossing the now damp blanket on the chair, and stepped inside the cabin, quietly heading toward the bathroom. Jessie was a huddle of blankets in the middle of the bed as he walked by. He paused for a fraction of a second, the urge to climb in there and pull her against him and feel her body next to his so damn strong it hurt. Instead, he grabbed clean clothes, shut the bathroom door, stripped, and turned on the shower, letting the hot water slide over him, hoping it would wash away the regret.

He didn't feel that much better after the shower, though at least he wasn't dragging as much. He might make it through the day. When he came out of the bathroom, Jessie was still huddled under the covers. It was barely past dawn, doubtful anyone would be up yet. He sat on the sofa in the one-room cabin and propped his feet on the worn coffee table, watching her sleep.

Rays of dawn spun a golden glow over the bed, highlighting her face. She squinted to block out the light, showcasing the smudges under her eyes. He wondered how much sleep she'd gotten last night. Probably not a whole lot. His fault. She deserved better. A guy who wouldn't make her unhappy. Didn't that prove he was making the right decision, or was he just rationalizing to make himself feel less like an asshole?

God, he was tired. He scrubbed his hand over his face, letting his eyes drift closed.

Diaz fought to open his eyes. They felt like they had sand in them. He lifted his head, palming the back of his neck. Blinking to clear away the haze, he sat up, realizing he'd fallen asleep on the sofa. Sunlight streamed into the cabin, making the wood floors shine. He turned to the bed. It was neatly made up, and when he looked around, there was no sign of Jessie.

He stood, went to the bathroom. The door was ajar, so he pushed it open. She wasn't in there. She'd left the cabin.

Hell. How long had he slept? He lifted his cell phone out of his pocket, then muttered a curse. Ten in the morning. He'd slept five hours. So much for doing fine without any sleep. He hadn't heard her get up and move around at all. She either walked around on cat feet or he'd been utterly dead to the world.

Probably a bit of both.

He put on his boots and walked up to the lodge to check on Spence. That's where he found Jessie, sitting next to Spence.

"I'll be back later," she said as soon as she spotted him.

She skirted past him without making eye contact.

"So what did you do to piss her off?" Spence asked.

Diaz shut the door. "I don't want to talk about it. How do you feel?"

"Like an axe went through my leg. Other than that, fine. Mark came in this morning to change the dressing. Said no sign of infection."

"That's good. Can you move at all?"

"Yeah. I can get up to go to the bathroom. Other than that, the doc says no movement for a day or so, which really sucks."

"Hey, it could have been worse. Your bike could have been totaled. Fortunately, the only thing that got hurt was your body."

Spence snorted. "True."

"I let Grange know what happened."

"Yeah? What did he say?"

"That you shouldn't go off by yourself anymore and that you're a dumbass, but he's glad you're not dead. Oh, and next time hang on to the bike."

Spence laughed. "Sounds like Grange. Make sure you follow

his advice and don't do what I did. Somebody didn't want me following that trail last night."

"I took care of that. We'll make sure next time we know exactly where they're going, and we can follow from a safe distance."

"What did you do?"

"I put GPS tracking devices on a few of those bikes that were out riding last night."

"Somewhere they won't notice?"

"They're microchips and well hidden. Trust me, they won't even see them. If they take off again without the entire gang, I'll be able to track them."

"Good deal. Wish I could go with you."

"If you're well enough when the time comes, you can. Until then . . ."

"You'll take Jessie." Spence gave him a stern look. "Don't do this alone."

Diaz nodded. "I'll take Jessie. But I still don't think she's ready for all this."

Jessie slipped in and closed the door behind her, shooting Diaz a scathing look. "How typical. You deciding what I can or can't handle. Are you sure you're not my father?"

Spence smothered a laugh. Diaz wasn't at all amused. "I think you of all people would know for a fact I'm not a blood relative, Jess."

"Touché, Diaz," Spence said.

Jessie sat next to Spencer's bed and shot him a glare. "What are you, the scorekeeper?"

Spence shrugged. "If the two of you keep going at it like scrapping yard dogs, somebody has to score the rounds."

"There's no scorekeeping required. We're finished," Jessie said, leaning back in the chair and crossing her arms.

"Awww, a lover's spat?" Spence asked, his gaze flitting between both of them.

"Don't fuck with me right now, Spence. I can and will hurt you," Jessie said.

Spence looked at Diaz, who shook his head.

"I put GPS tracking devices on Rex's bike and a few of the others who went out last night," Diaz explained to Jessie. "That way, if they go out again, we can follow at a discreet distance, hopefully not noticeable, and see where they're going. It'll be safer that way."

Jessie gave a curt nod. "Just let me know when we need to ride and I'll be armed and ready to go."

"Will do."

"What about Rex?" Spence asked. "We know anything about him?"

"I noted the tag number off his bike. Gave it to Grange to run a check on his registration, so we should hear something back today."

"Okay. Good."

"I need to go and . . . do a few things," Jess said, rising again. She turned to Spence. "You need anything?"

"Shot of whiskey and a hot woman."

Jessie laughed. "Can't help you with either, but I'll be back with lunch in a little while. In the meantime, try and get some rest."

"Yeah, yeah. That's all I've been doing. I'm already tired of resting."

"It's good for you."

She left without looking at Diaz.

"You hurt her," Spence said, casting accusing eyes at him.

"Yeah. But trust me, it's better this way. She'll get over it."

Spence shook his head. "You are one dumb son of a bitch, Diaz."

Diaz narrowed his gaze at Spence. "Don't get in the middle of this."

"It's obvious what's going on. She cares about you. You care about her. You're being noble, saving her from big, bad you."

Spence sounded a lot like Jessie. "You don't know anything."

"I know more than you think."

"Yeah? And what would you do if it was you and not me?"

"It isn't me, so it's not the same thing. You and I aren't the same, and you know that."

Diaz shrugged.

"Jessie's in love with you, man. And you're blowing it."

"I don't want to have this conversation with you, Spence." He didn't want to have it with anyone. "Stay out of it."

He started to walk to the door.

"I never figured you for a coward, Diaz."

That was the same thing Jessie said to him last night.

"I'm getting damn tired of hearing that."

"Maybe you should start listening."

Diaz clenched his fists, paused for a second, then opened the door and walked out.

His temper soared, his entire body heating with rage as he stepped out of the lodge into the crisp morning air. Even the cold outside didn't cool him down.

He needed a ride. Alone. He hopped on his bike, turned the engine over and let the vibration race through his bones. He closed his eyes for a few seconds, feeling the bike, losing himself in the sensation, before peeling away, spitting gravel in his wake. He rode away from the lodge, down the road until he hit blacktop, then really cranked it, letting the cold air seep into his pores, clear his head.

He didn't even know where he was going, just needed the solitude of the ride and the bike humming underneath him.

Spence was right. He was a coward. It still didn't change anything. What he was doing wasn't admirable. But it was the only
thing he could do. He knew what he was, his background, his
own temper. He might have control over it now. So had his father,
at one time.

Diaz was a ticking time bomb. And he was never going to ex-
plode on Jessie. Not on someone he loved.

Not ever.

So they could all go on thinking he was an asshole. That was
fine.

Jess would be safe.

He rode out of town, found a bar catering to bikers that sat on
a hill overlooking the river. He spent the day there, alone, content
with a seat by the window, loud music to drown out the noise of
his own thoughts, and a couple of beers to quench his occasional
thirst. When he got tired of beer he switched to bottled water, figuring by the time the sun sank he'd need a clear head. He kept an
eye on the time, wanting to get back to the lodge by dark, just in
case Rex, or Crush, decided to take a little night ride. It was late
afternoon when he hopped back on his bike to make the trek back
to the lodge. When he got there, they were serving dinner and everyone was piled into the dining room. Jessie was seated next to
Spence, who had managed to make it out of bed and sat at a corner
spot, his bandaged leg propped up on a chair. Stephanie fussed
over him on one side, Jessie on the other.

Lucky guy.

Diaz walked in and Spence waved him over.

"Hey, where've you been?"

Diaz took the empty seat across from Spence. Jess, as usual,
avoided eye contact.

"I took a long ride."

"Nice day for it. Sun's out."

"Yeah. Found a bar a couple of towns over. Just hung out and listened to music, watched the scenery."

"Good."

"Anything going on around here today?"

Spence shook his head. "Not a damn thing. Few of the guys went fishing down at the creek. Crush took a bunch of guys for a long ride, too. Some went ATVing."

Diaz nodded, then went to the buffet for food. The rest of the meal was mostly spent in silence, with him and Spence occasionally talking. Jessie spoke to Spence, not to him. Stephanie noticed, too, because she continually inched her chair closer to Spence's, no doubt thinking Jess was trying to muscle in on her guy. If Stephanie got any closer to Spencer, she'd be in his lap. In fact, she kept bumping Spence's leg, causing him to wince.

Jessie wasn't doing anything to clarify the situation to Stephanie, either. Then again, Jessie had made it clear she didn't think much of Stephanie.

His cell phone buzzed, interrupting the show. Diaz stood, saw the number as one of Grange's, so he stepped outside the lodge to take the call.

"Yeah."

"That tag number you gave me for Rex came back," Grange said.

"And?"

"Comes back as registered to Landon Mitchell."

"Who the hell is Landon Mitchell? He's not one of the guys in Crush's gang."

"No clue on this end. Name has no priors, so it doesn't show up in any of the crime databases."

"So the registration is stolen or fake?"

"That's what I'm thinking," Grange said.

"Okay. So we'll have to find another way to ID Rex. I'll see what I can do."

"Keep me posted."

Diaz hung up and pondered the situation. He'd have to talk to Jessie and Spence, figure out a strategy. He headed back inside, finished dinner, and waited for the crowd to thin out. Once it had, he told Spence he needed to talk to him. Alone.

Stephanie pouted, told Spence she'd wait for him. There was a dance in the lodge hall tonight. Right, like Spence was going to dance? Diaz rolled his eyes as he helped Spence into his room. He gave Jessie a look that he hoped made her understand he wanted to see her, too. She just had to get away from Stephanie's curious gaze.

Once he got Spence back into his room, they waited for Jessie to make an appearance. She did, shutting the door behind her.

"It was all I could do to get away from nosy Stephanie. She thinks I'm after you, Spence." She giggled and sat on the love seat.

"Good. Maybe she'll leave me the hell alone, then. The woman is starting to annoy me."

Jessie snorted.

"Okay, here's the deal," Diaz said, trying to bring the focus on the mission. "Grange ran Rex's bike registration and it came up bogus. That means we need to ID him another way. So I'm open to suggestions."

"That's easy," Jessie said with a shrug. "Pickpocket his wallet, check for his driver's license or any other identification he has on him."

"Easier said than done, cupcake," Spence said.

She propped her feet on the coffee table. "I don't know about that. I used to do it all the time. Bet I could get in his pants."

Spence choked on a laugh. Diaz frowned and said, "Not a good idea."

Jessie met his glare. "Why not?"

"Too dangerous."

She rolled her eyes. "Please. I can lift a wallet in my sleep. We're thieves, remember? I haven't forgotten something as elemental as that."

"And how are you going to manage it?"

"Easy," she said. "All I have to do is get his attention—get close to him."

"There is a dance tonight," Spence said. "Dark room, lots of bodies pressed in together."

"There you go," Jessie said, turning her gaze to Diaz. "It's perfect. A couple of dances, me rubbing up against him, I'll have him so distracted he won't know what's up."

"His dick will be what's up, darlin'," Spence said with a laugh.

Jessie laughed, too.

Diaz, however, didn't.

"Well?" she asked.

He couldn't tell her not to do it. There was no valid reason, other than he was already jealous as hell. Which had nothing to do with the mission, and everything to do with how he felt about Jessie.

If he told Jessie the real reason he didn't want her to do it, it would blow everything. He'd just told her he didn't care about her. Acting like a jealous lover wouldn't convince her of that, would it? And it wasn't like he could be the one sliding his hand in Rex's pocket. It had to be Jessie.

Fuck.

"Yeah, go ahead. If you get into trouble, give me some kind of signal."

"I won't have any trouble. It'll be like taking candy from a baby."

That's what he was afraid of.

BY THE TIME THE BAND HAD SET UP IN THE HALL, THERE WAS a thick crowd of people who had already made good use of the bar. Alcohol was flowing, it was noisy, and Diaz and Jessie had a tough time finding a table. Fortunately, Spence insisted on coming with them, so people cleared a spot for him to sit—a good table in front of the dance floor, with extra chairs so he could prop up his leg. You had to love bikers—they always took care of their own.

Diaz and Jessie pulled up chairs at the same table. Stephanie wriggled her way through the crowd, disappointed to find Diaz on one side of Spence and Jessie on the other. Her heavily painted lips formed a pout.

Tough shit. If they were lucky, maybe she'd get pissed and go away.

The band started up, kicking into a rousing rock and roll oldies set. Nearly everyone got out on the dance floor. Stephanie looked over at Spence and cast a hopeful look.

"Not on your life, honey," he said. "I'm sitting the night out. This is my dance partner tonight." He lifted his bottle of beer and grinned.

Stephanie threw herself back in the chair and let out a long, loud sigh.

Jessie snickered, then whispered something in Spence's ear, causing him to throw his head back and bellow out a laugh.

She was deliberately trying to irritate Stephanie. From the livid expression on Stephanie's face, it was working.

By the time the band had played three or four songs, they had spotted Rex, leaning against the bar talking with a couple of guys. Jessie kept her focus on him, making occasional eye contact.

Rex had been noticing, too. Hell, who wouldn't? Jessie wore tight jeans and a bright red midriff-baring top that hugged her breasts.

"I need a refill," she said. "Be right back."

She stood, moving with deliberate catlike grace over to the bar. Diaz's pants tightened, his dick clamoring to life as he remembered what it felt like to run his hands over such a beautiful woman.

She pushed her way in between Rex and his friends, turning her attention on the bald-headed, muscled Rex. He smiled down at her, and they engaged in conversation.

Maybe she'd lift the wallet and be done with it. Fast and easy.

But no, apparently it wasn't going to work that way, because she set her beer on the bar, took the hand that Rex held out, and the two of them headed for the dance floor.

Diaz leaned forward, trying to make them out, but they'd been swallowed by the thick crowd.

Shit.

He stood, moving to the front of the floor, trying to act as nonchalant as possible. He was, after all, just stretching his legs, taking a little walk.

"Wanna dance, honey?"

He looked down to find Stephanie there.

"No, thanks."

"Are you sure?" She leaned up against him. Or, he should say, she squished her breasts against his arm, making sure to rub her hard nipples against his biceps.

"Shouldn't you be sitting with Spence?"

"No. I want to dance. Spence is out of commission. And you look like you're eager to get out there."

"Your devotion to Spence is admirable," he said, not even attempting to keep the sarcasm out of his voice.

Stephanie didn't seem to take offense, continuing to undulate against him. "Similar to Jessie's devotion to you, I presume? She looks pretty hot and heavy with Rex out there on the dance floor right now."

He finally spotted them. Rex had hold of Jessie's hips, the two of them swaying in time to a mellow pop song. It sure as hell looked like they were crotch to crotch. Jessie held on to Rex's shoulders, looking like she was going to wrap her legs around him any second. Despite the jacking of his pulse, he shrugged and said, "Jessie's a free spirit. She can do whatever she wants."

"As am I. Spence and I don't have a commitment. I can do whatever, or *whoever*, I want." In a bold move, she cupped his crotch, rubbing her hand over his dick.

It was at that moment that Jessie made eye contact, noticed where Stephanie's hand was, and frowned. She swiveled and rubbed her ass against Rex's crotch. Was that a dig at Diaz, or so she could keep an eye on Stephanie? Diaz wasn't sure, but he was damned distracted.

And goddammit, he was getting very turned on. Not by Stephanie—she didn't do a thing for him. Jessie, on the other hand . . . anything and everything she did made his dick hard, even if she was doing it with or to another guy.

He grabbed Stephanie's hand and jerked her along with him. "Let's dance."

"Finally," she said.

He dragged Stephanie onto the dance floor, pushing his way

past the throng of dancers until they were only a few couples from Jessie and Rex. Jess didn't even try to ignore him, though she did give her attention to Rex. She turned, wrapping her body around Rex as they moved in rhythm to the music.

Diaz pulled Stephanie into his arms, pretty much ignoring whatever it was she did. She clung to him, rubbing her breasts over his chest, then down his stomach as she slithered over his body.

He didn't care. He watched Jess, felt Jess, every movement she made. It was her hands on his body—touching him, burning him, making his dick harden with every seductive sway of her hips. Jess turned away from Rex and he grabbed hold of her hips, guiding her back and forth across his cock, the same way Diaz wanted to do.

His breathing quickened, his heart jackhammering against his chest as he concentrated on Jess, on the music, the primal beat she swayed to. He was mesmerized as she twined her arms seductively upward like a rising flame. It made her shirt rise, baring more of her belly.

Rex palmed her stomach, his fingers inching under her shirt.

She smiled at Diaz, tormenting him with what he couldn't have, twined her arms around Rex's huge, muscled one, held him firmly in place as she rocked against him.

This was the worst torture he could endure, forced to watch another man with his hands on Jessie, knowing he had no right to object as she touched Rex intimately—his shoulders, his arms, his stomach, his hips, his ass, sliding over him like a snake slithering around his body. Rex held still, his eyes closed, his cock hard and straining against his pants, evidence of how Jessie turned him on.

Rex wanted to fuck Jessie. Would she say no, or, now that Diaz had pushed her away, would she take him on?

Stephanie moved against him, seemingly lost in her own dance of seduction. He was only dimly aware of his hands roaming over

Stephanie's body, the two of them moving in tempo to the slow beat of the song, but his full focus was on Jessie. There was only Jessie on his mind—his gaze was locked on hers. No other woman existed for him.

The heat inside him grew, a bonfire raging out of control as the music built in intensity, pounding against his body. Stephanie cupped him, purring against him as she stroked his cock with the palm of her hand. Jessie continued to dance around Rex, stroking his ass, dipping down to worship at his thighs, then slowly make her way up to wrap her arms around his waist, locking the two of them together to sway to the music. Her breasts were pressed against his back until Rex turned around, grabbed her by the buttocks to lift her. She wrapped her legs around him and laughed, tilting her head back as Rex danced her around in circles.

God, he wanted that, wanted her carefree laughter, wanted to dance with her in his arms.

The music died down, and Rex put Jessie down. He bent toward her ear, whispered to her. She smiled, held his hands, looked into his eyes, said something to him, and winked. Rex laughed, and Jessie walked away, out of the hall and out of the door.

Alone.

"Damn, that was hot."

Diaz knew Stephanie's comment hadn't been about Jessie. He looked down at the redhead, smiled at her. "Too hot for me. Thanks for the dance."

He turned and walked away, leaving Stephanie standing on the dance floor.

He caught up with Jessie halfway down the road leading to their cabin. They didn't speak until they stepped inside the door. She closed it, locked it, withdrew a wallet from the back of her jeans, and handed it to him.

Rex's, no doubt. She must have slipped it from him during their dance.

Diaz slipped the ID out and looked it over. "No Landon Mitchell. It says Rex James."

"So the registration on his bike *is* phony."

"Yeah."

"I need to get this wallet to him before he notices it's missing. I'll be right back."

She left and was gone about ten minutes, slipping in through the back door.

"Get it done?" he asked.

"Yeah. I left it on the floor near the bar. He'll think he dropped it there when he was paying for beers."

She was a good thief.

Hell, what man wouldn't have been distracted with a woman like Jessie sliding her hands and body all over him?

Even the walk in the cool night air hadn't eliminated the heated flush from her skin. Her cheeks were still pink, perspiration still dotted her chest.

"Enjoy the dance?" he asked.

"Yes. You?"

"No."

She arched a brow. "Too bad. Looked like Stephanie was having fun."

"I wasn't paying attention to Stephanie."

"Your cock thought otherwise."

"My cock was watching you."

She paused, her breasts rising with each deep breath, misery written all over her face. "This sucks, Diaz."

"Yeah, I know."

"I'm pent up, anxious, hot, and turned on. I need you."

Her honesty had always been the part of her that he admired the most, the part that made her so unlike any other woman he'd ever known. "Jess."

She took a step toward him, flipping open the button of her jeans. "This is about scratching an itch we both need to scratch. I'm clear on you not wanting to have a relationship with me. You want it that way, I'm fine with it. Let's make this about sex. Just sex. You do want to have sex with me, don't you?"

"Yes."

She lifted her top over her head, flung it onto the nearby chair. Her nipples were hard, whether from the cold or her state of arousal, he didn't know—didn't care. All he knew was that she took his breath away, coming toward him half undressed, her skin flushed with desire and need, the same need that made his cock rise up and press insistently against his jeans. The same desire that made his balls twist in a knot.

Why the hell should he hesitate? Jessie knew the score now, and she was offering sex without strings. He should jump on the chance to relieve them both.

"Are you sure this is what you want?"

She stopped with only inches separating them, her gaze showing no hesitation. "Quit asking me. I know what I want—you and me in that bed together. I need to come, Diaz. You got me all hot and bothered out there on the dance floor."

She reached for his belt buckle, opened it, then went for his zipper. When her fingers brushed his erection, he sucked in a breath. He was ready to go off, had been ever since her seductive dance at the lodge hall. She drew the zipper down, slid her hand inside. He hissed at the feel of her cool fingers encircling his cock, squeezing him.

"Made you hot, did I?" she asked, leaning into him, the tips of her breasts brushing his shirt.

"You know you did."

"Good. Because it made me wet to dance for you, to tease Rex like that."

"His dick was hard."

"I know. He rubbed it against me."

"He wanted to fuck you."

She stroked him, pushed at his jeans until they pooled to his ankles. "Yes. He told me he did."

"So why didn't you?"

She shrugged, captured his cock with both hands, rolled it between them until he was heavy, aching and needy. "I decide who I fuck. I already know what you can give me."

He started to undress her, wanted her naked, but she grabbed his wrists. "Oh, no. Not yet."

Instead, she sank to the floor, using her fingernails to scrape at his thighs as she did. Her mouth at the level of his cock, she took him between her lips, licking the wide crest, flicking her tongue over the liquid that pooled there before swallowing his cockhead and engulfing his shaft.

"Ahh, God, Jessie," he said, resting his hand on the top of her head as she sucked him with greedy abandon. Her mouth was wet, hot, her tongue swirling over his shaft, her hands moving over his balls, his cock, squeezing and stroking every time she pulled her mouth away. Seeing his cock disappear between her sweet lips was a mix of heaven and hell, delight and torture. His balls tightened, filled with the come he wanted to spill down her throat. But he so wanted to come in her hot, tight pussy instead.

"Come on, baby, quit teasing me," he managed through dragging breaths. "Let me fuck you."

She pulled his shaft from between her lips, stood, and backed away from him, drawing the zipper down on her jeans at the same time as she toed her boots off. He kicked off his jeans and boots, drawing his shirt over his head and following Jess to the bed. She drew the quilt back and climbed onto the mattress, lying back with her legs dangling over the side.

Diaz applied the condom, then lifted her legs over his hips, drawing her butt off the mattress.

"You have such a pretty pussy, baby."

She snaked her hand down over her belly, capturing her clit between her fingers. "Fuck me. Make me come. I need it."

Her harsh words ratcheted up his arousal. He drove inside her, his balls quivering as she gripped him in a tight vise, taking him on a wild, fast ride. Jessie continued to massage her clit as he fucked her, her face tight with strain as she worked herself.

He enjoyed watching her touch herself, loved this position where he could see the two of them joined, could watch his cock disappear between her plump, moisture-drenched pussy lips. She was close to coming, her back arched, her fingers moving faster.

But something was different. Her head was tilted back and her eyes were closed. He realized then what was different. She was completely disconnected from him, unlike the way they'd made love before. Other than his cock inside her, she wasn't touching him.

"Yes. Fuck me harder," she said, lifting against him, strumming her clit in a frenzy. "I'm close."

Her eyes were squeezed shut, one hand clenched in the sheets. He drove into her, feeling her walls close in around him, gripping him. Her lips parted and she let loose a low moan, shuddering as she came. He watched her—so beautiful when she let go like that—and then allowed himself to orgasm.

She panted, opened her eyes, offered up a satisfied smile that had zero warmth, then pushed back, separating them. She slid off the bed and went into the bathroom briefly, came back and grabbed her clothes to get dressed.

Diaz cleaned up and dressed, feeling utterly empty inside. He sat on the couch and slipped on his boots, refusing to look at Jess.

He stood, grabbed his jacket, and headed for the door, feeling the need to say . . . something.

"Jess, I—"

Her head jerked up. "Don't. Just don't."

He stared at her, the blank expression on her face, the utter lack of any spark.

And for a split second he wanted the old Jessie back. The one who spit anger at him, who laughed, who cried, the one he could pull into his arms and wring emotion out of every time he touched her.

But he had no rights to that Jessie. This was the game they played now, by the rules he'd set.

And he hated it.

FIFTEEN

Jessie watched Diaz walk out. As soon as he closed the door, she collapsed onto the bed, her eyes filling with tears. She swiped at one rolling down her cheek, angry at herself for feeling like this—for feeling anything at all. She'd thought she could handle it, had been so aroused that she'd let the physical sensations take over, figuring it would be enough to sustain her. She'd pushed back all her emotions, refusing to let herself feel them.

Holding back had been so hard, had wrecked her. She couldn't do it again. Maybe Diaz was capable of sex without feeling, but she wasn't. She put her heart into it as well as her body.

That had been the last time. And it had been unpleasant. Well, not entirely unpleasant. The sex had rocked her, of course. She'd come, but it had been distant, not at all like what they'd shared previously. Before, they had connected in more than just physical ways. A few moments ago it had been nothing more than two people fucking—getting off and going their separate ways.

She loved Diaz. She couldn't just fuck him. Maybe when she had more experience, she'd be better at using men for physical release. Until then she'd go back to her hand and her vibrator. It was less painful to her heart.

The door opened and Diaz walked back in. She blinked, hoping her face wasn't streaked with tears.

"Spence said Rex and a couple of other guys took off about a half hour ago."

Work was exactly what she needed to clear her head of emotion. She jumped off the bed and grabbed her boots, sliding into them and grabbing her jacket. "Why didn't he call?"

His lips lifted. "Said he did. My cell was on vibrate. In my jeans, which were on the floor."

"Oh."

"You ready to ride?"

She shrugged into her jacket. "Yeah. Is the GPS picking them up?"

He nodded, held up the tiny GPS tracking unit. "I've got a read on their location. It clips to my wrist so it'll be easy to keep track while we're riding, and I can keep it hidden under my jacket."

"Let's go, then."

They climbed on their bikes and revved them up. They hadn't taken off yet when Crush rode up next to them.

"Going somewhere?" he asked.

Uh oh.

"Yeah," Diaz said. "We're going for a ride."

"How 'bout some company?"

Diaz shook his head. "My lady and I need some private time."

Good thing Diaz could think on the fly.

"Not tonight you don't. I'm coming with you," Crush said.

"Excuse me? I just said we want to be alone."

"And I told you that's not gonna happen. Not after what went down with Spence last night."

"I think I can take care of myself, and my woman, without a babysitter."

Crush narrowed his gaze. "The two of you plus Spence are new to my gang. I feel responsible for what happened to Spence—it's never happened before. We ride hard, we play hard, we brawl . . . but I don't want trouble like that."

Diaz cocked a brow. "Are you saying what happened was Spence's fault?"

Jessie chewed her bottom lip. This wasn't going well. And with every second that ticked by, Rex and the others were riding farther away.

"It wasn't Spence's fault, Crush," she said, feeling like she needed to get involved. Maybe he'd listen to her. "Surely you aren't blaming him for being shot?"

"I don't know what to think. Rex said he and the others weren't anywhere near where Spence was last night. No one in my gang had been shot before you all joined."

"My friend was on the receiving end of that bullet," she argued back, thinking this was ridiculous. What kind of point was he trying to make?

"I just need to keep an eye on all of you, so if you want to ride tonight, I'm going with you."

Diaz hated that they'd lost this argument, but he didn't see any way around it. Crush was the leader of the Skulls, and as members they were obliged to do as he said. If he wanted to ride with them, Diaz was going to have to let him.

Maybe this was an opportunity to test Crush under fire, see if he knew anything, gauge his reactions. They could still follow Rex, and if they came up against anything suspicious, it would be a chance to see what Crush knew about it.

He shrugged. "You're the boss. Let's ride."

Diaz had the GPS and he intended to follow Rex's trail. If Crush tried to stop them or veer them away, he'd know why.

After they left the lodge property, they rode west down the main road, which was the same way Rex and his group had taken off in. He'd let Crush lead for a while, as long as they were heading in the right direction. Diaz kept close watch on the GPS unit, pinpointing Rex's location. They were still riding west.

When Crush turned north, Diaz and Jessie didn't follow. Crush turned around and pulled beside them. They stopped.

"I thought I'd show you this road that curved along the river," he said. "It's a nice night ride."

Diaz shook his head. "This is my ride tonight. If you want to come along, that's fine, but we're going my way."

Crush's narrowed gaze showed suspicion. Diaz didn't care. This whole mission was coming to a head and soon, so if Crush was going to show his hand, it might as well be now.

"You have somewhere specific in mind?" he asked.

"Maybe. Maybe not." He was hoping Crush would pick up on his resentment and think it was because Crush insinuated himself into this ride, and nothing more.

Crush studied him for a few seconds, then gave a curt nod. "Lead the way, then."

After about thirty minutes or so, Rex and his group had stopped. Soon they'd catch up and Diaz was going to have to figure out what to do with Crush, because Diaz and Jessie were going to have to find a place to park the bikes and determine what Rex and the others were up to.

Diaz turned off the main road and headed south, into a well-forested area, following the tracking device. He pulled off about a half mile back from where Rex was located.

"Why are we stopping here?" Crush asked, parking his bike.

Diaz held up his hand. "I saw something. Stay quiet and follow me."

Fortunately, Crush didn't argue, and Diaz wasn't about to explain that he picked up Rex on the GPS. Sometimes you just had to let things unfold, and this was Crush's test. Besides, Diaz and Jessie were armed and he wasn't about to let Crush get behind him in case Crush knew what was going down. He could handle Crush if necessary.

They crept toward Rex's group, Diaz monitoring the GPS. Crush wasn't even aware he had it on. Now that he had a clear path in mind and knew where Rex and the others were, he didn't need to use it, just followed due north, keeping as silent as possible, setting up behind some felled trees until he had clear sight of the group.

They had lanterns set up in what looked like a clearing on an old abandoned campsite.

"Hey, that's—"

Diaz held up his hand to silence Crush. If Crush was going to try and give away their location, Diaz intended to coldcock him with the butt of his gun. But Crush stayed silent and watched.

Within a few minutes there was a roar of engines, the sound heading their way. Diaz instructed them to get down as they waited to see who was approaching. More bikers maybe?

It wasn't bikes. ATVs, six of them, pulling into the camping spot. They turned off their engines and climbed off, approaching Rex and the others. Diaz pulled out his hearing device, as did Jessie.

Crush cast him a questioning frown. Diaz shook his head,

looked at Crush then back at Jessie, who nodded. Crush hadn't given them away, hadn't pulled a weapon, hadn't done anything to indicate he knew what the hell was going on here. Taking a chance, Diaz dug into his pocket and pulled out another ear device, motioning for Crush to stay silent as he handed it over.

Now they could all hear what was being said.

Diaz heard an unrecognizable voice first.

"Are you sure you weren't followed?"

"We're hardly amateurs, George," Rex said in reply. "We're alone, so quit worrying."

"Heard you had some trouble last night. Had to shoot someone."

Crush shot a glance to Diaz. Diaz held his hand up, a signal for Crush to remain quiet. Crush was either acting innocent, or he really didn't know about any of this. How could he not know? Diaz still wasn't convinced.

"Who told you that?"

"You think we don't watch you? We don't want no trouble. We do this deal straight up and without no law involved."

Rex paused. "There is no law involved. I told you, we've got it covered. It was just one of the new guys in the wrong place at the wrong time. He got too close so we scared him away. Now do you want the guns or don't you?"

Bingo.

"You got 'em with you?"

"You know we do. But I'm anxious to get rid of them. Have you got the money?"

"Yeah. We got the money. You just bring the merchandise like we set up and we'll make the swap."

No one else was talking but Rex and this George guy, so the two of them must be in charge of the deal. Diaz slanted a glance at

Crush. He held one hand over the ear holding the communication device. Otherwise, he hadn't moved. He looked shocked as hell.

Diaz still wasn't convinced.

"Tomorrow night. You bring the rifles and ammo. We'll be there."

"So will we. You bring the money."

"I got your money. Don't you worry. You just keep the law or anyone else from tailin' ya. You bring trouble with ya, boy, and you're all gonna be dead."

Diaz listened as they discussed the designated meeting place. They'd have to alert Grange so they could get the Feds assembled and in here for the takedown.

The ATVs took off and headed out. Diaz and the others stayed low. Diaz instructed Crush to stay down until Rex and his group took off on their bikes. When the roar of their exhaust faded away, they stood.

"What the fuck is going on?"

Diaz figured Crush would be the first to talk. He just wasn't sure he was ready to provide any answers.

Jessie had stayed quiet the whole time, too. "Is that what you expected to find?" she asked.

He gave her a short nod.

"Is someone going to tell me what the hell's happening here? Do you two know what's going on?"

"Yes."

Diaz turned a sharp gaze on Jess.

"Tell him. He doesn't know."

"He doesn't need to."

"Tell me what?"

"Diaz. It's obvious he's not part of this."

"We don't know that." The longer they stood in front of Crush talking about it, the more he was going to learn. It could be a setup. Crush could be acting, learning what he could about Diaz and Jessie. This whole thing could blow up in their faces.

"What the hell do you two know about what we just saw? What arms were Rex talking about? Who were those guys?"

Jessie held up her hand. "Crush, please. Just give us a minute to talk about this." She turned to Diaz. "Tell him. He can help us."

"We don't need help. And he can't be trusted."

"I think he can. Come on, Diaz, he doesn't know anything."

"Goddammit! Somebody better start talking or I'm going to go beat the shit out of Rex until *he* tells me."

Jessie turned to Crush. "We believe Rex and the others are working a deal to sell illegal arms to a group of survivalists."

Shit. There went their cover, and possibly this entire mission.

Crush went still, his eyes wide. "Say that again."

Jessie repeated what she'd told him. His gaze narrowed. "How do you know this?"

"We work for the United States government and we infiltrated your gang to find out who's selling arms to a known survivalist group here in the hills."

"Jesus, Jessie. Why don't you give him our Social Security numbers while you're at it." Diaz dragged his fingers through his hair and began to pace. He couldn't believe she'd told him. Grange was going to have his ass. What the fuck was Jessie thinking?

"Are you serious?" Crush ping-ponged his gaze between both of them. "You're government agents? Like ATF or something?"

"That's not important," Jessie said. "What do you know about this impending arms deal?"

"Nothing. Fuck." Now Crush joined Diaz in his pacing. "How the hell could Rex do this to me? We've been friends since high school."

"And you knew nothing about his activities?"

"No." Crush fisted the fingers of both hands. "I'm in the dark here. I need some answers. I thought these men were my friends—men I could trust."

Crush sat on one of the fallen logs, dropping his face in his hands. "What Steph said makes sense now."

"What did Stephanie say?" Jessie asked.

He lifted his head. "Six months ago after they broke up, she complained that Rex had gone off the deep end. She said he was going overboard with talks of moving to the hills, roughing it, living on their own where they could be free and protected. Steph said he'd changed and she wanted no part of it. I blew her off, figured Rex was maybe talking about building a log cabin some-place rural. I didn't think he was joining survivalists. I never made the connection."

"No reason for you to," Jessie said.

Crush lifted misery-laden eyes to Jess. "I should have listened to her. I should have asked Rex what was up, but I didn't want to get involved. Shit. No one plays me like this—no one uses my gang to front illegal arms deals or anything else."

Crush stood and started to walk away, but Diaz stepped in front of him. "Where do you think you're going?"

"Back to the lodge to mete out some goddamn justice. The Skulls will take care of Rex and the others."

Exactly what Diaz hadn't wanted to happen. He shot Jessie a glare. She glared right back.

"No. You're not going to do that."

"Don't tell me what I can and can't do with my people, Diaz."

Jessie moved to Crush's side, laid her hand on his shoulder to get his attention. "Crush, if you go to Rex right now and bring this out in the open, you'll blow everything we've worked so hard on.

I understand you want payback for Rex's betrayal, but our job is to grab those firearms before the survivalists can get to them. The last thing we want is for those guns to fall into the wrong hands."

Crush didn't say anything, just stared mutely through the trees.

"Please, think about this," she continued. "Work with us. Help us take down Rex and the survivalists. There's your justice."

Crush craned his head to the side. "You'd let me help."

Jessie looked at Diaz, who shook his head.

"Maybe. It depends. We'll have to talk about it, see where you'd fit in."

Diaz rolled his eyes. Clearly, he'd lost control of Jess, and this mission. He'd have something to say to her about this later. No way in hell was he involving Crush in this.

"I can't believe I didn't peg you all for Feds. Spence, too?"

Jessie nodded.

"Goddamn. You don't look like Feds."

Jessie grinned. "That's the idea, Crush."

"I want them out of my gang. I want them to pay for their betrayal, and I want it done publicly so the other Skulls can see what happens to traitors."

Jessie looked to Diaz.

"We'll take care of it," he said. Apparently he had no choice. His plans for this mission had been irrevocably altered. Staying under the radar was now out of the question.

But maybe, just maybe, Crush could be of some use. He led this gang. He had connections and ins they didn't have. He wouldn't burn his bridges with Crush just yet.

"One caveat," Diaz said. "You're the only one who knows who we are and we want to keep it that way. As far as the rest of the Skulls know, we're still the new guys. You spread the word about us and we pull you out of the picture. And by out of the picture,

I mean you won't even be in Arkansas. There'll be a convenient reason given for your absence. Verifiable, well documented, foolproof. And don't think we can't do it. One phone call and you disappear. Understood?"

Crush gave a short nod. "Got it. I'm less interested in who the three of you are than who my so-called friends turned out to be."

"Then we're clear," Diaz said.

"One more thing," Crush said, turning to Diaz. "I make a much better ally than enemy. I really can help you with this. Maybe you should listen to Jessie. I *can* be trusted."

"Jessie trusts you. I don't—not completely. You'll have to prove it. In the meantime, we need to head back. I want to fill Spence in on what happened, then I need to make some calls and we need to plan."

"You'll bring me in on everything," Crush said as they walked back to the bikes.

"Everything we're able to," Diaz said. "Some things you can't be privy to, and there's nothing I can do about that. But as far as the plans for how we take down Rex and get hold of those arms and see how many of those survivalists we can bring to justice, then yeah, we'll pull you in."

"Good enough."

Back at the main lodge, Crush came with them to talk to Spence. Initially, Spence looked surprised to see Crush with them, but after they told him what happened, he rolled with it.

"At least no one else got shot tonight," Spence said, moving around the room with a lot more ease than he had the day before.

"Hey man, I'm sorry about that," Crush said. "I had no idea."

Spence shrugged. "If you didn't know any of your people were involved in this, then it isn't your fault. You didn't fire the gun."

"Speaking of, how do you feel?" Jessie asked.

"Good. A little stiff, but I can walk, sit, stand, and I can damn sure ride by tomorrow. Even the doc said I could."

Diaz nodded. "Good. We need you. We'll figure out a plan in the morning. In the meantime, I need you to rest up—don't do anything stupid."

Spence pointed a finger at his own chest. "Me? Do something stupid? Please."

They left Crush and Spence at the lodge and returned to their cabin at the bottom of the hill. Once inside, Diaz locked the door behind him and turned to Jessie.

"Okay, tell me the plan," he said, dropping onto the couch and planting his feet on the coffee table.

She shrugged out of her jacket, heading toward him with a frown. "My plan?"

"Yeah. Since you seem to have taken over this mission as leader, I'd like to know what the next step is."

She took the seat next to his. "Diaz. Sometimes you have to go with gut instinct. Crush wasn't involved. It was obvious."

"And you shouldn't rely on blind faith without proof. People have died doing that."

"My instincts have never let me down."

His job was to train her. What better time than now? "Instincts aren't the same as evidence, as waiting until someone is proven innocent. You risked not only yourself tonight, Jess, but all the Wild Riders by revealing who we were."

She lifted her chin. "I didn't tell him who we were, only that we worked for the government."

"You told him too much. You shouldn't have said anything at all. You aren't in charge of this mission. You are, at best, what I would consider a junior on this assignment—an apprentice. This is your first case, a chance to learn from me and from Spence.

We've done more than a few of these and I'd like to think we know what the hell we're doing, even though we don't approach things the same way you might. I don't want to have to remind you again that you aren't the lead.

"You fucked up, Jessie. If we're really lucky, Crush isn't part of all this. If we're unlucky, then right now he's blowing the entire arms deal and we've lost. And if we lose, then the blame will rest entirely on your shoulders."

She opened her mouth to speak, then clamped her lips shut, turned away to stare down at her boots.

It was obvious she didn't like what he had to say. He hadn't liked saying it, but it was necessary. She'd overstepped her bounds. If it had been one of the guys he wouldn't have hesitated doing the smackdown. He'd have been ruthless, in their face, and told them in no uncertain terms where and how they screwed up. He couldn't treat Jessie any differently. She wouldn't respect him if he did.

"You're right," she said, surprising him. "I grossly overstepped my authority. I jumped in and made a decision that I had no business making. One that could have cost us this mission."

He wanted to comfort her, but that was the part of him that cared about her. He resisted, instead let her stew.

"I don't know what I was thinking," she continued. "I was so eager, so excited, and I really feel like I'm right on this, Diaz. Crush isn't involved." She folded her hands in her lap, went quiet for a few more minutes.

Finally, she shifted and turned to face him. "You're absolutely right. I screwed up. I'm sorry."

His gut twisted at the look of misery on her face. He wanted to gather her in his arms, smooth his hand over her hair, and kiss away her pain. But right now he was her superior, and making her feel better wasn't part of his job. If she was going to be a Wild

Rider, she was going to have to learn to take the bad with the good.

"Don't do it again. Let's just hope it's salvageable, that Crush really can help us."

She nodded.

There was a knock at the door. Jessie got up to open it, letting Crush through. He didn't come all the way in the room, just leaned against the wall.

"I don't know how many guns there are, but there's a stash of weapons hidden under a false bottom in Nate's RV."

Diaz stood. "How do you know?"

"Because I crawled under and found it. Nate was with Rex tonight. Figured if they were going to bring weapons with them, Nate's RV would be big enough to hide them. I started with the outside."

"Anyone see you?"

Crush shook his head. "They're all up at the lodge partying. Hey, I do have some skills. I know how *not* to get caught."

Jessie slid her hands in the pockets of her jeans and moved next to Diaz. "Any idea how many weapons?"

"Hundreds. I didn't stop to count, but there are guns, rifles, some automatic. Ammo, too. Some look like military issue. There's some other stuff locked up in dark green boxes. I'm thinking maybe explosives or maybe even missiles."

So not what he wanted to hear. "That's possible."

"Now that you know about it, what's the plan? You bring in the Feds and wrap things up?"

"It's not that simple," Diaz explained. "We drag in the Feds now to surround the RV, we lose the survivalists, the chance to bring in some of those tax-evading, scum-sucking antigovernment assholes. We want to take a few of them down, too."

"Oh, right. So what's the plan?"

"I'm working on it. I need to call in, make arrangements to bring the Feds in so they're ready to take these guys down tomorrow. What part we'll play in all that is uncertain at the moment. We'll meet up in the morning to talk about it with Spence."

"Okay. I'm out of here. I'll keep an eye on the RV tonight." Crush turned to the door.

"Crush?"

"Yeah."

"I might have been wrong about you. Thanks for the info."

His lips quirked. "You bet."

After Crush left, Jessie turned to him. "Thank you for that."

"Just because your instincts might have been on about Crush doesn't mean you can go off half-cocked anytime you want to."

She nodded. "I understand. But I do trust him. Do you now?"

"I'm beginning to. We'll see what happens as we move along in the plan."

"So what exactly is the plan?"

He shrugged. "I don't know yet. I'll have to think about options. We'll have one by tomorrow."

Diaz knew he'd get no sleep tonight. They had to get those firearms before the survivalists did, and he wanted to bring those guys in.

Which meant the plan had to be solid—no mistakes. All avenues and potential ways things could go wrong had to be covered.

He had a lot to think about.

Jessie went into the bathroom, shut the door, and turned on the shower. He made a call to Grange, gave him the time and location for the arms delivery, and discussed options. Grange said he'd have the Feds call him directly to arrange a liaison point for tomorrow, and then they could plan from there.

After he hung up he stared at the bathroom door. He heard the water running, thought about Jessie naked, and had a driving urge to join her, to say the hell with his determination to keep things impersonal between them when what he really wanted was to get really, really personal.

But after their last time together it would be such a bad idea. She'd been distant, emotionally removed from the encounter—hurt. He didn't want to keep leading her on just because his dick wanted some comfort.

He'd gone without sexual release before, had gone a long damn time without it, in fact. He'd survive being around Jessie and keeping things strictly business.

She opened the door, the smell of her pouring out of the bathroom. She appeared through the steam, her skin rosy pink from the shower. She wore sweats, her nipples outlined against the soft brown fabric of her shirt. He remembered what her skin felt like—soft, warm, pliant under his hands.

Despite his intentions, his cock twitched, began to harden, his gaze targeting her like a torpedo as she moved around the room busying herself with—well, hell he had no idea what she was doing. He was watching her body—the way she walked, the way her hips swayed, the sensuous stride of her legs, the way her breasts bounced with every movement.

She stilled, obviously becoming aware of his attention, because she slowly turned around to face him as he sat in the wingback chair.

She moved to the bed, pulled back the covers, and pushed the pillows against the headboard. She laid down on her side, half reclining, and looked at him, her intent clear as she laid her palm on the mattress.

Invitation. No words, no explanations, no recriminations later.

Maybe this was what they both needed. A little release of tension before the shit hit the fan tomorrow. But could he do this again, knowing what happened between them the last time? Could he remain detached? Could it ever be "just sex" with Jessie?

He stood, walked to the bed, stopped when he hit the edge.

"Are you sure?"

She nodded.

He wasn't going to ask again, because he did need this. And from the way she devoured his erection with her eyes, so did she.

He stripped off his clothes and climbed into bed beside her, laying his hand on the softness of her hip, then rolling his palm upward, raising her shirt up with his movements.

Bare skin. So soft and warm, fragrant from her shower. She watched him touch her, didn't move, but her breathing quickened. He pushed her onto her back, used both hands to push her shirt up and over her breasts. Her nipples were already tight buds awaiting his mouth. He swooped down and took one between his lips, intoxicated by the sweet smell of her skin. It was almost dizzying to be able to touch her and taste her again, when he thought he'd never be able to. And to feel her arch against him, to feed him her breasts, made his cock rock hard, pressing urgently against the mattress.

He wanted to be inside her, burying deep and fucking her with mindless abandon. But he wanted more than that, because he knew this was going to be the last time.

And it wasn't going to be "just sex." Not this time.

He moved to the other nipple, teased it with his teeth and tongue until it stood hard and erect, then kissed his way down her ribs and belly, flicking the little charm at her navel.

He was going to miss having access to her body, refused to think of this being someone else's playground someday. He pushed aside the warning bells proclaiming him a total dumbass for letting her go.

Not now, not when his hands were filled with her buttery soft skin, when he breathed in the scent of her tempting arousal just south of the teasing jewel of her belly button.

He slid down, swirling his tongue over her mound, feeling her body tense and arch as he drew closer to her sex. He repositioned himself between her legs, spreading them wide so he could see her, touch her, kiss the inside of her thighs as he draped them over his shoulders.

She was so beautiful, even here. He licked her pussy lips and she shuddered, let out a cry of delight, and fisted his hair as he moved his tongue over her clit and sucked.

He wanted more, licking his way down to her pussy. She was so wet here. He let out a groan as he slid his tongue inside her, not realizing how hungry he'd been for her until the taste of her flooded his mouth. She bucked against him in uncontrollable spasms, moaning his name as she came with unashamed screams. He held on to her, licking her, soaking up everything she had to give as she rode out her orgasm. This is what he loved about Jessie, the way she came apart. No hesitation, holding nothing back and giving everything to him. He continued to kiss and lick her pussy until she was tense and needy again, her fingers tightening in his hair. Only then did he let go of her, and only long enough to crawl up her body to capture her mouth in a deep kiss. She wrapped her arms and legs around him, holding him tight as she returned the kiss with fervor.

He broke them apart only long enough to apply a condom before pulling her in his arms and rolling her to the side. He wanted to lie with her, arms and legs tangled up. He slid his cock inside with a gentle push, watching the way her lips parted as he drove until he was fully inside her.

His cock throbbed, his balls tight, full and ready to burst. But all he could do was savor this moment of having Jessie in his arms, her body locked with his, the feel of her pussy gripping him, the scent of her filling the air around them.

Neither of them had spoken—they didn't need to. There was nothing to be said, only this moment to be shared between them. This contact they both seemed to need, and the understanding they had that this was the last time.

He moved, surging forward. Jessie answered by convulsing around him, her leg wrapping around his hip to lock him in place. With every movement her breathing grew harsher, louder, then turned to whimpers and moans. He breathed them in, memorized every sound, every expression, every subtle movement of her body until he couldn't take it anymore and started to fuck her with long, deep strokes, holding tight to her hip as he reared back and powered hard inside her.

Then restraint became impossible. He was going to go off, especially when he felt her tighten and tremors erupt inside her. She threw her head back and gasped, held tight to him as she trembled through her orgasm. He watched her climax, then he was unable to hold back and went with her, erupting from the base of his spine to jettison come in a torrent that left him gasping for breath and barely able to move.

Shaken, he held her close, realizing he didn't want to let her go, but knowing he had to.

Jessie sighed, stroked his back, and pulled away. She kissed him, traced her finger over his lips, and without a word left the bed and went into the bathroom.

Was that to make it easier on him, or on herself?

Christ, why was this so damned difficult?

When she came out again, she had her sweats on.

"I think I'll make some coffee. I'm not tired, and I figured you probably have to do some planning tonight."

He nodded on his way to the bathroom. "Good idea. Thanks."

He shut the bathroom door, stared at his reflection in the mirror, and raked his fingers through his hair. Yeah, he had to do some planning. For the mission.

That had to be his focus, though making love with Jessie had shaken him more than he thought.

He'd always been good about walking away, had never let a woman in. His heart was impenetrable, a solid wall of ice. He was incapable of loving anyone—or so he'd thought.

Jessie had gotten in.

Why was it so goddamn hard to get her out?

sixteen

BEFORE DAWN, JESSIE, DIAZ, CRUSH, AND SPENCE HAD GATH-
ered in a private room to discuss options. True to his word, Crush
had kept watch over the RV all night. He reported no activity. The
RV hadn't moved, and Rex had gone to bed without incident. Apparently a few words to a couple of his guys had put some eyes on
Rex. He was under close watch now and Crush assured them no
one knew why, and no questions would be asked. It wasn't the
first time Crush had some of his members watched, and no one
ever questioned the Skulls' leader.

Jessie didn't think any of them had gotten much sleep the night
before. They all yawned while nursing that first cup of coffee.
She'd tried to sleep, tossing from one side to the other in the bed
while Diaz paced, laid on the couch, got up, and paced more.

It wasn't lost on her that he hadn't gotten back in bed with her.

She ached for him, missed the feel of his big body snuggled up
against her. But distance between them was probably for the best.

Making love with him last night had been a spur-of-the-moment decision, a choice on her part. She'd needed it and so had he, that release of tension before the "big game," so to speak.

But now it was time she focus on her job. She'd been too eager in so many ways. Too eager for him, as well as in her involvement with the mission. Both had cost her dearly. It was time to take a step back and let Diaz run the show, job wise. As far as their personal relationship . . .

There wasn't one. And she was going to have to learn to live with it. She couldn't have impersonal sex with him. She'd learned that the hard way. Sex without reaching out emotionally meant nothing.

Last night she'd let all her emotions fly. It had been wonderful. But she'd also kept in the back of her mind that Diaz was never going to be the kind of man she could have a relationship with. It had been okay, while they were in bed.

But as soon as they were done, she knew it wasn't going to be okay. It was never going to be okay being without him.

So she was never going to sleep with him again. She'd just as soon walk away from him than continually batter her heart like that. It was best to simply focus on the mission, get through the end of this case, then get back to Wild Riders' headquarters and move on with her life.

Without Diaz, because that's the way he wanted it. She'd ask Grange not to assign her to a case with Diaz for a while. Then, with time and a little distance, maybe she could work with him again. Surely her heart would heal, and they could be friends. She'd move on, start dating, which is what she should have been doing all along instead of getting hung up on a guy who wasn't interested in a future with her. Once she fell in and out of love a few times, she and Diaz could both laugh about this.

Theoretically, it sounded great. Reality was going to be a lot different.

Enough. It was time to focus. Everyone was brainstorming and she'd barely been tuning in. She turned her attention to the guys.

"We could hijack the RV," Crush suggested.

Diaz shook his head. "The survivalists would never follow. They'd recognize the setup and it would just send them deeper undercover. We'll lose the bust that way, and we'll not only screw up the chance to bring in some survivalists, but Rex, Nate, and the others, too."

"So the best thing to do is just let the transfer happen?" Jessie asked.

Diaz nodded. "Yeah. I've already been in touch with Walt, our Fed contact. The plan is to set up in the prearranged drop location several hours in advance of Rex's meeting with the survivalists. The ATF is already planning to scour the area and make sure no one's around. We'll bury ourselves deep, hide vehicles, and be ready to jump on them as soon as they make the exchange. That way we catch both sides in the act of selling and buying illegal arms."

"When do we go?"

Diaz looked at Crush. "We're trained for this. You're not. This could get dangerous."

Crush leveled a glare at Diaz. "You can't kick me out of this now. I can handle myself. Besides, my guys are neck deep in this shit. I feel responsible. I want to see it through."

Diaz considered it. Bad move to bring in a civilian, but Crush seemed to know how to handle himself, and they might need another knowledgeable biker in case things went south. Besides, Crush already knew what was going to happen. Better to keep him close rather than telling him he had to stay here, pissing him off and risk having him show up at the wrong time and blow the whole operation. "Okay, but you so much as blink the wrong way and I'll knock you out. This is a Federal bust, and it's huge. They're going to crap bricks knowing we have a civilian in the midst of this, so you take every step glued to my side and do exactly what I tell you."

Crush nodded. "You got it."

"We already have tracking devices on Rex's bike as well as the others involved," Diaz said. "But I want to add one to the RV, too. I'm not taking any chances in case they make a last-minute deviation from the designated meeting place, especially since we won't be here to watch over them."

Crush nodded. "Sounds like you have it all planned out."

Spence snorted. "It's never as easy as it looks. The plan just sounds simple. And straightforward plans are typically the worst kind."

"Because a thousand different things can go wrong, and because human nature is utterly unpredictable," Jessie added.

"Exactly." Diaz stood and paced Crush's crowded room. They'd holed up in here because Crush assured them of privacy. "We can plan for different outcomes, but we never know what might happen. The one thing we have to avoid is detection. No one on either Rex's side or the survivalists' side can know we're there watching."

"Are we doing video?" Spence asked.

"Got it covered."

At Crush's questioning look, Diaz said, "We'll get the arms-for-cash trade on video. The Feds will need it for evidence, and I told Walt that we had video taken care of."

Jessie grabbed a pad of paper and a pen and started jotting notes. They had to secure the video equipment, make arrangements to sneak out early today so they could rendezvous with the Feds and get everything in place. Diaz put Crush in charge of making appropriate excuses for their whereabouts. Crush was going to tell people that he was leading Diaz, Spence, and Jessie on a ride to one of his favorite spots. That they would be gone for most of the day and well into the night. Before they left, weapons would have to be checked, loaded, extra ammo secured.

Jessie hoped gunfire wouldn't be necessary, but she knew they'd all do whatever it took. They'd also have to keep an eye on Crush, because he was a civilian. If something happened to him, it would be her fault. Yes, she trusted him, but it wasn't his job to put his neck on the line to help them reel in the bad guys.

Stupid move, Jessie. She knew better, she really did. She was going to have to stop being so eager and start taking a backseat to the mission leader in the future.

If she even had a future with the Wild Riders when this was over. She wouldn't blame Diaz at all if he reported her to Grange.

They spent the morning playing at being low-key. They put in an appearance in the lodge restaurant, chatted and drank coffee, acted as normal as possible. Crush made a big deal about talking with Diaz about taking a ride that day, one that would lead them north for a day into Missouri and last into the night. Before long it was time to pack up and go.

It was a little after noon when they arrived at the meeting destination, more than eight hours before the survivalists and Rex's group were scheduled to rendezvous. The Feds were already there, combing the area. They stashed and covered their bikes, making sure they couldn't be spotted from the road. Walt met up with Diaz and they exchanged information.

"I've got teams clearing the area as far back as five miles, making sure no one is in the woods," Walt said. "Weather forecast is shit for tonight, low ceiling and heavy rain possible. With all these hills and trees it's too dangerous for choppers, so we'll get no air support."

Walt was tall, well built with deep blue eyes and midnight black hair closely cropped and almost hidden underneath an ATF ball cap. All his men were dressed similarly in camouflaging dark clothes.

The place was crawling with agents scurrying around, making very little noise, saying hardly anything, but everyone seemed to know what they were supposed to do and where they were supposed to be. Their vehicles were already long gone, everything happening on foot. These guys were good.

"You four can move up to the front with me," Walt said. "You have video, so we'll need you close to the action."

Diaz nodded and they followed. There was only one discernible path visible from the main road and wide enough for Nate to bring the RV through. Other than that, it was dense forest all the way. Vegetation littered the forest floor, making the walking hazardous.

"This is going to suck at night," Jessie muttered, picking her way over fallen limbs and rocks. "If we have to take off after these guys, we're going to trip and fall on our asses."

"By then we'll be hitting them with lights, so that should help your footing," Walt offered.

Yeah, it would help some, but how much? She hoped it was a full moon tonight. Then again, as she tilted her head back and looked up at the canopy of trees overhead, she realized they'd be lucky to get anything through that thick foliage.

This was going to be interesting.

They discussed the perimeter, where to set up and how. SUVs had been hidden, with drivers stashed behind the wheels, ready to block the main road and all available exits at a moment's notice. No way could they park nearby because they'd be seen, but Walt assured them that they had vehicles at the ready and could reappear within moments. Jessie assumed they knew what they were doing.

They settled in about twenty yards behind the clearing, well hidden behind a large, mossy rock and a thick copse of trees. To the north was a cliff and a steep drop down to the river, so no chance of the survivalists coming up that way. The only way they'd have to move in was from the east and from the main road, and the ATF agents weren't set up there. Everyone was buried in the forest, deep out of sight.

Jessie leaned against the rock and grabbed her bottle of water out of her pack. She turned to Spence, who let out a grumbling curse while settling in.

"Are you doing okay?"

He gave a quick nod and a reassuring smile, squeezing her hand. "I've handled worse than this, darlin'. I'm gonna be fine."

She had no idea what was worse than being shot, and wasn't sure she wanted to know what else Spence had been through.

Now all they had to do was wait. She looked at her watch. It was six o'clock.

They had three hours left.

Stakeouts sucked. Too much time to idle, reflect, and think. Jessie hated inactivity, much preferred doing something.

Diaz had settled in next to her. They were sitting on damp ground, leaves over them. She was starting to cramp.

The skies turned dark and a cold misty rain began to fall. *Great, just great.*

Jessie zipped her jacket all the way to her chin, pulling the collar up, thankful she'd remembered to put on her thick socks. It was going to be cold tonight, made even more so by the dampness in the air.

"Cold?" Diaz asked.

"Did my chattering teeth give me away?"

He laughed, pushed closer toward her. "I'd lie on top of you to keep you warm, but then I'd lose all focus on the mission."

She snorted, then turned her head to look at him, sucking in a breath at his dark eyes studying her.

"What?" she asked.

His lips curled. "Nothing."

Yeah, she was definitely going to have to ask Grange not to assign her cases with Diaz anymore. Her stomach clenched and she felt all warm and gooey inside. Just looking at him made her brains scramble—but at least she was warmer now. *Bonus.*

The hours passed slowly. They talked about the mission, and Walt helped pass the time by telling them about some other stakeouts he'd been on. Some were dicey and action packed, others complete clusterfucks, and some, like this one, were hours spent just sitting and waiting. His world was fascinating though, and he'd made some high-profile busts.

Finally she heard sounds. Engine sounds. The loud roar of pipes. It was time.

"Get into position," Walt said, alerting his team via his comm.

They dropped down as bikes entered the clearing, engines shut off, and whispered voices echoed in the empty forest.

It was Rex and the other bikers from Crush's gang. Diaz signaled for them all to keep hidden. Jessie checked her watch. Straight up nine o'clock. Rex was prompt, no doubt eager to get his payoff.

The RV came in a few minutes later. Nate pulled up into the camp spot and cut his engine, followed right after that by several ATVs and pickup trucks. The survivalists. For a while it was chaos, loud engines, talking. Diaz lifted his thumb, and they slowly raised up and peered around the rocks and vegetation to take a look at the action.

It was the same group from last night, only this time they'd brought a few more. About twenty men, from what Jessie could count, all heavily armed.

Jessie took the camera out of her bag.

"Let me do it," Spence whispered. "I've got a clear angle here."

She handed the camera to Spence and he started filming. The truck and ATV headlights had been left on, giving them plenty of light to see everyone.

The survivalists were an unruly-looking bunch. They wore dark hats pulled low over their eyes, sported full beards—no way to even recognize faces. All of them were dressed in hiking boots, camouflage pants and jackets, no doubt so they'd blend in with the forest, all nondescript in appearance.

And those rifles the survivalists cradled were definitely not any kind you'd buy in a gun shop. Jessie was no weapons expert, but they looked like military issue. Wherever they'd gotten them, they had to have been obtained illegally. These guys were prepared for war. A shiver skittered down her spine as she thought of the possibilities. This was serious business, and she felt ill prepared to face these people with nothing more than a forty-caliber pistol. She'd wager that Rex, Nate, and the other bikers were armed, too. She was suddenly very glad to have the ATF with them.

With the comm devices in their ears, they could pick up what was being said. The survivalists approached the RV. The man who'd done most of the talking last night—George, she thought was his name—was there again.

"Are they in here?"

Rex nodded. "There's a false bottom built in, almost like a storage room. Guns and ammo."

George spit out a wad of chewing tobacco. "Good."

"You got our money?" Nate asked.

" 'Course we do. We're honest businessmen. We make a deal, we stick to the terms." George surveyed the area. "You sure you weren't followed?"

"I'd hardly pass the test to get into your group if I were dumb enough to be tailed."

Rex wanted to join the survivalists?

"We'll see how smart you are," George said, stepping forward and crouching down in front of the RV. He crawled under, remaining there for about five minutes before reappearing, wiping his hands off. "Damn genius idea to create that false bottom. Hardly noticeable."

Nate beamed a smile. "Thanks."

"We could use someone with your smarts in our ranks. You interested in joining the real militia?"

Rex elbowed him, and Nate stumbled, "Uh, yeah. I mean, sure. Yes, sir. I'd be real interested in joining up."

George nodded, spit again. "We'll have to check you out, then. You got family?"

"Ex-wife is all. She sure as hell wouldn't miss me if I disappeared."

"Good enough. We'll talk about you later. Let's get this unloaded."

Now the action was really beginning. Jessie wondered how long the ATF would wait before moving in. She glanced over at Walt, but he was watching intently, making no sign to move in. He had a comm device strapped to his shoulder, his rifle at the ready, but he appeared relaxed, listening. Spence was filming, getting all of this on tape, which would make great evidence when they arrested all these guys and this went to court.

The bikers and survivalists pitched in to unload the arms from under the RV into the waiting pickup trucks.

Jessie tensed, pulled her weapon, waiting for the signal so they could go in and take these guys down.

As soon as the trucks were loaded, Rex and George met up in

front of one of the pickups. George pulled a duffel bag from the cab of the truck and handed it to Rex.

"Two hundred fifty thousand, like we talked about. It's all there."

Rex nodded and accepted the bag.

"That's it," Walt said, then gave the signal through his communicator. "Move in, now!"

Flash grenades detonated in the clearing, to blind the survivalists and bikers. ATF burst out from all directions, ordering everyone to freeze.

Then the sound of gunfire exploded.

Jessie blew out a breath, leaped from her hiding place, and headed out at a dead run, following Diaz's lead.

Game on.

seventeen

DIAZ LED HIS TEAM AS CONFUSION REIGNED AROUND THEM. Gunfire rang out, so loud he could barely hear his own voice as he shouted orders.

"Stay low and grab for cover!" Diaz shouted, concerned only for his team at the moment. He snapped his gaze to Crush, satisfied that Crush had a weapon of his own. "You, stay back," he ordered. Crush nodded and took up position behind him as they moved in behind the lead row of ATF agents.

Their job wasn't to handle the corralling and arrests, but to provide backup. They'd done their part, but now that they were knee-deep in this melee, no way was Diaz going to stand around with his thumb up his ass and just watch it all go down. Nor was he going to put his team in the line of fire. Survivalists usually didn't surrender, which meant there was serious danger ahead. Gunfire was everywhere, ricocheting off trees, bark flying past their heads as bullets hit nearby. Diaz was thankful the ATF had brought a damn army with them.

"Stay behind these trees. Don't enter the clearing. We'll go in if help is needed."

But then the unmistakable sound of bike engines drew his attention away from the battle and toward the main road.

"Do you hear that?" Spence moved in behind Diaz.

"Yeah."

"I think our friends are trying to make a getaway."

"Not today, they're not." The ATF were engaged, their big black SUVs already having moved into the camping area to block the exit.

Diaz and his team had a much better chance of catching Rex and the others. "Head back to the bikes," Diaz said on the run. "We're going to have to follow them. I don't want to lose these guys."

They hustled back to their bikes, uncovered them, and hopped on, using the GPS unit to track Rex and his guys. They cut into the woods, taking it slow but deliberate.

Just as he figured, the bikes had waded through the forest and back out onto the main road.

Goddammit, this wasn't going to happen. They'd worked too hard to let these guys get away. He cranked the throttle and sped up, the others tucked in right behind him. They hadn't made it far along the road before Diaz caught sight of Rex and the others.

The rain made the narrow stretch of two-lane road even more treacherous.

Diaz caught up, moved beside them, his intent to buzz past them in order to slow them down. Rex tried to slam into him but Diaz was faster, swerving around him and hitting the brakes to move back behind him. They were careening around curves so fast Rex and the others wouldn't be able to use their guns.

When they hit a fork in the road, Rex and two of the other guys shot left, the other three right. Diaz signaled to Spence, and Spence and Crush went to the right, while Diaz and Jessie followed Rex and the other two.

The road Rex had taken was going to dead-end up ahead at the river. Despite the falling rain, Diaz spotted a wide sandbar and an upward slope peppered with grass and scrub. Nothing else. Rex took his bike up and over the edge, down the grassy hill and then started paralleling the river.

Where the hell did he think he was going? Rex's friends followed, and so did Diaz and Jess.

Diaz spotted the bridge up ahead, knew that's where Rex was headed. He throttled up and pushed past the two bikers, intending to cut them off before they hit the bridge. Jessie moved quickly, too, using her bike to wedge between the other two and Rex.

Rex made it to the bridge, but Jessie had managed to veer off the other two. Diaz had no choice but to follow Rex over the wooden planked bridge. He couldn't let him get away, but he didn't like leaving Jessie alone to deal with the other two bikers.

He had to think of the mission first. Jessie was armed. She could handle it, right?

Bullshit. He'd get to Rex later. He wasn't leaving Jessie to deal with two bikers.

A shot rang out and he skidded in the middle of the bridge as he applied the brakes, turning his bike a hundred and eighty degrees. One bike was down on the sandbar, and in the falling rain he couldn't make out who it was. Was it Jessie or one of the other bikers? He shot a glance to the end of the bridge, saw Rex's taillights disappearing in the rain and darkness.

Shit.

You didn't leave a team member in danger. Cardinal rule of the Wild Riders, especially when the big deal went down, and this was definitely the big deal. He was responsible for Jessie, a junior member of the team. He wasn't going to leave her, no matter how much he wanted to drag Rex in.

He hit the throttle, heading back toward the fallen bike. It seemed to take forever to get there, like time had slowed to a crawl. He squinted through the rain, which now came down in sheets, trying to make out the bike and the fallen rider lying beside it. The closer he got, the harder his heart pounded.

What if it was Jessie? What if she was shot, bleeding, hurt bad? Or worse?

Adrenaline pumping, he flew off his bike as soon as he was close enough and ran to the fallen biker. It was one of Rex's guys, shot in the shoulder and out cold. Relief flooded him, followed immediately by confusion and renewed fear.

Where was the other biker? Where was Jessie? He scanned the area, but didn't see a damn thing. After determining the biker's injuries weren't life threatening, he grabbed a set of handcuffs out of his bag, cuffed the biker's hands behind his back, alerted the Feds to his location, the fallen biker's status, and what was going on, then climbed back on his bike, raking his fingers through his hair.

He breathed in, out, trying to settle the panic jumbling in his gut.

Then he heard it, whipped his head around at the rumbling sound of motorcycle engines.

He grabbed his GPS and followed the signals, figuring if she was tailing one of Rex's buddies then the signal would lead to her, and it had to be the closest one since he'd heard the bike. He maneuvered out of the sand and up the grassy embankment, locating a road in the rain-filled darkness, following that and his tracking unit. The sound of his own bike's engine drowned out the possibility of hearing their bikes, but he concentrated on his GPS unit, determined it was going to lead him to Jess. He refused to consider any other possibility. He had to find her.

The signal pinpointed him moving in on one of the units, then showed that the bike had stopped. Diaz slowed, not wanting to tip his hand. Whoever he was tracking wasn't moving any longer. That was either good or really bad.

He spotted a gravel pit up ahead, and that's where the signal ended.

Shit. Definitely not good. Piles of crushed rock made great camouflage. Who knew where they could be hiding? He slowed the bike to a crawl as he rode around each hill-sized pile of gravel, searching for a bike or people. There were lights on at the crushing center, but it was closed, locks firmly attached to the steel entrance doors. He continued on, searching for any signs of the bikers or Jess. The only good thing about the rain was it made great bike tracks in the mud. He spotted a line from one of the doors—they'd probably tried to get into the factory and realized they couldn't, and took off. He followed the bike tracks, leading his bike slowly along, keeping an ever watchful eye out for—

He was rocketed off his bike by something slamming into his left shoulder. White-hot pain knifed into him, sending him sprawling into the thick mud. Momentarily dazed, he blinked to clear the fog of pain and confusion, fighting to breathe, knowing he'd been shot but no idea how bad. He flexed his fingers on that side, relieved to know they worked. He rolled over, using his fallen bike as cover, and with his good arm reached into his pocket for his own gun. A quick scan of the area showed nothing. His arm hurt like a son of a bitch and he felt the trickle of cascading blood, but there wasn't a damn thing he could do about it at the moment, only hope that he wouldn't bleed hard enough to pass out.

Then he heard it—a slight scream, a smothered gasp. Instinct told him it was Jessie. It came from the side of the building, about twenty feet away from where he lay. Unfortunately, if he got up and made a run for it and someone happened to be leaning against the corner of the building, he'd make great target practice. Getting shot again wasn't high on his priority list.

Then he heard a groan, followed by a loud curse, and Jessie shot out from behind the building, running toward him like her hair was on fire. Shots rang out, but she flew behind his bike, landing with a spray of gravel over both of them.

In a panic, afraid she'd been shot, Diaz returned fire, then turned to her. "Are you all right?"

She nodded, her face bruised and dirty. "I'm fine. You?"

"Took a bullet in my arm, but I'm okay."

Her eyes widened as she reached for him. "Oh God, Diaz. Where? How bad is it?"

He shrugged her off, focusing his attention on the side of the building. "Not now. I can handle it. We need to get out of this crisis first. What's going on back there? How many guys? Did Rex meet up with the guy you were chasing?" He pulled out his cell phone, punched in the number to send an alert to Walt. Hopefully Walt would pick up on Diaz's GPS and send a team to their location.

"Just the one guy. Haven't seen Rex," she said after Diaz pocketed his cell.

"Do you have your gun?"

She shook her head. "He took it from me."

"There's another gun in my saddlebag if you can reach it."

She dug her hand under his bike to get to his saddlebag. "So this guy . . . I think his name is Dave? Anyway, he ran me down

and kicked me off my bike, then grabbed me and hauled me behind the building when he heard your bike coming."

Diaz's blood pressure rose at the visual of someone hurting
her. He itched to get his hands on Dave.

"I kneed him in the nuts and gave him an elbow to the chin
and came running out here."

Diaz smiled. "Good girl."

"He's also contacted Rex, who's supposed to meet him
shortly."

"Glad to hear that." Diaz had hated losing Rex. "But first,
we've got to get out of this open clearing. We're sitting ducks
here." Plus, Diaz didn't like hiding behind a tank full of gasoline.
That was just asking for a fiery, explosive death. There didn't seem
to be anymore bullets flying in their direction, so Dave was probably lying low, waiting for Diaz to make the next move. He might
have run off, too. Or maybe he was out of bullets. They should be
so lucky.

Diaz swiveled around, spotted the gravel hills behind them.

"Let's get away from this bike. We can use those gravel mounds
as cover."

Having taken the gun from his saddlebag, Jessie pocketed the
extra ammo and nodded. "I'm ready when you are."

Using his noninjured arm to push himself into a crouching
position, he gave the signal. Jessie sprinted, and Diaz fired in con-
tinual bursts at the corner spot on the building while he was on
the run. He got in front of Jessie in case any bullets came flying at
them. It seemed to take forever, but Diaz knew it was only seconds until they were safely behind a tall gray mound.

They waited. Either Dave had left or wasn't going to waste
anymore ammo shooting at them.

"You need to let me see your arm," Jessie whispered.

"It's fine. I don't think the bullet penetrated." The pain was down to a dull throb now, and the bleeding seemed to have slowed. "I think the thickness of my jacket probably slowed the bullet."

Jessie slanted a dubious look in his direction. "If you pass out on me from blood loss I'm going to kick you."

His lips lifted. "Duly noted."

She settled against the gravel, gun pointed toward the building. "So now what?"

"We wait."

They didn't have to wait long. A bike's throaty hum echoed through the quiet.

"Rex's coming in behind the building," Diaz said. "I'll bet your Dave has left his post to meet up with him. We'll take the left side of the building, see if we can sneak up behind them. Let's move while they're distracted with meeting up."

Diaz pushed off and Jessie was right with him as they made a left around the hill, staying low to the ground. Diaz motioned for Jess to stay put while he made a dash to the side of the building. If anyone was going to take a hit, it was going to be him. He made it, then signaled for Jessie, who sped to his side. They flattened themselves against the cold concrete wall of the gravel plant. Diaz listened for sounds, Rex's or Dave's bike, anything that would signal their location.

He looked to Jessie, who shook her head.

Dammit, they were going to have to hunt for them, which would put them out in the open and just as vulnerable as the bad guys. But they had no choice. They couldn't just stand there and wait for Rex and Dave to come to them, as convenient as that would be.

He caught Jessie's attention and cocked his head to the right, inching his way across the wall toward the other end of the building. Jessie followed, staying close, her gun raised and ready.

The plant was well lit with halogen lights hanging from the roof, shining a beacon over the pits and surrounding area. It was both a good and bad thing, because it would make it harder for Rex and Dave to hide from them, but also make it more difficult for Diaz and Jessie to hide under cover of darkness, too. Which meant he'd have to figure out a way to search for them without illuminating themselves under the lights like rock stars at a concert.

He paused at the corner between the side and back of the plant. Behind them was nothing but gravel. To the west were shrubs and then fence. If they pushed off and circled west, hidden behind the vegetation, they'd be out of the lighted area. They could move in darkness that way, only lit for a few seconds as they dashed off into the night.

Diaz pointed the muzzle of the gun toward the bushes. Jessie nodded and he held up three fingers, counting down to zero. He took off at a run, Jessie right on his heels.

No shots rang out as they made their way behind a thick bush. *Good.* If they were really lucky they hadn't been seen. Diaz hoped Dave had told Rex they were hiding out front, and that's where they were looking. Now they had a chance to take the advantage.

Diaz kept them low and behind the shrubbery, moving beyond it and into the nonlit part of the yard. Though flat and with nothing to hide behind, it was dark. The rain had picked up again, but at least that meant cloud cover and no moonlight.

He wished whatever machinery they used in the plant wasn't so noisy. Didn't they ever shut it off? A low humming noise, constant. It meant he couldn't listen for footsteps, for whispers, for anything that would signal Rex's whereabouts.

But the sound of a bike? Yeah, that he could hear, and did. Two of them, in fact. He spun around at the sound of one behind them, its headlight on high beam and barreling straight at them.

"Move!" he shouted at Jessie. She skirted out of the way and he pivoted, pointing his gun and firing. It missed, but gravel sprayed up and into the face of the rider, causing him to swerve and lay down the bike. Apparently not hurt, Dave leaped off the bike and took off.

Oh, no. Not this time. Diaz went after him at a dead run, caught up, and made a flying tackle.

Son of a bitch, that made his arm hurt. He pushed the pain inward, rolled Dave over, and landed a hard punch to his jaw.

Huh. Dave's jaw must be made of glass, because he was out cold. That was easy. Diaz stood, kicked Dave over onto his belly, and cuffed him, conscious of the sound of Rex's bike in the distance. He rose, turned, and realized Jessie wasn't nearby.

Shit.

Rain poured down his face, obliterating his ability to see more than an arm's length in front of him. He slogged through the mud and gravel, following the sound of Rex's bike, seeing the headlight swerving left and right.

She was running, heading for the bushes.

With Rex barreling after her on his bike, toying with her, revving his engine then cutting it back.

Fuck!

Diaz gave it everything he had, watching in horror as Rex drew closer to a running Jessie. He was almost on top of her, his intent clear.

He was going to hit her.

Fury boiled inside him and Diaz ran harder than he ever had, closing the distance between them, those last few feet sucking up every ounce of oxygen left in his lungs. His boots sank in the mud, his entire body felt like it weighed thousands of pounds as he made his way closer to an advancing Rex.

He wasn't going to make it in time. He stopped, raised his gun, hoping like hell he could get the shot, that it would slow Rex down before he hit her.

Just as it seemed Jessie was going to be swallowed up by Rex's front tire, Diaz fired. Jessie took a diving leap over a huge bush. At the same moment the bullet hit Rex's bike and Rex swerved. The bike skidded, and Rex went down. Diaz went running, leaping over the fallen bike and body tackling Rex.

Damn lucky for both of them that the rain had softened the ground. Impact had been hard enough. Diaz was up in a flash, fury over what Rex had tried to do to Jessie keeping his adrenaline pumping. He reared back and slammed his fist into Rex's face, satisfied at the bone-crunching sound, the blood flying from Rex's nose.

But it wasn't enough. Not after he'd seen Jessie literally running for her life.

He heard cars approaching. The ATF, no doubt. Diaz heard shouting, but he was oblivious. Rage drove him and he continued to pummel Rex, who tried to crawl away on his belly like the snake he was. Diaz picked him up by the back of his jacket and landed another hard punch, tossing him back to the ground.

Red haze blinded him and he could think of only one thing—the look of utter terror on Jessie's face as Rex barreled after her.

"Come on, motherfucker! It's easy to run down a defenseless girl, isn't it? Now get up and fight like a man."

Rex rolled over onto his stomach, groaning, refusing to get up.

"Oh, no. You don't get to quit that easy." He kicked him over onto his back, lifted him by his jacket again, intending to stand him on his feet so he could beat the crap out of him.

"Diaz. Stop!"

He heard Jessie's voice, but he was focused only on Rex, wanted him to beg for mercy. Even then, he had no intention of stopping. He wanted Rex to pay.

"Diaz. It's over. The Feds are here."

Jessie stepped over Rex, pushed Diaz hard in the chest. "Diaz!"

He blinked, his heart jamming like crazy against his chest. He focused on Jessie, the look on her face.

"The Feds are here. Let them finish this."

Her voice was soft, but he saw the look in her eyes. And he knew what she saw.

She saw what he'd done.

He looked down at his hands, covered in blood, then down at Rex, passed out on the ground, his face a bloody pulp. He was beating an unconscious man.

Christ. He inhaled through his nose, fighting back the bile rising in his throat. He turned, walked away from Jess, grabbed a handkerchief from his back pocket to wipe off the blood.

"I need to go find Walt, give a report," he said.

"I'll go with you."

He started to object, then gave a quick nod. *Work. Focus on work.* That was good.

Anything but the unconscious body of the man he no doubt would have beaten to death if Jessie hadn't stopped him.

As he'd guessed, the bullet wound wasn't bad at all and they patched him up on scene. The medic told him he'd be sore for a couple of days, but fine.

Despite the wild gunfire, no one with the ATF had been injured. Spence and Crush had rounded up the others in Rex's gang and held them for the agents to pick up.

Rex and his crew were now in custody. The location of the survivalist camp was still unknown, but the Feds were satisfied they had been able to arrest at least two dozen of them at the scene of the arms transaction. It was typically damned near impossible to smoke any of them out of hiding, or to get anything on them other than tax evasion. Now they had them on illegal arms dealing, and that was a big offense. As far as the government was concerned, this was a good bust.

After Diaz informed Walt that he would file a detailed report in the morning, Diaz, Jessie, Spence, and Crush made their way back to the lodge. It was time to pack up and take their leave of the Devil's Skulls.

Crush was going to take care of informing his gang about what went down with Rex, Nate, and the others. He also said it was time to clean house with the Skulls, root out anyone else sympathetic to the survivalists. That wasn't an element he wanted in the Skulls. He was still pissed as hell about his gang being used that way.

Crush was going to be busy.

"So this is it?" Crush asked, leaning against the wall of Diaz and Jessie's cabin. Spence had already packed up and checked out of his room at the lodge and was now seated on Diaz's sofa.

"This is it. Other than some paperwork, we're finished here. The Feds will want to take a statement from you and possibly some of the others, see what you can tell them about Rex, Nate, and the rest of them."

Crush nodded. "Yeah, they told me. I'll do what I can to help. I still can't believe this was going on right under my nose. Really pisses me off."

"They didn't want you to know. They're good at hiding their activities," Jessie said.

"I guess."

"But we got them," Spence said. "And you helped."

Crush grinned. "Yeah. This is probably the most fun I've had in years on one of these rides."

Spence laughed. "Don't get to take down criminals very often?"

"No, not often."

Diaz went over to him and held out his hand. "You did good. We couldn't have done this without you."

Crush shook Diaz's hand. "Like I said. I enjoy adventure, and this is one to tell the grandkids someday."

"Just don't use our names in the story," Jessie said with a wink.

"I'll be purposely vague."

Diaz zipped up his bag, and they all walked outside.

"Anytime any of you want to ride with the Skulls, you're welcome to join in. You're members now and you always will be."

Diaz grinned at Crush. "Might just do that. I need to get away now and then. And I like this area."

"Give me a call. I'll ride with you anytime."

They said their good-byes and headed out. Rather than wait until morning, Diaz wanted to ride back to Wild Riders' headquarters tonight. Spence and Jessie agreed there was no point in lingering at the lodge.

He figured they were all anxious to get back. Everyone had things to do. The mission was over.

It was time to go home.

Time to get back to reality.

And definitely time for a reality check. If anyone needed one of those, it was Diaz. He needed to talk to Grange.

Then he needed to talk to Jessie.

eighteen

Home. Jessie was happy to get back to Wild Riders' headquarters. It was always good to see Grange and whichever of the guys happened to be hanging around at the time.

Now, though, she wished it was just her and Diaz. She wanted some time alone with him, to talk to him about what happened that last night with Rex. She knew it bothered him. Like so many other things bothered him.

But they hadn't had a moment alone since they got back two days ago. First he'd been holed up with Grange, then busy filing reports. She had to give her report, too. If it wasn't one thing it was another.

She kicked the wastebasket in her room, stood, and began pacing, her arms crossed.

Diaz was avoiding her. It didn't take a rocket scientist to figure that out. He wasn't being subtle about it, either. Oh sure, she knew they'd had that whole conversation about there being nothing between them, about how there could only be the mission and they couldn't have a personal relationship. But that was all his doing, not hers. And she knew why. She got his reluctance. She understood.

But there were a few things Diaz needed to understand, and she was tired of him making all the rules. It was time for her to start making some.

While he'd been busy the past couple of days doing his damndest to avoid her, she'd also been busy. Thinking. And when she did her thinking, she thought hard. She'd finally figured out the puzzle of Jessie and Diaz, and how it fit. How they fit. And they *did* fit.

Time for Diaz to realize she wasn't going away just because he willed it.

But first she had to talk to Grange. Diaz wasn't going to like that, either, but too bad. They weren't on a mission any longer and she was free to do whatever she wanted.

She slid off the bed and went downstairs to Grange's office, rapping lightly on his door.

"What?"

She smiled at the gruff tone of his voice. It never failed to amuse her. "It's Jessie."

"Come on in."

She stepped into his war room and took a seat in the chair across from his desk, waiting until he finished up whatever he was keying into his computer.

"Okay," he said, finally looking up at her.

She studied his face, the lines streaming out from his eyes, the years of wear on his skin that told of so many battles he'd fought and won. More than physical battles, too. She'd never admired a man more than she admired General Grange Lee. And he was the only father figure she had ever known. She trusted him with her life.

"I'm in love with Diaz."

True to form, he didn't even blink. Nothing anyone said could ever shock or surprise the man. "You are, huh?"

"Yes."

"Does he love you back?"

"I believe he does, yes. But he keeps pushing me away."

"Because . . ."

"His parental history. His father."

"Ah." Grange steepled his fingers and looked over them at Jessie. "He's afraid of hurting you."

She nodded. "Which he won't. I know him. Probably better than he knows himself. He's incapable of hurting me."

"He's not perfect, Jessie. He does have some issues."

"I'm fully aware of that. But his issues aren't with me. He has never, would never, hurt me. He needs to understand that."

"And how are you going to convince him?"

"Oh, I have an idea."

"Do I want to know what it is?"

She grinned. "Probably not."

He shook his head. "So why are you telling me this?"

She stood, went around his desk, and kissed his cheek. "In case you hear a lot of yelling and screaming. I didn't want you to worry. I can handle Diaz."

As she was heading out the door, she heard his low chuckle. "If anyone can, Jess, it's you."

She was glad Grange had such confidence in her. That confidence flagged when she reached the door to Diaz's room. She raised her hand to knock, then paused, sucked in a breath.

Come on Jessie. You want this. Don't let him bully you into running away.

She rapped hard three times.

No answer. Figured. He probably knew it was her, or maybe he was intending to ignore everyone.

"Diaz?"

"I'm busy, Jess."

She turned the knob and opened the door, shutting it behind her.

He was seated at his desk, staring at his computer. He turned and glared at her.

"What part of 'I'm busy, Jess' didn't you get?"

"I decided to ignore you." She stepped into the room and took a seat on the side of his bed. His glare didn't get any friendlier. *Tough.* She wasn't leaving until they had it out.

He heaved a great big sigh that she was certain was all for effect, then pushed his chair around to face her. "Fine. What is it?"

"I want to talk about what happened with Rex."

He swiveled his chair back around to face his computer. "I don't need psychoanalyzing, but thanks."

Rolling her eyes, she stood and moved to his desk, planting her hip against it. "I'm not psychoanalyzing you. I think you're upset by what happened."

"You do. And what do you base this on?"

"The fact that I know you, that I can read your body signals. You've been tense, quiet, you haven't said much around the guys, and you haven't talked to me since we got back."

"I've been busy since we got back, and I don't need to hold hands with the guys. And you and I are hardly BFFs, Jess."

She fought a grin. "BFFs?"

"Or whatever the kids call it. I try to stay up on the lingo. Is that wrong?"

"No, it was accurate. And why can't we be . . . BFFs?"

Another sigh. "Jess, really. I've got a lot of work to do."

"You're avoiding me, Diaz—all because you beat the hell out of Rex."

"No. Because I've got to file reports, work with the federal liaison on this case so we can get our part closed. Paperwork. As mission leader, that's my job."

"It's more than that." She crossed her arms and stared him down, refusing to believe that paperwork had anything to do with his mood since he returned. She knelt before him, stroking the top of his hand, softening her voice. "Talk to me, Diaz. Please."

His gaze narrowed, then he let out a sigh. "He tried to kill you. What was I supposed to do?"

Now they were getting somewhere. "I appreciate you defending me. You saved my life, you know." She squeezed his hand. "I haven't even had the opportunity to thank you for that."

He jerked his hand away and stood, moving to the window. "It's my job to keep the members of my team safe. That's all there is to it."

She stood and followed. "Is that why you went after Rex so hard? Because you were keeping a team member safe?"

"No. Yes." He raked his fingers through his hair. "I don't know. Get out, Jessie."

She came closer, breathing him in. The scent of him never failed to arouse her. Her nipples tightened. He noticed. Animal passion fired up silently between them, hanging in the air, invisible, but like a steel chain holding them in place.

He stared her down, his gaze hard and unyielding. "I already told you this will never work between us."

"Because you're afraid you'll hurt me."

He didn't speak for what had to be a full minute, the longest minute of her life. She refused to move, refused to say anything until he did.

"Yes, dammit. Because I'm afraid I'll hurt you. You saw what I did to Rex, what I did to that other guy during initiation. I have that violence in me, Jessie, and someday I'll turn it on you."

"You don't use it against someone you love, Diaz. You've never hurt me."

"It's only a matter of time."

This was where she had to throw the gauntlet down. This was where she had to test him.

She eased back, exhaled. "Maybe you're right. Maybe I'm wasting my time and making a fool of myself chasing after you."

She saw the confusion in his eyes, and knew she had to follow through. "I'm tired, Diaz. So damn tired of throwing myself at you and having you push me away. I'm a full-grown woman and I have a woman's needs and desires. It's damn time I find someone who'll fulfill those desires for me."

She pushed off the desk and moved toward the door.

"Jessie, what are you talking about?"

"You asked me before why I remained a virgin for so long. I told you because I was picky. I think it's time I stop being so picky. You taught me to love sex, Diaz. And you taught me about love. I've decided I want them both in my life. If you refuse to give them to me, I'm going to find someone who will."

She opened the door to his room, walked out, and headed to her own.

It was a gamble. A risky one.

She fought back tears when he followed her to her room, pushed open the door she tried to close in his face.

"What the hell are you doing?"

She lifted her top off and tossed it to the floor. He quickly shut the door to keep prying eyes from getting a peek. She went to her closet and found her leather corset, the one that made her breasts spill over the top. As she put it on, she turned to him. "I'm going to go out and get a life, Diaz. Do you mind?"

His jaw clenched in that dangerous way she found so sexy. He didn't say anything as she zipped up the corset and went in search of her leathers.

"So you're going to dress in your sexiest clothes and go find you a man, huh?"

"I don't know. I just need to get out. Whether I find a man or not remains to be seen."

"Where are you going?"

"Not sure. AJ and Pax are in from their mission. They said something about a new biker bar in downtown Dallas. Thought I'd go with them tonight."

"AJ and Pax are party animals."

She slipped on the leather pants, watching the way his eyes darkened as she zipped up the side. Now for her boots.

"AJ and Pax can take care of themselves. And so can I." She sat on her chair and added her high-heeled boots to finish off the outfit, then stood, went to the mirror to apply lipstick.

"Christ, Jessie, dressed like that do you know what guys are gonna think?"

She whipped around and advanced on him. "Look, Diaz. I don't need a father. Never had one, never missed it. I need a man who'll love me, who wants to be with me. I'm never going to chase after a man again. If one wants me he can goddamn well come to me and tell me all the reasons why I should let him have me. Now get the hell out of my way. I'm tired of being cast aside. I'm going to party."

She pushed him aside and stormed over to the elevator, grateful it was open and waiting for her. She jammed the button and rode it downstairs, then stalked across the main floor, ignoring the gap-

ing stares of Spence, AJ, and Pax as she hit the security code opening the lower level elevator leading to the parking garage.

"I'm hitting that new club downtown," she threw over her
shoulder. "If anyone wants to come with me, let's go. Otherwise,
I'll be back later."

She didn't wait for replies, just stepped into the elevator, took
it down, and exited outside. The cool air helped clear the fog of
anger out of her head.

Diaz didn't care. He wasn't going to follow.

Like so many men she'd heard about before—he didn't want
her, but he didn't want anyone else to have her, either.

That was just too damn bad, because she was dead serious. She
refused to sit around and wait for him any longer. She'd done her
best to try and make him feel better.

Sometimes your best wasn't good enough.

Sometimes you had to know when to throw in the towel and
surrender.

"YOU'RE JUST GOING TO LET HER GO OUT—LIKE THAT?"

Diaz stared at the closed elevator door. He'd made it down to
the main level, watched Jessie leave. Now he stood with Pax and
AJ, who glared at him with expectant looks.

Why the hell were they looking at him? "I'm not her keeper."

Pax hit him with a narrowed look. "Dude, unless you're blind,
it's obvious she has a thing for you."

"Yeah," AJ added. "A thing called love. So what are you going
to do about it?"

It just figured that Grange picked that moment to walk out of
his office and into the main lounge. "What's going on?"

"Jessie just walked out of here, pissed as hell and dressed to kill," Pax said, folding his arms and leaning against the elevator door.

Grange lifted a brow and looked at Diaz. "Is that so?"

Diaz rolled his eyes. "What?"

Grange shrugged. "Nothing." He looked to Pax. "Where's she headed?"

"Some new club downtown we told her about."

"You're going with her."

That wasn't a question. That was a command. Pax and AJ headed for their rooms. "Yeah, I guess we are."

"Don't. I'll do it."

They both stopped. Stared at Grange, then at Diaz.

"Are you sure about that?" Grange asked.

He knew what Grange was asking.

"Yeah. I'm sure. Pax, give me the name and address of the club."

Within an hour he'd showered and driven to the new club on the outskirts of downtown. Trendy, lit up with neon, and absolutely packed. A line formed all the way down the block, with a mean-looking bouncer taking names at the door. Fortunately, AJ knew the guy and had already called ahead and gotten Diaz an in. He walked right up to the front, much to the dismay of the younger set lining the sidewalk who groaned and booed at him as he was granted entry through the black double doors of Hot Shots.

Music blasted his eardrums as soon as he stepped in. Loud, with a bass beat guaranteed to make you want to jump on the dance floor and shake your ass.

If you were into that kind of thing, which he wasn't. He searched for and found a long, black bar with well-padded armrests, ordered a double shot of Jack Daniel's, and downed it in one gulp. The burn made his eyes water, but it helped. He turned and searched the packed club. Bodies crowded every available space. People mingled around, some standing, others occupying seats at the booths and tables. The rest gyrated on the oversized dance floor, packed together like sardines and bumping up against each other.

If he was going to find Jessie, he was going to have to take a walk.

As he did, he realized pretty quickly that this place was nothing more than a meat market. Women sizing up men, their eager, hungry stares making it all too evident what they were shopping for. And the men were just as obvious, leaning in, suggestive, groping and grasping if they could get away with it. Enough alcohol was flowing that a lot of them could.

Had he ever been this young and stupid? Yeah, sadly, he had been. As he made his way through the press of bodies, he got plenty of looks from girls about Jessie's age. Women scoping out his body, throwing off signals that they were open to his approach. Some even stopped him, touched his jacket, asked if he wanted a dance or if they could buy him a drink.

He wasn't interested. Not in them, anyway.

Tables and booths were spread throughout the club, the dance floor set right in the middle. That's where he found Jessie, undulating between two guys as a sexy, suggestive song played. They splayed their hands across her stomach and back and she swung her hips between them both, her arms raised above her head, her eyes closed as she swayed back and forth to the music. Her lips parted, her tongue darted out to sweep across her bottom lip.

One guy put his hand on her throat to draw her face toward his. Jessie opened her eyes, laughed, and tilted her head away from his. He tried again; she palmed his chest and pushed him off, turning away from him to dance with the other guy, who wrapped an arm around her waist and brought her close to his chest.

Diaz inhaled, fought back the rising fury brought on by seeing hands all over her.

He had no right to be angry. Jessie wasn't his. She could do whatever she wanted, with whomever she wanted to do it with.

He'd laid down those rules, pushed her away time and time again because it was the right thing to do.

But goddammit, that wasn't what he wanted.

He pushed his way through the crowd and toward Jessie. She spotted him when he was a few feet away, kept on dancing. In fact, she turned her back to him, reaching behind her to pull the second guy closer.

That wasn't going to work. Diaz tapped him on the shoulder. He looked up.

"Get lost."

Since Diaz was about a foot taller and forty pounds heavier, the dude apparently decided it wasn't worth putting up a fight. He shrugged and left the dance floor. When Diaz offered a menacing stare to the one in front of Jessie, he took a hike, too.

Jessie turned around to face him. "What the hell are you doing?"

"Dance with me."

"Fuck you." She started to push past him, but he grabbed her arm.

She looked where he held her, then up at him, her eyes blazing fury even in the darkened club. "Let me go, Diaz. Now."

He released her arm and she stalked off the dance floor. He followed as she grabbed her jacket off a barstool and went out the front door to the parking lot.

He'd parked the Camaro next to her bike, so he stood in front of her.

"Jess, we need to talk."

"I'm talked out. I need you to leave me the hell alone."

He refused to get out of her way so she could get on her bike.

"Isn't this what you wanted? For me to follow you? Okay, you got me here, so we're going to talk."

"It's not what I wanted. I don't want to talk to you. I don't want to do anything with you anymore. I'm through trying to talk to you only to end up nowhere. Go back home, Diaz."

They'd drawn a crowd, including some beefy guys, no doubt bouncers from the club. They made their approach. *Great.* Just what he didn't need right now.

"This guy bothering you, ma'am?"

A tall, thick, bald-headed dude approached, his arms nearly as wide as his neck.

"Get lost," Diaz said. "We're talking."

"Okay, that's enough." The bald guy stepped between Diaz and Jessie. "You need to get out of here and leave the lady alone."

"The lady and I are fine. We don't need your interference."

The bald guy got in his space. Diaz took a step forward. If this guy wanted to rumble, then Diaz was all for it. He could already feel the heat rushing through his veins, priming him for battle. And he was just damned irritated enough to want to pummel this Neanderthal. Jessie didn't need protecting. Not from him.

But Jessie pushed her way between the two of them, tilted her head back, and locked eyes with Diaz.

"Don't do this. Please."

He was about to move Jessie out of the way, but there was something in the way she looked at him that made him pause. Her eyes, so clear, pleading with him, finally reaching through the thick haze of anger, reminding him that he did have something to lose by letting his anger take control.

Her.

This had to end. Not just for her, but for himself.

He took a step back, raised his hands, palm side up. "Sorry, man," he said to the bouncer. "I don't want a fight here."

Diaz had never backed away in his entire life. It pained him to do it now—made him feel like a coward. But he had to.

For Jessie. For himself. There was nothing to win here, and everything to lose.

He gave her his hand, held it out, and for some odd reason he felt as if it was his heart that he held there for her to either take or walk away from. Yeah, stupid thought, but there it was.

Her lips tilted upward, she slid her hand in his. "Let's go."

He nodded to the bouncer, who nodded back and turned to walk away, shuffling the gathering crowd with him.

It was over.

"Let's take a ride."

"Okay," she said.

He opened the door for her and she slid into the passenger seat. He got in, started up the engine, and drove.

They rode in silence. He knew exactly where he wanted to take her. The night was clear, the moon high and bright without a cloud in the sky, the only sound the revving purr of the Camaro's engine. He pulled into the park, deserted this time of night, found a nice spot—well secluded by draping willow trees—and pulled over, cutting the engine.

Now that they were here, he found it hard to find the right starting place. He stared out the windshield at the willow branches swaying in the breeze.

She wasn't going to talk first, not this time, and he knew it. This was up to him. He might as well start with the most important things first.

"I don't want you to be with anyone else."

She didn't answer.

"I don't do relationships, Jess. I never have. I know it's not an excuse, but it's all I have. I don't know how to handle loving someone, because I've never loved anyone before." He paused, turned to face her. "But I do love you. Remember when I told you that nothing scares me?"

She nodded.

"I lied. The possibility of hurting you someday scares the hell out of me."

"You won't hurt me. Not the way you think. The only way you hurt me is not giving us a chance."

He nodded. "I realize that now. Losing you scares me even more. I love you, Jessie."

Her eyes closed, drifted opened again. He saw tears glistening there. God, he'd made such a mess of this.

"So I'm going to screw up," he continued. "I'll probably screw up bad. I didn't want to fall in love with you. I didn't want to fall in love with anyone."

"Are you sorry you did?"

She had turned away to look out the window, not even facing him. Her voice sounded so small, like it hurt even to say that.

"No. I can't be sorry for loving you. You've changed me. You've made me think about who I am, about the man I want to be, about a lot of things I never would have thought about if I hadn't fallen in love with you. I'd never want to take that back."

She shifted to face him. God, she was so beautiful, her face shaped like a heart, her lips moist and full and so damn kissable it made his stomach hurt. And her eyes—so full of expression, so full of emotion she never could hide from him.

"I'm messed up, Jess."

"I don't expect you to be perfect."

"It's more than that. I have a problem. I've already talked to Grange about it."

She shifted, half turning in the seat to face him. "Do you think I don't know that you have issues with anger? Of course I realize you have a problem. But your problem doesn't extend to me."

He tilted his head, frowned. "What do you mean?"

"How many times have I pissed you off?"

His lips curled. "Plenty."

"Have you ever come after me when you were angry? Have you ever raised your hand to me?"

He tilted back, the very thought of physically hurting her making him sick to his stomach. "Hell no."

"Exactly. And you wouldn't. It isn't in you to hurt me. It isn't in you to hurt anyone you care about, Diaz. You *aren't* like your father, and it's time to stop carrying that burden—his burden. It's not your cross to bear. He did what he did, but it's not who *you* are."

He wanted to deny what she said. He'd spent his whole life thinking he was just like his old man. Hell, his father had told him often enough that he was just like him.

But Jessie was right. He wasn't like his dad. He'd never hurt Jessie, or any woman, or anyone he cared about.

"You're right. But I still blow up too easy, I still have trouble controlling my anger. It's affecting my work."

"Are you going to do something about it?"

"Yeah. Grange said I can take some counseling. He didn't seem too worried about it."

"Good."

"Do you—would you like to go with me?"

Her eyes widened. "You'd want me to?"

"Yeah. I would. It would help if you were there. I'm not really good at saying how I feel. Maybe you can help me with that part."

Her eyes filled with tears. "I'd love to go with you."

This was weird. Sitting here with Jessie, making plans like they were a couple. Though he guessed they were now. Something else he didn't exactly know how to handle. He supposed he was going to have to figure it out.

"You look lost."

He glanced at her. "Yeah. I kind of am. I told you I don't do relationships. Where do we go from here?"

She shrugged. "I have no idea. It's not like I'm an expert at this."

"Great. The blind leading the blind."

"You could make a great start by kissing me," she said.

"Yeah I could do that, couldn't I?" he replied with a grin.

But when he leaned over, he realized that the damn Camaro had bucket seats, and a console with a stick shift between them. Still, he managed to brush his lips across hers. As soon as he touched his tongue to hers, the flavor of her burst into his mouth, making his mouth water. She tasted warm and spicy, like cinnamon, like everything that he'd ever wanted. He leaned farther, cupping the back of her neck to draw her deeper into the kiss, eliciting a moan in response. She drew closer to him, her hands grasping his jacket and holding on tight. He felt her tension, her need, wanted to draw her onto his lap so he could feel her whole body against him while he kissed her. He wanted more, a lot more than he was going to get in this car.

"Let's go home," he whispered against her mouth. "Where I can get closer to you." Where he could undress her, take his time to really show her how he felt.

She shook her head. "I don't want to go there. Too crowded.

Too many people interrupting us. This is fine." She reached behind her and shifted her seat forward, then climbed into the backseat. "Come on back here with me."

The Camaro wasn't the most spacious car, and he wasn't exactly a small guy, but she was right. Wild Riders' headquarters wasn't the best place to be alone. Here wasn't exactly convenient, but they had as much privacy as they were going to get.

Jessie was already peeling off her jacket, revealing that sexy corset she'd teased him with earlier. Her breasts spilled over the top, making his mouth water for a taste of her buttery soft flesh. She positioned herself on the seat and spread her legs, palming her pussy.

"When you dressed in that outfit earlier, I wanted to put you over my knee and spank you for even thinking of going out in it."

She arched a brow. "We'll have to explore the spanking thing later. Right now I need you, Diaz. Get back here."

With a groan that was either frustration or need, he forced his big body into the backseat with her. Cramped, uncomfortable as hell, he wasn't sure he cared, though, because he was closer to her now. He grabbed her around the waist and pulled her on top of him.

"You smell good," he said as she leaned against his chest.

"You have too many clothes on." She pushed at his shoulders, helping him discard his jacket, and flung it into the front seat. Then she buried her face in his neck, licking across his throat. "I've missed you," she murmured against his skin. "I've missed the way you smell and the way you taste. I especially miss the way you feel. So hard against me." She surged against him and he damn near lost it.

"You keep doing that and I can't guarantee much restraint." His cock was already hard, aching and straining against his jeans.

He rocked against her leather pants, holding on to her hips to position her sex against his hard-on.

"I don't need or want you restrained around me," she said, lifting up to rest her hands on his shoulders. She slid forward, deliberately teasing him by rocking against his dick. "I want you wild and out of control, especially with sex."

He inhaled, breathing in her aroused scent. He pulled her forward and reached for the zipper of her corset. Jessie kept her gaze locked with his as he drew the zipper down, pulled the corset away, freeing her breasts. He tossed the corset on top of his jacket and filled his hands with her soft globes. They were warm, her nipples puckering as soon as he brushed his palms over the tiny pink buds. Jessie arched against his hands, a silent signal for more.

"I have calluses on my palms," he said, but he didn't stop rubbing her breasts.

"I know. It makes my nipples tingle. Do it some more."

He did, sliding his palms over each nipple until her breath caught and she gasped, her legs trembling beneath him. He liked her reaction, wanted more, so he moved his hands to her back to bring her breasts to his lips. He nuzzled between them, loving the softness of her skin against the harsh roughness of his. She laughed, the sound magnified against his ears. He licked the valley between her breasts. Even there she tasted like the sweetest honey, and he didn't think it was her soap. It was simply Jessie. He moved his head, took one nipple in his mouth and sucked, flicking the tight bud with his tongue.

Jessie moaned, grasped his head to hold him in place as he licked and nibbled the taut bud. "I can feel that in my pussy."

That's what he liked to hear. Jess was an incredibly sexual woman. Life with her was going to be phenomenal. He couldn't believe he'd almost let her go. He was so damn lucky that he'd been given a second chance to build a life with this amazing woman.

When she slid over his dick again, he growled, pushed her off his lap and onto her back on the seat, unzipped her pants and pulled them down, needing to have her naked and on top of him. While she wrestled with kicking the leather off, he jerked down the zipper of his jeans and grabbed a condom from a pocket, ready for her. Waiting for her.

JESSIE COULDN'T GET HER PANTS OFF FAST ENOUGH. SHE WAS wet, her nipples tight, on fire from Diaz's mouth. As she straddled him, her legs trembled. She was such a mess. She'd never felt such a sense of urgency, her entire body zoned in on Diaz, her pussy quivering with the need to feel his cock inside her.

Diaz held on to her waist and eased her onto his shaft. She slid down, engulfing him, feeling him expand inside her. She closed her eyes and focused on the sensation as his cock dragged over her sensitive tissues until she was seated on his thighs. She opened her eyes to find him staring at her with such an intense look it made her belly quiver. His lids were half closed, his head tilted to the side. With his dark good looks half shadowed, he looked like the devil himself, and he couldn't be any sexier than at that moment. He spread the fingers of both hands over her hips and brought her forward, dragging her clit across his pelvis. She sucked in a breath and held it at the rippling sensation, like being pulled across warm sand.

Then he pushed her back, at the same time lifting his hips to thrust inside her, and pull her forward again. She laid her palms across his chest, dug her nails into his skin, lost in the sensations, lost in him.

Being part of Diaz had always taken some of her sanity. She was so attuned to her body when he was inside her. It was much more than just physical contact—he read her body's reactions and adjusted his movements to give her the highest pleasure. Only a man who cared deeply would do that for his woman.

His woman. She was his woman now. She cupped his face with her palm, tingling at his coarse stubble.

"I love feeling you inside me. The way your cock swells, gets bigger the more you thrust."

"You're going to make it swell more if you keep talking like that."

She grinned, leaned forward to capture his mouth. God she loved his mouth, the way he kissed her. He palmed the back of her neck, held her there while he ravaged her lips with his, using his tongue to dive inside and tangle with hers, leaving her breathless. His kiss spoke of sex, of love, of the deepest emotion and things he couldn't yet say. But she knew the emotions he couldn't voice, and it made her tighten inside—all this joy, this revelation, having this man and knowing he was hers.

She pulled away, grasped his arms, and rode him, letting him grab her butt to lift her up and down. She gasped as she drew closer, watched his face, the way his frown tightened as he concentrated, his jaw clenched, the sweat beading on his forehead—it all ratcheted up her own pleasure.

She whimpered, felt herself unraveling. "I'm close. I need to come."

He nodded, his fingers digging into the flesh of her buttocks. His thrusts became harder now, deeper, and she held tight to his forearms. She waited for him to slam into her, to catapult her over the edge.

Instead, he used measured, relentless strokes, dragging his cock over that spot inside her that shattered her.

Her orgasm sent her reeling, crying out, and falling forward as she ground against him, shuddering through the waves of pleasure that penetrated every part of her. Her toes curled and even her scalp tingled. Diaz wrapped his arms around her back and groaned into her neck as he climaxed, burying deep and nearly cutting off her breath as he held her. She didn't care. She'd never felt so cherished.

Damp with perspiration, they clung together. The position wasn't the most comfortable, but Jessie didn't want to disengage. Not with Diaz stroking her back, kissing her neck, his heart beating against her chest.

"I love you," she whispered.

"I don't know what I did to deserve that."

She pushed off his chest to sit upright. "You didn't have to do anything other than be yourself. You deserve to be loved. So do I."

He nodded, his expression softer now. "I'm starting to believe that." He swept his hand over her face. "I love you, too, Jess."

They parted, dressed, and climbed back into the front seat.

"Now what?" she asked.

"I guess we go back to headquarters."

He didn't look happy about that. "What's wrong?"

"We're going to have to get our own place. I can't chase you around at headquarters and rip your clothes off and have you on the kitchen table with Grange and the guys hanging around all the time."

She laughed. "No, I guess you can't." Ridiculously giddy with happiness, she said, "So, I guess we'll go apartment hunting?"

He grimaced. "Yeah. I suppose it's time I set down some roots."

"Oh, the sacrifices a man makes in the name of love."

He leaned over and pressed his lips to hers in a kiss so tender it made her ache inside. He barely pulled away, whispering against her mouth. "Anything for you, Jessie. Anything."

Keep reading for a sneak peek
at the next book in
Jaci Burton's steamy series,

RIDING ON INSTINCT

Coming in 2009.

SPENCER KING WALKED A CIRCLE AROUND AGENT SHADOE Grayson and shook his head, deciding immediately that this assignment was going to fail.

"No way in hell is anyone going to believe she's a stripper."

As he stopped in front of her, she arched one perfectly manicured brow and narrowed her brown eyes. She was pretty, but nothing about her screamed "stripper."

"Excuse me?"

"Sorry, darlin', but you're not the right man for the job, so to speak."

She crossed her arms. "And why is that?"

"Well, look at you. Loose, dark pantsuit with God only knows what kind of body underneath it, hair in a bun without one strand out of place. Your face is pinched so tight you look like you have a stick shoved up your ass."

"Jesus, Spence, use a little tact."

Spence glared at his boss, General Grange Lee. "When have I ever used tact?"

"Good point." Grange turned to Shadoe. "I'm sorry, Agent Grayson. The guys around here aren't polite."

"I don't need polite, General Lee. I'm just here to get the job done."

Spence leaned against the sofa arm and shook his head again. "You aren't gonna get it done looking like that. Strippers wear less clothes than that goin' to church on Sunday."

"This is regulation Department of Justice uniform . . . what is your name again, Mr.—"

"Spence. Just call me Spence." He directed his attention back to General Lee. "Grange, this isn't gonna work."

"It's going to have to. We've been given the assignment, we'll work it out."

Spence slid fully onto the couch and planted his booted feet on the coffee table. "Whatever. But who's going to teach the prim schoolteacher over there how to be sexy?"

"I am not a schoolteacher. I'm a trained field agent."

He grinned. "Yeah, but you ain't no stripper."

She pivoted and faced Grange. "Really, General Lee. This is ridiculous."

Spence thought so, too. He could think of a hundred women who would make better strippers than Miss Prim and Proper there. Of course those hundred women *were* strippers, so that's probably why. What dumbass in Washington thought up this co-lossal clusterfuck of an assignment?

"We have a DEA agent out there selling secrets to the Colum-bians," Grange reminded him. "Our job is to find and detain him. We'll make this work."

Spence shrugged. "Whatever you say, boss."

The others began to trail in—all part of Wild Riders, a secret government organization charged with operating under the radar, assisting the government in less-than-legal ways. Spence loved his job. He got to steal and do illegal things that suddenly became—legal.

"So, another assignment?" Mac asked, his new wife Lily in tow. Jessie and Diaz came in with them. They piled up on the sofa, Lily pushing at Spencer to scoot over.

"So it seems," AJ said, coming in with Rick to stand behind the sofa.

Paxton followed.

"Agent Shadoe Grayson of the Department of Justice. These are the Wild Riders." He made them all introduce themselves, then asked her to take a seat, motioning to a space left over on the sofa where Spencer sat.

Spence noted with more than a little amusement that she took the vacant chair next to the sofa. Oh yeah, she was going to be all over the men at the strip club. She couldn't even stomach sitting close to one man. He resisted rolling his eyes, not wanting to hear a lecture from Grange.

"Okay, here's the deal," Grange said. "For some time now, the DEA has been aware that every bust operation in the New Orleans area has been foiled, as if the Columbians have received advance knowledge. They know they have someone inside feeding them information, and every time they try to set up their own sting, the rogue is nowhere to be found."

"Probably because the agent knows everyone in their department, knows when they're being followed or if there's a plant," Mac suggested.

"Exactly," Grange confirmed. "Which is why we've been brought in. The rogue doesn't know us."

"But wouldn't they know Agent Grayson?" Lily asked.

"No. She's new."

"Great. A rookie," Spence mumbled.

Shadoe glared at him. Spence smiled.

"Agent Grayson might be new in the field, but she's very good at her job. Don't underestimate her. And she has some . . . special talents that the Department is thrilled to make use of."

"Such as?" Rick asked.

"I have a photographic memory," she answered.

"Oh, cool. So you can remember everything you read and hear?" Jessie asked.

Shadoe nodded.

"Bullshit." Spencer didn't believe anyone could have a photographic memory.

"*No way in hell is anyone going to believe she's a stripper. Sorry, darlin', but you're not the right man for the job, so to speak. Well, look at you. Loose, dark pantsuit with God only knows what kind of body underneath it, hair in a bun without one strand out of place. Your face is pinched so tight you look like you have a stick shoved up your ass.* Should I go on, Spence, or stop now?"

"Well, goddamn. She just repeated everything I said to her right before y'all came in."

"No shit?" AJ asked.

"No shit," Spence replied, then looked back at Shadoe with a nod of appreciation. "I stand corrected, darlin'. You've got the skills there."

Those weren't her only skills, either. Because when her lips lifted in a hint of a smile, he saw a spark flash from those brown eyes of hers that rocked his balls into a quiver of awareness. Damn, she was pretty. Even with her severe clothing, no makeup, and hair all pulled back, there was definitely . . . something. Maybe she wasn't a total lost cause.

"Can we move on now, Spencer, or do you want to bullshit all day?"

Spence nodded, realizing he'd pissed off Grange. "Sorry, General."

"Okay. We have intelligence that this rogue is coming in to meet with his—or her—Columbian contact in New Orleans sometime within the next couple of weeks. We don't know who either is, but with Agent Grayson's assistance, we hope to nab the rogue."

"What's the plan?" Lily asked.

"Agent Grayson and Spencer will be going undercover at the Wild Rose Club in the French Quarter."

"Oooh lah lah! One of the finest strip clubs in the city," Rick said.

Grange nodded. "Agent Grayson will be undercover as a feature stripper, Spencer as her bodyguard."

"Oooh, can I strip?" Jessie asked.

"Oh, hell no," Diaz said.

Jessie affected a pout. "I never get to have any fun."

AJ snorted. "Your day will come, sweetheart. I'm sure there are thousands of guys out there who'd love to see you naked."

"Over my dead body," Diaz said.

She grinned at that. Spencer shook his head. Jessie was the baby of the bunch. She'd been with the Wild Riders since Mac rescued her from a really bad situation when she was a teen. She was more little sister than partner to them, and they all protected her. She'd grown up, though, had finished her first assignment a few months back with Spence and Diaz. Jessie and Diaz had fallen in love on that case, making the two of them working together in the future a sticky situation. But since Mac and Lily managed it, Spence supposed Grange could work it out with Diaz and Jessie, too. Spence was just glad he didn't have to deal with those kinds of entanglements. Fucking was one thing. Love was something entirely different and not in his vocabulary.

"Anyway," Grange said, wrangling their attention again, "all of you will be there, interspersing with the crowds, in and out of the bar scene. Agent Grayson here has memorized every single face in the agent books. She's the only one who will be able to identify the rogue agent when he or she makes an appearance. Our job is to grab the agent when Shadoe identifies him or her."

"After she learns to strip," Spence added.

Shadoe didn't even look at him, but her fingernails tapped on one crisp pant leg. He smiled at her irritation.

"I have an expert coming in to assist you with that, Agent Grayson," Grange said.

"Please, everyone, call me Shadoe. The 'Agent' thing gets a little old and formal, and as Spence seems so fond of reminding me," she said, this time shooting a pointed look in his direction, "I need to loosen up."

He winked. She rolled her eyes.

This was going to be fun.

SHADOE UNPACKED, RATHER FURIOUSLY, JAMMING HER THINGS IN the two-drawer dresser in the tiny bedroom provided for her by General Lee. At least she could take out her frustrations on her clothing instead of the huge hulk of a man who'd infuriated her from the start.

Spencer. Why did he have to be the one she was going to work with? The other guys seemed nice, at least. Spencer was an arrogant ass who'd clearly already determined she couldn't do the job. As if she hadn't come up against hundreds of guys just like him—starting with her father. She'd made the colossal sin of being born a girl, and her father had never forgiven her for that.

She'd show him, and she'd show Spencer, too. She could do this assignment. And when she rose to the top of the ranks at the department, she'd tell her father to shove it, too. Her gender did not preclude her from becoming successful in law enforcement.

Just because all her father's brothers had graced them with sons and her father had only managed to produce one daughter did not make her a mistake, did not make her less than worthy to carry on the Grayson tradition of being prominent decorated officers.

Her father was an ass. So was Spencer.

She'd parade down Bourbon Street stark naked if she had to, but she'd nab the rogue agent.

A knock forced her to hurry and shove the last of her things in the drawer. She opened the door to find one of the men of her thoughts taking up most of the doorway.

God, he was imposing. Impossibly tall, tan, stunningly gorgeous, if she had to admit it. Eyes the color of the ocean, with a square jaw that bore a hint of unshaven stubble. If she was the kind of woman to swoon over a good-looking man, she'd be a puddle on the floor by now.

Good thing her career took all her time and she didn't focus on men and sex.

Though her body was doing a pretty darn good imitation of libidinous longing at the moment. She ignored it. "Yes?"

"Your stripping instructor Maria was delayed. She won't be here until tomorrow. But Jessie's offered to help loosen you up. She's waiting for you in the workout room."

"Okay."

"I'll show you the way."

"Fine."

"And I'd change into something less . . . anal-retentive . . . if I were you."

"Gee, thanks. I was planning on it." She waited. He didn't move.

"Do you mind?"

"No. Go ahead." He still didn't go away. Nor did he stop smiling. God, that was irritating.

"Geez, you're dense." She shut the door in his face, shook her head, and dug out a T-shirt and sweats, changing in a hurry. When she opened the door again, he arched a brow and gave her a tilted-head once-over, but didn't say a word.

Good, because she did know how to drop-kick a well-over-six-foot-tall giant, and she wouldn't at all mind giving him a demonstration of *that* right there in the hall. She was in a mood.

He took her down to the ground floor and into a good-sized gym.

Jessie was waiting for her in a back room, dressed in cropped spandex workout pants and a tight T-shirt. And holy shit, did the girl have a body on her. Shadoe immediately felt inadequate.

Maybe Jessie should be the one stripping, because she was gorgeous. Platinum blond spiky hair, face of an angel, and a body made for sin.

"Hey!" Jessie said with enthusiasm when she spotted Shadoe. "I figured since Maria was going to be late, you'd want to loosen up a little bit and maybe start working on some dance moves."

"Sure. Thanks for working with me."

"Are you kidding? I'm jealous as hell you get to strip. It sounds like a blast."

"Don't even think about it, Jess."

The deep baritone voice of Diaz came out as a warning, but Jessie only blew him a kiss and grinned.

"He belong to you?" Shadoe asked.

"Body and soul," she said. "But you can ignore him. He goes Neanderthal and jealous on me at times. It just means he loves me. And I'm still jealous that you get this juicy assignment."

"Oh, right. Not exactly the best assignment I could have hoped for, but I'll live through the humiliation."

Jessie put her hands on her hips. "You're joking, right? Stripping is power, honey. You'll have men drooling at your feet, willing to do anything you say for the tiniest glimpse of skin. You'll be in utter control. Don't ever forget that."

"You know, for someone so young, you're very wise."

Jessie laughed. "I just know who holds the clout in that kind of situation. Growing up with all these guys, I've learned a lot."

Shadoe glanced at Spencer, who was leaning against the wall. His expression was noncommittal, but she could well imagine the protective instincts of all those men taking care of a teenaged Jessie. General Lee had given her cursory background information on all the Wild Riders. Impressive lot, all of them, having worked their way into their positions after coming from nothing.

She supposed teaching the girl street smarts and learning about guys through living with them wasn't a bad thing at all. Shadoe wished someone had let her in on a few of those secrets, because as far as men were concerned, she was mainly clueless.

"Let's stretch a bit, then we'll get to movements."

They went down on the floor and did some basic stretches. Shadoe was aware of Spencer still hovering near the door, but she tried her best to ignore him and concentrate on Jessie. She figured he'd get bored soon enough and leave for something more exciting, like wrestling on television. Or maybe a game on Xbox.

No such luck. By the time they had finished their stretching and Jessie went to put music on, not only had Spencer pulled up a chair, two more of the guys had come in to watch, though Diaz was shooting them looks that could kill. They seemed to be ignoring him.

"Hey guys," Jessie said with a wave. "We're going to work on some dance moves. Want to join in?"

"I'd rather have the hair on my balls plucked out with tweezers," Paxton said with a grimace.

"Don't look at me," AJ said. "Two left feet, remember?"

Spence stayed silent. Diaz kept glaring.

"Pussies," Jessie replied, then laughed and turned back to Shadoe. "Let's get started."

The music was slow and sexy, and Shadoe followed Jessie's lead.

"First thing you have to do is relax your body. Breathe in and out," Jessie said, her chest rising and falling as she deeply inhaled and exhaled. "If your body isn't relaxed, you'll be out there dancing around like you have rigor mortis."

Shadoe snorted. "Good point." She did the deep breathing as Jessie instructed.

"Ignore the audience. Concentrate on the music and how it makes *you* feel. Because you're the only one who counts. It's just you and me dancing."

Shadoe focused on the music, relaxing, breathing, watching only Jessie. Jessie had a way with her body and the music, sliding her hips back and forth. Slight, but oh so sexy.

Jessie reached out and grabbed Shadoe's hips. "Honey, you are one tight ball of tension. Let it go. This is fun stuff. Loosen your hips and let them slide. Back and forth, back and forth. That's it. Now raise your arms over your head and swing your ass a little."

It was difficult for Shadoe to let go. Jessie was right—she was always tense, always on the job, always thinking, planning, plotting . . . working.

But . . . this *was* work, wasn't it? And her focus was on being the best. So she had to be the best at this.

"Come here," Jessie said, bringing herself up hip to hip with Shadoe and taking Shadoe's hands in hers. "Now, move your body in time with mine."

They were breast to breast, hip to hip. This made it much easier to follow Jessie, undulating her hips in a side-to-side rhythm. Oh, yeah, now she was getting it. She settled into the music, letting her body relax, flow along with Jessie's. Jessie pulled back, then Shadoe moved up close to her again until their breasts were touching. Then Shadoe would move back and Jessie would rock her hips against Shadoe.

"Oh yes, now you've got it. That's hot, babe," Jessie said. "Keep doing it."

This was fun. And Jessie was right, dancing like this was hot.

When she turned, there were several sets of equally steamy eyes riveted on them, anticipation written all over their faces.

Jessie was right. There *was* power in this. And she hadn't even taken her clothes off yet.

"FUCK ME, THAT'S HOT AS HELL," CU SAID IN A TIGHT WHISPER.

"I don't think my dick's supposed to be getting hard, but it is," Paxton replied.

"You'd better all be staring at Shadoe or you're dead," Diaz said.

Spencer said nothing, but his throat was dry, his cock like steel, and his balls quivered. Watching Shadoe and Jessie dance together was one hell of an erotic scene. Though he wasn't focusing on Jessie at all.

Now that she was out of her loose pantsuit, he realized Shadoe had a body. Not the knock-your-eyes-out-of-your-sockets body that Jessie had, but the woman definitely had curves. Nice breasts pressing against her T-shirt, an indented waist and hips made for a man's hands. And legs. Long legs. He wanted to see those legs she hid under the sweatpants, dammit. A woman could have tits like mountains and he wouldn't care. He was a leg man.

And he was wrong—she *could* move. She learned quickly, and though he could tell she was a novice, once she was given instruction, she was a quick study. If Maria could teach her a few moves, she might make one hell of a stripper.

If she could actually handle it, and that was the key. Could she handle it? He'd have to find out before they put her up on stage.

He knew exactly how to do that.

He waited while she and Jessie practiced awhile longer. The other guys left, obviously unable to stand the girl on girl torture any longer. It was just Diaz and him. He already knew Diaz wouldn't leave until Jessie did.

When Jessie finished up, Shadoe indicated she was going to hang out and practice for a while. Jessie winked at Diaz as she walked by and left the gym. Diaz walked out right after her, but Spencer hung back, watching. Shadoe was immersed in the music, clearly oblivious to his presence.

He stood and walked toward her. She was sliding her hips back and forth in front of the mirror, her eyes open as he approached.

Maybe she wasn't oblivious, because she locked gazes with him, yet continued to move, raising her arms over her head. He stopped behind her.

"Stripping is more than just shaking your ass, you know," he said.

"I'm fully aware of that."

She continued to move. She had a really nice ass. His dick continued to pound. He didn't try to hide the fact he had an erection, either. He stepped beside her, and her gaze drifted down. She had to notice.

She did. Her gaze shot back up to his face.

"Yes, watching you and Jessie dance got my dick hard. Does that bother you?"

This time she stopped, turned to him, swallowed before answering. "No."

"Good. Because as a stripper you're going to be getting a lot of guys hard. Get used to it."

She grabbed a towel from the back of the chair and wiped her neck. "There are a lot of things I need to get used to, but I'm not innocent, Spence."

"Could have fooled me."

"I'm twenty-eight years old. I've had sex before."

"How many times?"

She stilled. "That's really none of your business."

He laughed. That answer told him a lot. "Oh, a woman of the world, are you?"

"You're an ass."

"Yes. But I need to be able to cover yours, and you need to be able to pull this off. So I'm not going to let you pretend to be something you're not. If you can't do this, you should stop now."

"I can do this."

"Prove it. Strip for me right now."